Praise for *Francie's Got a Gun*

One of CBC's Best Canadian Fiction Books of the Year

"I loved every character in [*Francie's Got a Gun*]. In beautiful prose, Snyder unfurls Francie's story through a chorus of perspectives, illuminating the hopes, flaws, disappointments, small preferences and large ambitions within a community. Together these voices propel the narrative toward a devastating, beautiful, and pitch-perfect conclusion. Carrie Snyder has pulled off a magic trick with this novel—it is a literary feat."
— Emily Urquhart, bestselling author of *Beyond the Pale*

"At once tense and tragic, sweet and tender . . . [*Francie's Got a Gun*] is a strong, complex novel, with a myriad of layers that elevate [it] to a timeless novel."
— *The Miramichi Reader*

"*Francie's Got a Gun* is a tender, pulsating novel about a girl and a supporting cast of characters drawn with such complexity and rawness you feel as though you are inhabiting not only their worlds but their living, breathing bodies. Carrie Snyder has—by some miracle—succeeded in writing a novel that has its own heartbeat."
— Tasneem Jamal, author of *Where the Air is Sweet*

Praise for *Girl Runner*

Shortlisted for the Rogers Writers' Trust Prize for Fiction

"*Girl Runner* is a witty, poignant, and finely plotted novel that offers us a character possessed of the wisdom that arises only from a life well-lived."
    —Jury Citation, Rogers Writers' Trust Prize for Fiction

"An exquisitely crafted, deeply imagined novel . . . [that] unfolds with the sure-footedness of an elite runner."
    —Cathy Marie Buchanan, author of *The Painted Girls*

"Extraordinary, accomplished . . . a wonderful story of a free spirit forced to make difficult choices . . . [It] grabbed my hand on page one and never let go."
    —Sara Gruen, author of *Water for Elephants*

"A beautiful, thoughtful homage to those forgotten women who stepped outside the boundaries of what was allotted to them, and a testament to the struggles and sacrifices that paved the way for the female athletes who followed."
    —*Quill & Quire*

Francie's
Got a Gun

Francie's Got a Gun

CARRIE SNYDER

VINTAGE CANADA

VINTAGE CANADA EDITION, 2023

Published by Vintage Canada, a division of Penguin Random House Canada Limited, Toronto, in 2023. Originally published in hardcover by Knopf Canada, a division of Penguin Random House Canada Limited, Toronto, in 2022. Distributed in Canada by Penguin Random House Canada Limited, Toronto.

www.penguinrandomhouse.ca

The author acknowledges the support of the Canada Council for the Arts.

Canada Council   Conseil des arts
for the Arts   du Canada

LIBRARY AND ARCHIVES CANADA CATALOGUING IN PUBLICATION

Title: Francie's got a gun / Carrie Snyder.
Names: Snyder, Carrie, author.
Description: Previously published: Toronto: Knopf Canada, 2022.
Identifiers: Canadiana 20210350539 | ISBN 9780735281936 (softcover)
Classification: LCC PS8587.N785 F73 2023 | DDC jC813/.6—dc23

Book design by Kelly Hill
Cover image: Sue Oldfield / Getty Images

Printed in the United States of America

2 4 6 8 9 7 5 3 1

Penguin
Random House
VINTAGE CANADA

For first friends

The trees you planted in childhood have grown too heavy. You cannot bring them along.

—Rainer Maria Rilke (translated by Anita Barrows and Joanna Macy)

Begin

Do fragments make a whole?

You wake in the early hours before your alarm sounds, and you wish you had someone to tell about this feeling washing your body. Of terror. Nameless and blind and hauling you back through time. What was it like to be you, when you were unformed and whole, innocent and brave, when everyone watched and nobody saw?

Breathe, breathe, breathe, you remind yourself.

Breathe in. But also, breathe out.

You are curled tight on a futon on the floor, dim dawn light filtering through the high, uncovered window. You can hear the birds.

You remind yourself who you are: a strong woman, tough, ambitious. You've left behind childhood. You've earned the degree you could afford, and a job, and you talk to your mom and your brother, or text with them, regularly, and you've been training your body since you were a kid, and this summer, on the weekends, you're back to competing in road races, a half-marathon, a triathlon, whatever you can sign up for and afford to get yourself to.

You're never going to win, never going to be the best, but that's not why you do it.

Why do you do it?

You set one hand on your stomach and one hand on your heart.

You stretch out flat on your back. You could say that your body has a spirit or a soul, but when you search for it, try to see it, it cuts out, like a firefly flickering on and off and gone in the night.

You're not old, you've barely begun. Your capacity for growth feels infinite, but limited to your body.

Maybe you're okay with that, maybe you're not. Maybe you're torn, like your muscles, day in and day out, seeking endurance through suffering.

But what if you don't want to suffer? What if you're done with all that? What if you want to rest, to relax, to forgive, to turn toward everything and everyone with hope and open arms?

What then? What now?

If you keep running through the same story, can you come around to a different end?

ONE

Gun Run

A lot of things were going wrong, all at once.

Francie couldn't feel her hands or lips or feet. She knew that the air was warm, thick, almost wet, and she knew that her jeans were sticking to her legs, like she was swimming not running. Her arm, hanging from her shoulder, was so heavy—she knew that was the gun, but she couldn't feel it in her hand. It was as if in one sudden move—lurching forward, wrenching away—Francie had become someone else, another girl entirely, maybe not even a child, a stranger. Was it possible to split in two? To float above herself, like watching another person?

Floating and watching, floating and watching.

She had no pity, only curiosity, for this other girl, running, running, running. The girl—the other Francie—was a pretty good runner, but her feet were tangled in sagging cuffs, flapping sneakers, and she couldn't see so well, overgrown bangs, hair in her eyes, her heart was going to hammer through her throat.

The floating Francie could watch, and wonder, without having to feel the crackle of fear, its electrical snap. The terrible thing that it seemed they had all been waiting for, silently, numbly—almost expecting—had happened, suddenly and all at once.

Now, she had to run.

There was no other choice but to hide and to run, to run and to hide. It was like playing a game, but the game had no rules. It's okay, she told herself, watching from above, it's okay, because you've got the gun, now, you've got the gun, not him.

But she didn't want the gun.

A lot of things were going wrong.

The hot June afternoon. The tangling jeans. The neighbourhood behind the school that she didn't know at all, with streets all hushed and grand and empty, smooth paved blackness turning round and round, as if to confuse her. She ran like a rat dropped into a maze.

The gun.

She forced herself to feel it in her hand, to wrap her buzzing fingers around it, tightly enough not to drop it by accident. It looked small, but it was heavy. Blunt-nosed, a snout like an angry little animal, one you could not make friends with or adopt or bring home, no matter how you tried.

But Francie wasn't running home. She wasn't running anywhere, just away. The thought was almost enough to break her apart entirely: the floating Francie imagined what it would look like if the Francie who was running, hot and red and lost, down the middle of a silent street, was to shatter, break into all her parts—an arm, a leg, and then a kneecap, a toe, and into smaller and smaller bits until she was nothing at all. Invisible, scattered like dust.

But that Francie did not shatter. Did not stop. Not quit.

———

She heard the sound of a car or a truck turning into the street behind her, but she didn't look back, not even a glance. To look back would be the end. And this was not the end, not the end of Francie. The floating Francie suddenly saw through the other Francie's eyes, and it was like being pulled inside a tunnel, a quick tightening of vision, sharpened onto a still point of light ahead, everything else fading into a blur.

She could hear her breath, harsh, wheezing. Like a car with a bad muffler. Or was that the truck, the red pickup truck with the broken window, behind her?

Like in a dream she would dream over and over, Francie saw herself veering onto perfect green grass, soft with the click of soaking sprinklers, she was at the top of a steep hill, she was plunging down. Inside her head a small whine was sounding, like an alarm. It seemed to grow stronger, louder, it wanted to break through, it wanted her to let it loose, to scream.

But she couldn't let it loose.

She had to be silent. Silently screaming through a mist of cool water that rose as if by magic from beneath dark-green grass beside a house of steel and glass, an enormous house as big as the houses Dad used to build—bigger, even. Down, down, down through wood chips and fresh plantings of tiny bushes and crawling vines, terraces held by huge smooth rocks. Francie skidded and jumped, trying to stop the hand with the gun from catching her as she stumbled, close to the house, glimpsing decks that jutted like shelves overlooking a seemingly endless lawn, wide and rolling.

Open space.

The tunnel burst wide. Not safe, exposed.

She'd slipped to her knees, fallen onto patio stone, her elbow ached, the elbow attached to the hand with the gun raised. Anyone could see it. One breath, two, shallow, raw, lifting her to her feet, tipping her forward, as she sensed rather than saw a woman wearing headphones and pushing a vacuum across an interior floor; sensed, dreamlike, the woman pause, notice her, step to the shining wall of windows, and in that single flashing frame become a shadow from which Francie was fleeing, away into the open, across this wide, smooth-shorn green field.

A golf course. A cart rolling to the top of a hill and stopping, the men like tiny action figures climbing out, moving around.

The gun hung from the hand that did not feel like Francie's hand.

She saw herself lift it and slide it under her t-shirt, to hide it against her stomach. Now it was harder to run, awkward, and she had the sensation again of swimming rather than running, swimming, something she wasn't any good at, flailing and sinking under the surface.

The gun felt cold against her stomach. Her stomach felt empty, even though she remembered sitting at her desk at first nutrition break and chewing on the butter-and-jam sandwich Grandma Irene had made this morning. Her backpack felt empty too, bouncing on her shoulders, even though she remembered zipping the lunch box into it before walking down the hall, obeying the secretary's too-familiar call over the loudspeakers: "Will Francie Fultz please come to the office. Francie Fultz to the office." Mrs. G in front of the whole choir, flinging her baton on the gymnasium floor, waving her arms: "Francie, this is impossible! You can't leave now! The concert is tonight, and this is our only dress rehearsal! What could be more important?"

Well, this, Mrs. G.

Francie was wearing her favourite t-shirt, black with a sparkly cat formed of glued-on jewels, not real, and below the cat, the word *LOVE* spelled out in jewels too, also not real, except in an imaginary world. The shirt could be turned inside out for the concert, which Mrs. G said they could do, if they were desperate. The choir should all look the same, dressed head to toe in black, "like professionals," Mrs. G said. When Francie drew the cat shirt over her head this morning, so soft and stretchy, so shiny with jewels, she heard Mrs. G's voice saying, *if you're desperate*, and she didn't think Mrs. G knew what that word meant—*desperate*.

Francie scrambled through a wide, sandy pit in the grass. She was too much inside herself suddenly. She wasn't floating anymore.

Her sneakers were full of sand.

A hole opened up behind Francie's eyes.

She could see Dad slouched in the torn-up dirt. Bleeding. Like he was going to kill someone, like he already had. But that wasn't over, that was now. That just happened, was still happening. She could see his face, red and wet, his eyes leaking, but not real tears. "Here, take it," Dad said. "Now get the hell out of here."

A lot of things were going wrong.

Her eye was full of sand, where her hand wiped it by accident. Not the hand with the gun.

"Fore!" Pastel shirts, pink faces under white ball caps, heads bobbing as the golf cart zoomed down the hill. The action figures were becoming real.

Francie ran toward a wall of bushes. The bushes were thick. Wriggling on her belly, she crawled in deep.

It wasn't just Dad she kept seeing, slouched in the torn-up dirt. It was Mikey. Him too. Seeping, slumped, fallen into the gravel and dirt. Lying there. He looked at her with his sad brown eyes as she took the gun, and ran right by him.

Dad had said he wasn't going to see Mikey, ever again. Dad said it was over, they'd never work together again, he was giving up on Mikey, but that was a different day, a different construction site, out in the country. That was May, that was the day Mrs. G had passed around the sign-up sheet where you could write your name if you wanted to sing a solo. Francie's hand shook so hard that she had to dig the pencil's tip into the paper to write the letters of her own name so that Mrs. G could read them later. Alice was watching. She whispered, "You'll get a solo for sure!" Francie passed her the piece of paper and the pencil, and Alice hesitated, but didn't write down her name. Francie knew she should have whispered encouragement to Alice too, but something ugly and small and argumentative inside herself held back the words.

Alice passed the paper and pencil to the next person in the row, and too late Francie whispered, "Maybe we could get a duet?" But maybe Alice didn't hear.

The loudspeaker was crackling: "Will Francie Fultz please come to the office, Francie Fultz to the office."

"Not again!" Mrs. G had lowered her baton, and Francie looked at the floor. "Where do you think you're going now?" But how could Francie know?

Dad was there to surprise her, like he liked to do, he was waiting for her in the office, leaning his elbows on the counter while the school secretary turned pink with laughter. As they walked to his car, Dad winked at Francie just like he'd winked at the secretary. He said, "You have a very important meeting with your very important dad."

"But I was in choir practice," said Francie.

"What—you want to go back? I can take you back."

Francie shook her head no. "I might get a solo," she said, mostly to herself.

As they drove out of town, onto a familiar country road, Dad switched on the radio, he smiled at her: "Wait'll you see this place, kiddo, it's gonna be a palace."

Then she knew they weren't going to Grandma's house, they were going to see a building, or part of a building, under construction. She rested her forehead on the window, and watched for horses in the fields, maybe even a wild mustang galloping and bucking. The fields were light green and the ditches were soft with dandelions and other flowering weeds.

At the construction site, Dad parked in the gravel beside the road and climbed out, walked around the hood of his Caddy, rapping the shiny gold with his knuckles. "Wait'll you see the dimensions on this place!"

Through the window, Francie saw a horse running smoothly along the fenceline, hooves drumming the ground, tail sailing. Away from them. Dad opened Francie's door and cool, fresh air blew in. Francie looked down at her sneakers. The grass in the ditch was wet.

Dad was wearing a blue jacket unzipped over a white t-shirt, bare hands stuffed into pockets. The lane was long, sharp with newly poured gravel.

"Imagine what this is going to be!" said Dad. The construction site didn't look like anything yet, but that's how everything started, Dad said. "You start with nothing but a good imagination, and watch out—you'll make big things happen!"

The running horse was a speck against a far stand of trees. Francie imagined being the horse, galloping, kicking, its tail streaming out behind its heels, like a wild mustang.

Dad was coming along slowly, his right foot dragging behind him through the stones. His boots were dark leather, Francie had watched him rub them clean with a rag and wax them with polish, sitting in the front hall on the bench where Mom piled cloth shopping bags and whatever wasn't junk that came in the mail.

Dad was as tall as a giant. His bad leg swung from his hip, it didn't bend at the knee or ankle. He didn't always have a bad leg. It got hurt last summer and Mom didn't need to tell Francie not to talk about it. No one did.

Francie hummed the song they'd been singing in Mrs. G's music portable, a struggle song, Mrs. G called it.

They were coming to the end of the lane, a sea of churned-up mud. Dad pressed down on Francie's shoulder, squeezed, and pushed off, moving toward a big machine that was chewing up dirt, dropping it by the bucketload into the back of a waiting dump truck. Another truck idled behind that one.

"Now this is a big operation, this is the big time, kiddo," said Dad.

A man hopped down from the cab of the second truck. He was holding a brown paper coffee cup in one hand, and he shouted over the rumble of the engine: "Hey, it's Lucky!"

Dad was looking around for her. "This is my girl, Francie."

But the man didn't like that. "*Hombre*," he said, "this is no place for kids."

"Francie's a pro. Great kid," said Dad, setting his hand on top of her head.

Francie didn't take her eyes off the stranger. He was looking at her too, examining her unhappily. He lifted the cup to his lips, took a swig, and spat it on the ground. "Cold," he said.

He came up close to Dad and tapped him on the shoulder, leaned in. "Are you sure you should be here, amigo?"

"What's that supposed to mean?"

"I heard Mikey's on to you. I heard he knows what you're selling."

"Mikey who? Mikey my buddy, my partner, my brother? Don't you worry about Mikey."

The man dumped out his coffee into the dirt. "Surprised you'd come around, that's all," he said. He tossed the cup and it caught in the breeze and rolled away.

Uh-oh.

Dad said: "You think you know Mikey so well, Mikey sells a clean site, and when we say clean, we mean fucking pristine!" Dad put his hand on the man's chest, and the man took a big step backward. A smile played on the man's lips, like he didn't know much. He didn't know what her dad could do, Francie thought, already running, running to pick up the cup.

The cup lifted and danced, but Francie leapt and caught it. The jaws of the big digger swung over her head, and she heard the man shouting, but not Dad.

Little stones rushed down into the freshly dug hole, but she wasn't going to slip in, she wasn't going to fall. Dad was calling her, calm and slow: "Come on back now, Francie, there's a girl."

She scrambled to her feet and ran back to them, the big machine gone quiet overhead. Dad's eyes were watering.

"*Dios mío*, that was too fucking close!" The man was yelling.

"Watch your language." Dad wasn't yelling.

"What's your name again, kid?" The man's voice was high, shaky.

Francie looked at Dad and he nodded, so she said, loud and clear, "Francie."

"How old are you, Francie?"

"Ten," she said.

"Ten. Ten. Yeah, I got a ten-year-old at home. Grade four? Grade five?"

"Grade four," said Dad, but Francie shook her head, dropped her voice to a whisper, "Grade five," just to put it on the record. She was looking at the field where the horse was running, up near the road again, and a truck was turning into the lane. A red pickup truck, moving slow.

Dad was patting around his jacket pocket. "While I'm here, anything I can do for you today?"

"I told you to watch your back," the man hissed.

"If you don't want anything, just say so."

"I don't want anything." The man put his hand up over his mouth, like he was covering a cough. "Mikey's here."

"Mikey's here? I didn't see his truck."

"Turn around."

Dad glanced over his shoulder. "Well, speak of the devil."

Francie saw the horse jogging along the fence at the same pace as the pickup truck. Sure enough, it was Mikey—she remembered last summer, when he'd come over to the backyard with hot dogs and buns, and Mom kept saying Dad's accident wasn't Mikey's fault, nobody was blaming him. Mikey almost broke the picnic table, the whole bench swooped low under his weight, and Francie remembered he'd wiped his face with his paper napkin, till it was crumpled and sopping, and Mom gave him the whole pile. Come back any time, Mom had told him when he left, and Dad said check with him next time before passing out invitations, and why'd she say that, anyway.

"Because he's our friend."

"He owes me," said Dad. You couldn't see anything wrong with Dad's leg when he was sitting down, just when he tried to stand up.

"Okay," Mom had said. "If you say so."

"Francie," Dad said now, his eyes watering, "I need you to do something for me."

He took her hand and opened it. "Run to the tree line and throw this away. I'll time you." She looked to see what it was: a plastic sandwich bag with foil packets inside.

But Mikey keeps a clean site, she thought.

"On your mark, get set, go!"

The field looked grassy and smooth, but it wasn't. When her foot stepped in a hole, Francie crashed sideways, and hoped Dad wasn't watching. She popped back up and kept running. Arms pumping. She felt the wind lift her hair like she was the horse, galloping. At the trees, she stopped at a wire fence, orange with rust that flaked off on her fingers. She stuffed the bag into the paper cup, crumpled it up, and threw everything over the fence.

When she turned around, Mikey's red truck was parked beside the porta-potty, looking across the field toward her. Dad and the men looked like dollhouse people. Like she could pick them up and move them around with her fingers. But where would she put them?

She was real, everyone else was pretend.

Dad and the men made a small circle that broke apart. Their shouts were faint, and travelled out of sync with their movements: first she saw the truck's door slam, then she heard it.

Francie didn't want to go back. She kicked through the yellow-headed weeds that grew beside the rusty fence, walk-ing toward the field where she'd seen the horse—and there it was, moving toward her, too. A good shiver rippled up Francie's neck. Moving as quietly as possible, she ripped up a handful of grass, and slid it through the fence. The horse's lips brushed her open palm, and Francie felt a million feelings she wanted to feel rushing through her body, and none she didn't want to feel. Like a million colours, a million soft threads rushing under her skin, binding her up with bravery, keeping her safe. She stepped softly beside the fence, and the horse came along with her, watchful too, moving like they were attached by an invisible cord, till Francie came closer and closer to the bare dirt of the construction site.

"Hey, Francie, honey, you okay, everything okay?" Mikey was calling to her. The horse stopped, alert. Mikey began walking toward them, and Francie could see his shoulders lifting and falling as he breathed in and out, heavily.

She knew whose side she was on. She didn't have to tell Mikey anything.

The horse trotted in a tight circle, slashing its tail, and Francie ran, then, up the gravel laneway. She was too fast for Mikey to catch her!

Dad was ahead of them, already getting into the car. Francie climbed in and slammed the door, yanking hard on the handle to manage it.

"Where'd you put that stuff I gave you?"

"The cup?"

"And the other stuff, in the little bag."

"I threw it away, like you said."

"Ah." His bad leg was trembling.

The glove compartment hung open, and Francie shut it. Dad turned the key and the engine roared.

"What's the difference between an enemy and a friend?" Dad said.

She had to be careful with him.

He said: "When a friend stabs you in the back, it hurts more."

She could see Mikey walking back toward his red truck, parked on the dirt beside the field.

"We won't be coming back here again, promise you that."

Dad cracked the window and moved the gearshift down to drive—Francie knew, because once he'd let her sit on his lap and move the gearshift, and steer. But only once. When she was little, before his leg got hurt. Before.

Francie knew, if she looked, that horse would be gone. So she didn't look. If she didn't look, the horse would be there forever.

The leaves on the bushes were slippery but sharp. It was impossible to crawl without using the hand that was holding the gun.

Throw it away! Francie thought.

But when she thought this thought, she couldn't breathe. To breathe, she had to squeeze her eyes shut tight and forget where she was. First, she saw Alice, as if they were walking together, and then running, running like they were riding on horses, through the woods.

Alice's horse was small, a rainbow-coloured pony, like the one on Francie's lunch box. Francie's horse was tall and strong, bright black tail swooshing out behind its hooves as it ran. Not an imaginary horse at all—the horse in the field, watchful and wild. No one would ever tame that horse. Except for me, thought Francie. Her eyes popped open.

If only Alice was here, then the gun might not be real. If this was a story Francie was making up, an adventure, Alice would keep her from floating away, Alice would know,

Alice would catch hold of Francie's elbow and lead them back home when the story was over.

Alone, on her own, Francie might get lost in it forever.

Alice, Dad, Mikey, Mrs. G, Grandma Irene, Mom—nobody knew where she was.

I don't know where I am!

She slithered out of the bushes on her belly—she was through to the other side, out into the sunshine and heat. The first thing she heard was a car, coming this way. Or maybe it was a truck, a red pickup truck, but Mikey wouldn't be driving it, Mikey was lying on the ground looking at the sky.

Don't look! Francie jumped to her feet, her mouth shut to keep from screaming.

She felt the air move around her—*whoosh*—as she ran across the street, which had no sidewalks, just grass, curb, pavement, curb, grass. She wasn't screaming, that was the sound of a horn, of tires screeching as the car swerved. Not red, black. Small. Fancy wheel rims. Dad always pointed out the fancy rims.

"What the fuck, kid, what the actual fuck?"

But Francie was away, on the other side, veering onto the first side street she saw, a boulevard. Bright, spiky flowers in pretty pots on porch steps. Window boxes planted with geraniums. Grandma Irene's favourite. *But the flowers are poison, watch out!*

Ahead, a busy street, like the one she and Alice had to cross to get to school—oh! Same street? Different spot! Big trees, four lanes of traffic, no lights here, no crossing guard. The hand with the gun was safe underneath her sparkly shirt, and Francie looked both ways this time, and when she got a break, she ran. She knew this street, she knew to turn left to go home, keep going straight to get to Alice's house.

Everything reminded her of Dad. She kept looking for him, like she wanted to see him, like she expected him to drive up beside her (in Mikey's red truck?) and roll down his window and say, Hop in, kid!

No! She didn't want that.

The world closed around her like a lid snapping shut.

She could be in two places at once, here and there, and there was as vivid as here, before as vivid as now. Francie saw Dad open the bathroom door, white light shining out, it was the middle of the night, she had to pee. He was so awake, was it morning? Was Mom asleep in their bedroom, or was she at work? Dad stepped out of the bathroom and past where Francie stood in the dark hall wearing a t-shirt as a nightgown, down to her knees. He walked to the front door, wrenched it open and slammed it shut, slammed it, and it crashed and swung open, and he crashed it again, again, till it was broken. Slamming it till he was gone. His boots had left black marks on the linoleum floor in the bathroom. Mom wouldn't like that. Mom must be at work, not here, if she was here, she would get up, she would go check on Sam, he'd started to cry, woken by the sound of the door crashing. Francie still had to pee. She felt grit under her bare feet as she moved like a sleepwalker to the broken door and saw Dad backing his car down the driveway, very fast, window rolled down even though the night air was cold. He was still wearing the blue jacket unzipped over the white t-shirt, like he'd slept in his clothes, or hadn't slept at all. Sam was screaming. Francie had to pee. The door wouldn't close.

Slowly, the world opened again. Slowly like a lid lifting, and Francie was out in the open, exposed, breathing the real air all around her.

She could see someone jogging after her down the side-walk, a lady's voice calling out, "Hey honey, is everything okay? Shouldn't you be in school?"

Francie stopped and half turned, so the lady wouldn't see the gun.

She felt her feet plant themselves solidly on the ground. All in one breath, she said to the lady, who'd stopped too: "It's a half day at my school, so I'm going to my grandma's house for the afternoon."

"Oh good! As long as you're okay . . ." The lady took one step closer.

"Thank you for asking," said Francie, her feet holding the ground. "I'm fine."

Francie turned and walked for a few paces, her heart beat-ing, pounding, leaping till she couldn't stop herself. She was running, again. This time, the rule was that if she looked back, the woman would still be there. If she didn't, the woman would disappear. Rules were funny that way. They shifted and changed. Alice didn't always understand. But Francie did.

She did not look back.

She had a feeling that she was going to the woods.

The quickest way to get to the woods was past Alice's house. Straight ahead, and one more turn onto the street that had a pothole shaped like a mouth—*here*—cracked pavement, the sidewalks jumbled and broken. Francie slowed, turned down the little alleyway that ran in between backyards—a shortcut. She would go to the woods, she would get rid of the gun.

There was Alice's house. The back of it. The long yard and the scraggling apple trees and the falling-down deck, and the bright-yellow siding. Francie stopped. She knew Alice would still be at school. But Sally would be home.

Sally, who didn't believe in locks on doors.

Sally, who didn't have a real job.

Sally, who loved birds and dogs and cats and chickens and green shoots popping out of her garden patch, even if they were just weeds. "Isn't it WONDERFUL? Isn't it AMAZING? Isn't this a GIFT?" Sally loved June the best in June. She loved mornings the best in the morning. She loved bugs screeching at twilight the best at twilight. Sally loved everything the best.

But Sally didn't really like Francie, Francie knew.

Francie stood in the alley, looking at Alice's house. She was so close. She could climb over the crumbling stone wall and run through the weedy grass, slide the glass door at the back of the house that opened into the mud room, the kind of room that didn't exist in Francie's house. Fake wood on the walls. Freezing cold in winter. An extra fridge with drawers of crunchy apples and carrots, bottles that looked like pop but were full of homemade beer, a big bowl covered with a towel that might be full of cookie dough or sauerkraut. You just never knew.

There would be a cat sleeping on the broken rocking chair in the corner. Dust from the kitty litter box, and the smell of something softly rotting, rolled under a shelf and forgotten. If you got down on your hands and knees, a layer of fur matted the pink carpet. And Sally would be singing loudly as she marched up the basement stairs with a basket of wet laundry in her arms.

Sometimes, Sally seemed like a big kid herself, hair braided into pigtails, surrounded by her pets: cats, dogs, chickens, children.

If Sally found Francie hiding in the mud room, and Francie showed her the gun, what would happen?

Would Sally find it in her to love Francie the best?

The alley was narrow and shaded, with ruts in a double track. Tiny weeds grew through the gravel. A cat hopped onto the moss-covered wall and looked at Francie, like it had been sent to give her a message. One of Sally's cats, the black-and-orange tabby with fur that swirled across its sharp little face like a bandit's mask—not the nice one, one of the mean ones who scratched everyone, even Alice. Possum was its name.

Francie stretched out her hand to pet its soft little head.

Slash! The paw darted out faster than a flash, and Francie stared at the back of her left hand, cut with four fresh lines. She felt nothing, and all at once the raked lines got hot, and itchy. Tiny beads of red popped onto the skin.

She was this close, and this far, from safety.

The back door was sliding open, but Francie's feet were quicker than the rest of her, already running. She did not wait to see Diego the dog bolt across the deck and leap into the yard. She did not wait to hear him barking for Sally, who was surely coming out of the house behind him, exclaiming: What's all this fuss, Diego? What are you trying to tell me? What do you know that I don't?

TWO

Broken Door

Alice and Francie were climbing the tree in front of Alice's house. Its branches hung over the sidewalk and street and its leaves were newly enormous and shady and strong and green—partway through May, and it seemed like they might stay this way forever.

Francie wasn't talking.

Alice wanted to crush a leaf between her fingers. She could feel the feeling of the leaf mashed and torn against her skin. But that would be bad, because leaves were alive, they were life. Alice tried very hard not to step on ants, because ants were life, and she cried when her mom, Sally, swatted a housefly, because flies were life. What about grass, what about flowers picked and put into a jar, what about carrots, salad, bread? What was Alice supposed to eat? Life was very confusing.

The fat, fluttering leaf was within reach, tender and pliable, and Alice's fingers wanted to snap it right off! Why did her fingers want to do something her heart knew was bad?—Alice thought about how her heart knew things that the rest of her did not, and she wanted to ask Francie if Francie's heart was also full of confusing, true messages, but Francie had pulled away, into herself, one arm twisted around the tree's trunk, her cheek pressed to the bark.

Alice touched her own cheek to the bark, but it felt too scratchy. Francie's bare feet swung just above Alice's head. They'd tossed their socks on the grass below and their shoes inside the house, shedding layers. Shedding school. Shedding Alice's mom, Sally. Slipping free.

Francie was Alice's best friend and Alice was Francie's best friend. Both had messy hair tangled at the back, both wore jeans and t-shirts that smelled like laundry hung to dry on the line, but Alice had brownish skin and thick, wavy black hair, and Francie had pinkish skin and thin, scraggling brown hair. Dishwater blond, according to Francie's mom, Marietta, whose hair was the exact same colour.

Francie was older than Alice by three months. This mattered to them both, but it was better not to discuss it because it would only lead to an argument.

Francie's foot dangled near Alice's face, the big toenail split where Francie had stubbed it on an uneven chunk of sidewalk. A bit of blood. But that wasn't what was bothering Francie, Alice knew—Sally was bothering Francie. Maybe Francie had been bragging? Just a bit? But Alice might have bragged too, if Mrs. G, the choir director, had told her: "You sing like an angel." Such surprising words, sweet as sugar. It didn't seem like Francie was really talking to anyone as she'd repeated the words on their walk home from school, and again in Alice's kitchen, holding up Sally's silver mixing bowl for Alice to fill with snacks: "You sing like an angel."

"Who sings like an angel?" Sally demanded, coming into the kitchen. "Who said what about who?"

Francie muttered. She slumped.

"Don't mumble," said Sally. "Enunciate."

Alice was standing on the counter, the cupboard doors swung open, a bag of chocolate chips in one hand, pretzels in the other. The chocolate chips made a pinging sound as they hit the bottom of the mixing bowl. Alice rooted around for the multicoloured mini-marshmallows, and said, because she knew her mom wouldn't quit asking till she knew: "Francie got a solo in choir."

"Well aren't you quite something," Sally said to Francie. Sally wore woolly rainbow socks and Birkenstock sandals, she looked like a large, colourful raft. But Alice knew her mom was as likely to push people off to swim for themselves as to save them.

Alice poured the pretzels and marshmallows into the bowl. Francie held the bowl steady, staring straight ahead, not looking at Alice.

"Throw some almonds in there and it's almost healthy," said Sally. "It isn't good manners to repeat a compliment. But maybe you don't know that."

Francie's face flushed, but she didn't acknowledge Sally at all. Diego the dog—a scruffy wolfhound—snuffled around Francie's feet, his tail bashing against Francie's leg in a friendly way. *Smack, smack, smack.* Francie lifted the mixing bowl higher. Diego was a very big dog. Francie was scared of dogs, Alice knew, especially Diego. But this wasn't something they talked about because it would only end in argument.

Alice sprinkled the last of the marshmallows on the floor, and Diego took the bait.

"I wonder what an angel sounds like," said Sally.

"Mom!" Alice jumped off the counter and landed as hard as she could in her sock feet, rattling the old house to its rafters. She grabbed the silver mixing bowl and pulled Francie away, away from Diego, away from Sally, both of them harmless in their hearts, but greedy.

On the sidewalk, Alice stopped to stuff her pockets with treats from the mixing bowl. Francie was already climbing, as fast as she could go, her toe bloodied, but Alice took her time, she climbed more slowly, floating not scrambling.

The tree was like a lake in the sky.

You could climb into it, be held by it, it moved all around you, but separate from you.

"I'm sorry," Alice said to Francie's foot. She wasn't sorry about the toe, she was sorry about Sally. "Do you want some chocolate chips?" Alice stood on the branch and her hand met Francie's reaching down. The chocolate was warm from her pocket, melting on their fingers.

"I like how you sing!" Alice's voice came out scratchy. She felt defiant, unbreakable as a green twig.

Francie licked her palm, and hummed a low, growling note.

Footsteps below. The neighbour with two yappy dogs coming along the sidewalk, muttering to herself. The dogs went directly for the snack bowl, collars pinging against the metal, and from inside the house Diego began flinging himself against the front window, barking wolfishly. He could have swallowed both tiny dogs in one gulp. Was it wrong to imagine it? Well, maybe not, but it was wrong to *enjoy* imagining it. Alice couldn't stop herself grinning.

Down below, the smaller dog squeezed its haunches and the neighbour bent to pick up squiggles of poop, tying them into a small plastic bag.

"Oh my!" Her eyes traced the girls' path up the tree trunk and found their hiding spot. "I'll bet you can see the whole world from up there!" It was the kind of thing grown-ups said, like, Do you know how lucky you are, or, Enjoy this while it lasts, or, What I wouldn't give to be bored again. The woman chuckled even though nothing was funny. She yanked a sock from the mouth of one of the dogs and dropped it beside the snack bowl—one of Francie's socks with the little rainbow on it—and she warned them as she went: "Be careful now! Don't fall!"

"Go higher!" Alice felt fierce.

Climbing was easy, you just didn't think about it. Like floating.

Alice's thumbnail wanted to press into the tree's trunk, the bark was thinner here, newer. She wanted to push her nail into the tree's smooth grey skin and leave a cut like a crescent moon, but the tree was life. "The tree is a person!" she shouted, her voice thin as a breeze.

Francie had stopped climbing.

Alice wanted to go even higher, to the very tip of the top, but the branch under Francie's foot squeaked and creaked as the tree shifted and the girls' hair lifted in a squeal of wind, chilly. The sun disappeared, blanketed by clouds lowering over them.

Below, the front door opened, slammed shut.

"Alice!" Sally called. Sally didn't care if the neighbours heard. She bellowed a three-note melody—"*Eee-oh-eet!*"—to which Alice had been trained to respond, no matter the circumstances, "*Eeet-eeo!*"

Sally charged across the lawn and shouted up at them: "The Suzuki-Olsens are coming for dinner, I'm running to the store. You need to practise your violin, your sister is in charge. Her only job is to make you practise. Get down here now and practise before the Suzuki-Olsens come."

"Who are the Suzuki-Olsens?" Francie asked Alice. Alice knew that Francie was suspicious, jealous of anyone who might like Alice as much as Francie did.

"They're okay, but they only have boys," she said.

Climbing down was easy for Alice, but Francie always got dizzy.

"Don't look down," Alice reminded her, but Francie said she had to, to see where to step, and Alice knew this could turn into an argument, so she didn't say anything more.

At the lowest branch, Alice swung round, let go, and landed in a crouch, her hair falling softly around her face. She pushed it out of her eyes and looked up at Francie, toes and fingers gripping the trunk, digging in. Francie slithered down and arrived at the lowest branch.

"My dad is sick," Francie said. Her voice came out booming and crackly, as if projected through the loudspeakers at school. She collapsed flat onto her belly on the branch and hugged it tight. "He had to leave in the middle of the night. Maybe he's sick. Or maybe he's not."

Alice was a bit afraid of Francie's dad. This could be part of a game, or it could be real, Alice never knew with Francie. She didn't ask any follow-up questions.

"Jump," Alice said, feeling calm. Francie closed her eyes. Everything was very still for a moment, like Francie might stay like this forever, and then she tilted and rolled, her hands locked around the branch. She swung for a split second in the air, her body jerking into a vertical line before the weight on her hands yanked them apart and she fell.

Alice bent down over Francie, who had landed in the silver mixing bowl. The remains of the snack spilled across the grass. When Francie sat up, Alice picked a crushed pretzel out of her hair, and ate it.

⁓

Kate was drawing loops in her journal, writing the same name over and over again. *Emma.* She sucked on a strand of hair and idly twirled it on her finger. No big thoughts arose.

Diego was sleeping across her legs, twitching like he was starring in some heroic dog dream. Kate liked the feeling of his weight on her, pinning her down, his warm smelly dog breath, but that wasn't a big thought she wanted to keep. They were on the "good couch," the one Diego wasn't supposed to sleep on, but Mom was out, and besides, rules in this house were loosely enforced: rules about chores, rules about hygiene, rules about curfews and bedtime and keeping your room clean. Arbitrary. Totally unfair, totally dependent on Mom's mood.

Stacked beside Kate were her biology textbook and binder, a pocket book of sudoku puzzles, and her pencil case, in which were stored a series of small folded notes from a boy she liked but not like that. Peter. He was one of the boys in grade nine who hadn't started growing yet, he was actually shorter even than Kate, which was maybe what she liked about him. Also he made her laugh. Also he wasn't hairy and loud and dripping with body spray and arguing for her attention and the attention of other girls in classes where Kate actually needed to focus or else she'd get lost.

Kate hated being lost.

She liked being the expert. She didn't mind telling someone else what to do, how to do it, explaining, knowing all. She and Peter were in a constant battle for supremacy, another reason she liked him, not liked-him liked him, just liked him. Like, he was funny. He *got* her. Why did it have to be weird?

She wrote: *Who am I and what am I doing here?* then slammed the journal shut and shoved it under the biology textbook.

Kate's sister Alice and her friend were coming inside and Kate was supposed to be in charge. She could hear her sister's little friend whispering excitedly, which annoyed her for no reason, and the annoyance of being annoyed was extra annoying! Kate stabbed at the back of her hand with the pen and began drawing loops across the bumpy bones. Blue ink. Black would look better.

Maybe I should get a tattoo.

"We could live in a tree, for real," she heard the friend whisper, and Alice said, "What about the bathroom? Where would we go to the bathroom?"

Okay, so Kate's little sister was weirdly obsessed with bathrooms.

The girls came into the living room, Alice still going on about bathrooms: "I wonder why there's no bathrooms in books."

"'Cause no one wants to read about it, that's why," Kate said. The blue loops on the back of her hand had turned into letters, *Emma*, so she began covering them over with flowers.

Alice paused in thought. "They also never tell in books what happens when kids lose their teeth."

"I saw the fairy again," Kate said, adding: "Not the tooth fairy." She doodled a vine that looked like it was strangling the flowers, which was not what she was going for. Ugh.

"Where? For real?" Alice was so excited, Kate almost felt bad. Almost.

"Backyard."

Alice frowned, puzzled. No, disbelieving. Skeptical. *We're getting too old for this*, Kate thought, but she couldn't help herself. She both did and didn't want to be too old for this.

"We looked there lots," Alice said sternly.

"We found the egg, remember? The tiny little egg!" That was Francie, the annoying friend, whispering again! Standing behind Alice like she was hiding from Kate. Kate didn't know why this irritated her so much. She started adding spiky leaves to the vine, and thorns. From upstairs came a loud whooping and thumping: Max and his friends, playing video games. Their family didn't have a television, because Mom wanted them to read books instead, but they had two different gaming consoles, and a Game Boy, and a powerful desktop in the corner of the living room; Dad would sometimes sit there all night, lit by the blue glow, with his headphones on, playing with his friends like a giant teenager. It was the only time he was loud, swearing and laughing in Spanish. The rest of the time, Mom did the talking. This was what Kate's family was like: boring, she thought. It was like they were all playing roles assigned to them by . . . well, like, by society, or something. She thought about writing this in her journal. A big thought? Kate had about ten to twelve big thoughts daily. Peter was the recipient of some of her big thoughts, neatly looped in handwriting on a scrap of paper she'd pass to him in class, and he'd write back with his own big thought, or crushing diss.

"The egg! The egg!" Francie kept whispering.

"What egg?" Kate looked up from the back of her hand. The drawing was a legit mess. Well, she wasn't an artist, per se. *Not my strength.*

What is your strength? Peter was asking inside Kate's head.

Francie burst out: "The fairy egg! It had a blue shell and it was broken on the ground."

"Okay, so here's the thing," said Kate. "Fairies don't lay eggs." Immediately, she regretted her tone, she regretted crushing the kid's hopes, she felt bad. She didn't like feeling bad. Ugh!

Alice pointed at Kate's hand. "What's that?"

"It's a tattoo," said Kate. "Aren't you supposed to practise your violin or something?"

"First, Francie has to practise her choir solo," Alice said.

"Oh yeah? What's the song?"

"'Wade in the Water,'" Francie said, in an unexpectedly loud voice.

"Yeah, I know that song."

"Can you help?" asked Alice.

Sigh. Other people didn't have little sisters and little brothers with little annoying friends. Other people weren't left in charge of said irritants. Other people weren't expected to be polite and tolerant when their little sisters started ordering them around—"Mom said you had to help!"—not that Kate minded all that much when Alice got up on her high horse, like their mother would say. It was kind of funny seeing Alice try to boss someone around.

Actually, she was pretty good at it.

Because you weren't expecting it from her. It was like taking orders from a mouse.

"What kind of help?" Kate reached for the biology textbook but grabbed the sudoku puzzles instead.

"Sing the chorus. Like the choir."

Mmmm. "And what are you going to do?"

Alice opened her violin case. Francie crowded in behind Alice, looking equal parts frightened and excited, and Kate felt renewed optimism about the way the afternoon was going. Alice snapped a sponge onto the underside of her violin with a rubber band and ran her bow across the strings. It made a weirdly appealing sound that prickled the hair on Kate's head.

"Sing the first line," Kate ordered Francie. After all, she was in charge. *That's my strength.* "Sing. Go on."

Now, Kate listened. She listened as she scanned for patterns in the sudoku boxes and thought about the way Emma had come into drama class today with part of her hair dyed pink.

Alice and Francie were trying their best to get it together. The violin sounded okay and Francie's voice sounded okay, but they couldn't find their rhythm.

"It's kind of a hard song," said Kate. "Try clapping or something."

"You're not even singing! You're supposed to sing the chorus!"

Kate said, "Actually I'm in charge, not you."

"Sing!" Alice's voice got very squeaky when she was upset.

Kate couldn't focus on the scanning of the numbers in boxes. She grabbed the journal and read her most recent big thought: *Who am I and what am I doing here?* Ugh. She began covering over the words with more of those spiky flowers, the only kind she seemed to know how to draw.

"*Wade in the water! Wade in the water children!*" That sounded better.

The boys' feet came slithering and stuttering down the stairs, voices trampling over each other, sounding more like a crowd than three twelve-year-old boys.

And I'm in charge!

Passing through the living room, one of the boys (not Max) burst into a mocking falsetto, and Kate burned him with her glare. She felt suddenly protective, but Francie and Alice didn't seem to notice, they were deep into the song, really going for it now. They didn't need Kate. They didn't need anyone. Lucky them. That was a nice feeling, Kate knew.

In the kitchen, Max slammed a cupboard door. "Who ate all the marshmallows?"

"*See that girl all dressed in red?*" Francie sang.

"*Who's gonna trouble the water?*" Kate sang in reply— without even thinking!

"*She must be scared, but she never said!*" Francie sang.

Yeah, those weren't the lyrics.

It was the kind of song that could go on and on, it didn't want to stop. Its end kept jumping back to its beginning. Kate's dad, David, came shuffling into the living room, on his way from bedroom to kitchen. He'd been here in the house all along—note: not in charge!—here yet not here, his most likely location when he wasn't on campus to lecture or to attend committee meetings. He had a little office set-up in the master bedroom, but who knew what he did in there. Probably, mostly, napped?

It used to be believed that mathematical genius peaked before the age of thirty, Sally liked to say, but David is forty-two and he still hasn't peaked!

She said it so often, Kate wasn't sure whether it was meant to be a joke of some kind, a punchline, or whether she was dead serious, a true believer. Sally was a difficult person to pin down. Kate had everyone figured out except her mother—but she wasn't interested in figuring out her mother, she just wanted to ensure she didn't *become* her. By accident. Apparently this happened. You had to watch out.

"David needs a safe place to retreat to. Sometimes his

brain just shuts down," Sally would say, as if he wasn't even in the room. Honestly, it was kind of messed up, wasn't it?

Kate's dad patted Diego's head absently as he passed by, not registering that the dog was on the good couch. Soon he was back with a glass of orange soda. He stood and listened to the girls, tapping time with one foot. He was wearing white sweat socks and soccer shorts.

The song was beginning to fade. Kate didn't bother joining in on the last chorus.

"*See that boy all dressed in blue? . . . He can't swim, what can he do!*"

"Ummmmm . . ." Kate's dad cleared his throat.

Francie trailed off, the violin trailed off.

"I like it," said David, "but I think that I might not have heard all the words correctly."

"Francie makes up her own words sometimes," Alice explained.

"I see, I see."

"For the concert, I'll sing the real words," said Francie.

"Do you know the real words?" Kate wondered, but Francie didn't answer. There was no way she knew the real words.

"I have to go home." Francie sounded breathless.

Kate didn't say what she could have said then, that they'd sounded pretty good, that they'd gotten it together, that the kid had an interesting voice. It wasn't pretty and it wasn't even exactly in tune, but it was *different*. It was *unlikely*. You'd remember its weirdness. "You're supposed to practise your own songs, actually," Kate told Alice.

"Who left my mixing bowl on the sidewalk?" Here came Sally, bursting through the front door. "Someone come give me a hand with these groceries!"

Francie ran to help. Weird kid.

Kate's dad wandered toward the front hall, but turned instead to go into the bedroom. The door shut quietly, so he was thinking about that, about making his escape. Kate gave Diego a quick shove off the good couch, and he looked at her with sad eyes. Betrayal. "Life's hard, dumbo."

Francie staggered by carrying a couple of grocery bags that looked like they might snap her arms off, and Kate said to Alice again: "You're supposed to practise your own songs."

Somehow, Alice managed to ignore Kate *and* follow her instructions. She started with scales, which made her sound dutiful and obedient. And got her off the hook for whatever Sally had planned for them.

"Kate!" Too late. "Help Francie put things away. She doesn't know what she's doing!"

"The bags are too heavy," said Francie, standing in the kitchen.

"Well, you made it this far," Sally told her.

Kate didn't think her mother knew that Francie wanted to cry just then. But how did Kate know? Kate knew, she just knew. Feelings swirled in the air and Kate caught them, whether she wanted to or not, and she had to decide: hold on or let go?

Could she use them for something powerful? Was this a thought on the cusp of becoming big?

"Move!" Sally waved her arms at Max and his friends, who were sitting on the wide windowsill at the end of the table, finishing the bag of pretzels. "You can't stay for supper," Sally announced in a general way. "We're having guests. They're very strange, the husband works with David and the wife writes poetry." Sally clapped her hands. "They're vege-tarians, so I'm making fish!"

"Ummmm, Mom . . ." But Kate didn't bother finishing.

She slid her journal into the pages of the biology text-book and picked up the textbook, her pencil case, the other things, and zipped them into her backpack, which she'd tripped over when standing up.

Diego was nosing inside the bags Francie had dropped on the floor, while Francie waved a bunch of kale at him, weakly; and Kate decided she liked the kid alright. Little weirdo.

Diego had found the fish.

"Get out of here!" Sally grabbed for the bag and shouted, probably at Diego, but if Kate were a kid, like Francie, would she know Sally's shouts weren't meant for her? It seemed like a long time since Kate had been a kid.

This could have been Kate's moment to drift away, but Sally sensed the silent gliding. "You, wash the kale."

Francie held it out to her, its leaves thick, black-green, ribbed and veined like the leaves of a tropical tree. It looked inedible. Kate was surprised when Francie met her eyes. The kid's feelings came rushing at her, an ambush of feelings.

Did this kid hate her? That wasn't fair. What did this kid want?

"Got it." Kate grabbed the kale. The kid was still looking at her.

"There are fairies that lay eggs," said the kid.

"There are?" Kate was caught off balance.

"Yeah," said the kid, "there are fairies that lay tiny little blue eggs."

"Right. Okay."

The problem with feelings was that sometimes they ran the other way. Sometimes they poured from you into someone else, and you couldn't stop it from happening. It was like the kid was daring Kate to hurt her, to be cruel, to tell her not to believe whatever it was she wanted to believe. This wasn't about fairies laying eggs. It was about who got to tell you what you were allowed to believe, to feel, to do, to be. Now that was a big thought.

The kid was leaving now, and Kate let herself feel what she was feeling, her own feelings bouncing back at her, off the kid, pouring into her bloodstream like a torrent of confusion and vigour and *caring*.

Dammit!

Kate felt the heat of everything she was feeling rush through her. It rushed through like a storm, possessed her. The kid was tying her shoes in the front hall, and Kate held the kale like a sword and pointed it at her mother. "You, on guard!"

⤫

Luce was on the couch. Marietta couldn't see him, but she knew he was there.

"Hello?" she called, pushing through the side door. She was lugging a cloth bag of groceries, fresh off the bus, pulling Sam in the umbrella stroller up over the threshold. "Hey, I could really use a hand here!"

Her uniform reeked of spilled chicken noodle soup slopped down its front. "We don't pay for laundering," the daytime supervisor told her, as if Marietta had requested a special favour. "It's in your contract."

Marietta couldn't remember signing any contract. She was fairly certain, however, that she didn't have a clean uniform waiting for her at home, it was trickier to get to the laundromat with these random night shifts at the new place.

The landlord had promised them a washer and dryer when they'd moved in, years ago. Marietta would settle for a washer, forget the dryer, she already hauled home the wet clothes to hang on the line. Hell, she thought, I'd settle for an old-fashioned hand-operated wringer. She remembered, all in a useless flash, that those machines were called mangles. A mangle. Why did she have to keep every last detail? *Empty it, empty it, empty it out.*

Mangle reminded her of the front door. Another meaning of the word. Mangled. Broken, wrecked, fucked. She'd found it like that yesterday morning when she got home from her night shift: the door hanging oddly on its hinges when she'd pushed it open, and no matter how she'd rattled the handle and muscled against it, it wouldn't close. While she was standing there in the front room, trying to make sense of it, Luce had come in the side door carrying a cup of takeout coffee, promising he'd fix it.

"But what happened? What happened to the door? Why were you out? Did you leave the kids here alone?"

"Just for a minute," Luce promised.

Luce promised.

"Should've picked up a coffee for you too," he said, and he poured half into a cup for her, and they sat at the table and he told her again about this project he was working on with Mikey, it was going to be big, and Marietta couldn't believe it, she couldn't believe him!

"This has to stop, Luce, this needs to end, you have to be real with me."

Luce hadn't said he was in any kind of trouble, but he never would. As long as his car was running, he thought the world would keep spinning in whatever direction he pleased.

She knew he was home now.

"Luce!" Marietta hated hollering, hated how it hurt her throat and her head. How it vibrated through every nerve in her body, rattling her to the core.

Sam began to cry. "It's not you," she told him, thinking, Breathe, just breathe.

She moved her foot and the side door swung shut, bumping her hip as she bent to unstrap Sam. He didn't nurse anymore. She had to quit breastfeeding when she took the night job, lining her bra with cabbage leaves to dry up the milk: a waft reminiscent of cabbage rolls pouring forth when she removed her bra after a long shift. She had to stop herself telling the old men what she had in there as she tended to their nighttime needs. Like a dirty joke, maybe they would have appreciated it; did she really want to know?

Sam was almost a year; still, Marietta felt she'd cheated him, or, perversely, he'd cheated her by letting go so easily. By not seeming to mind. By forgetting how he'd needed her. Francie was two and a half when she'd weaned, not that it made a difference, Marietta thought, sitting on the bottom step of the abbreviated staircase that led to the kitchen. She pushed off the flimsy canvas tennis shoes, her feet hurt—

Everything you are saying to yourself right now is negative! Stop complaining! Attitude of gratitude! She hated that phrase, superficial, fake . . . But she tried, she spoke out loud, quietly, gritting her teeth: "I'm thankful for . . . all of this . . ." She thought she heard a stirring from the front room, maybe Luce could hear her whispers louder than her shouts.

She knew he was here.

His car was parked in the driveway, and he never walked any distance anymore, not since the accident. They were coming up on a year now. What changed him wasn't the physical injury so much as how it all messed with his head.

Early on, she'd tried to help him bathe. He was in pain, naked on a stool in the shower, pretending nothing hurt. "I'm practically a nurse, this is nothing to be ashamed of," she told him. Just saying the word, *ashamed*, naming it, she shouldn't have.

"Too late," she whispered now.

She pulled Sam into her lap and unbuttoned his jacket—the babysitter had put it on wrong, skipping a button, he looked lopsided. He looked neglected. His cheeks and chin were dirty. The babysitter had several new kids today, crowding around underfoot, older than Sam; she wasn't licensed. But she had her first aid, Marietta asked to see the certificate. Marietta wasn't a thoughtless mother.

If you have to tell yourself that, it means you probably are!

Luce came into the kitchen and silently moved the cloth bag of groceries from the floor to the table.

"Where's Francie?" said Marietta.

He didn't know. He didn't even know what time of day it was, she could see it in his eyes.

"What happened to the door?" She couldn't help herself, repeating all the wrong questions.

He wasn't going to answer her.

"Did you fix it? Did you call the landlord?"

"I'm not calling the landlord, okay."

This was home, this one-storey postwar cottage built on a little rise of a hill above a busy four-lane street. It had probably been a quaint two-lane road when the house was first built, but now the street hummed with the steady flow of traffic, worst at commuting hours. The number seven bus stopped directly in front of their house. Strangers waited there on the sidewalk, all day long and into the night, dropping their glowing cigarettes, rocking their strollers, talking on their phones.

They'd moved into the house a few years ago. It was their first home that was a house. That spring, Luce dug up a sapling from his mother's property, wrapped its roots in burlap, and drove it here in the trunk of his car. He planted it in the front yard, didn't ask the landlord for permission.

The tree didn't make it.

The next spring, Luce tried again. Again, the little scrap of branches and twigs and fragile green leaves withered and yellowed and died.

Luce had been waiting on these two dead trees to grow suckers off their roots ever since. A dead tree wasn't really dead, he said. Sometime this spring, like every spring, Luce would grab Marietta and drag her out there to show her the sprouts of tender green growing out of those two dead trunks. What was she supposed to say?

"Change Sam's diaper, he's soaked."

Marietta handed Luce the baby, began unpacking items from the cloth bag, started sweeping the linoleum. She was thinking how Luce used to be able to pick her up, lift her right off the ground, not just when they were wanting each other but those other times when she was weeping and needing him to hold her—

Stop it, already. Don't make it worse.

In high school, Luce was a runner, eating up the miles in cross-country, his long legs loping, looking for all the world like this was easy for him. It was never easy for Marietta. She ran after him, after him, after him.

You can't tell another person how to be. But what about yourself?

"Changed," said Luce, coming back into the kitchen holding Sam, who was dressed in a different t-shirt. Luce leaned down to kiss Marietta's neck and Marietta sighed and turned toward him, not away.

"You smell funny," he said.

Marietta remembered the spoiled uniform and the other one that might not be clean, and that she had a shift tomorrow morning.

She pushed him away. "I have to make dinner. Take Sam outside. I don't think he gets enough fresh air at the sitter's."

She didn't ask: What did you do all day? She had her own secrets—or just the one, *and not what you'd think, Luce, not what you'd guess, if you noticed and thought and guessed anything about me at all.* She hadn't been to the bathroom since her break at two o'clock, yet she'd made time for a stop between work and picking up groceries; she'd let Sam stew in his juices at the babysitter's, just so she, Marietta, could hunt for a breath of calm in a room at the library full of other women with their eyes closed, chanting words in a language none of them understood, all of them hunting for themselves, for a scrap of themselves that still belonged to them alone. Could it be innocent when it felt so illicit?

Now, catching herself in the bathroom mirror, Marietta laughed. *You've been out in public like this! Don't look! Don't look at the fright queen!* She wanted to close her eyes and stay here, feeling the water warm against her hands, her forehead resting on the mirror, leaving a greasy print, she saw, when she drew away. That would never do.

Marietta spritzed the glass with a homemade solution of vinegar and water that she kept under the sink, and she wiped the mirror clean.

The clock on the stove read 6:07. Francie should be home by now. Marietta could call over to ask Sally if Francie was there, where Marietta knew she would be, she always was, but something in her resisted. She didn't need the judgment, thanks very much.

It's not like they were friends, she and Sally. It's not like Marietta told Sally things, and the things Sally told Marietta were the things she told everybody.

Marietta used to tell Mikey things. He listened, she missed him in their lives. She could have told Mikey about the door, for example. But not Sally. Definitely not her mother, who'd escaped with her third husband to Florida. Maybe Luce's mother. No. Better not.

Marietta scrubbed potatoes in the sink, leaving the peels on.

She was drying her hands when she heard Francie's raucous voice coming from the backyard. That girl had a pair of lungs on her. A good feeling, a lightness came into the day: everyone home!

Marietta turned the burner on high and walked to Francie and Sam's room. She pulled the slatted blind by its string, latching it open, so she could watch them play in the tidy backyard. There were things Marietta had that Sally did not: a tidy yard, a clean house. Marietta was certain that Sally had never gotten on her hands and knees to scrub the kitchen floor, let alone washed the walls, the baseboards, the handles of cupboards, cupboard doors, pulled everything out and repapered the shelves.

Marietta watched her children play.

Francie trotted a loop around the grass with Sam on her back, while Luce pretended to time them. Really, he was just staring at his phone. He sat on the top of the picnic table, scavenged from a neighbour's trash and carried home between the two of them, Luce and Marietta. After Francie was born. Long before the accident. Between pregnancies. She'd been pregnant a few times, two live births, plus the other times (Luce lifting her off the ground, holding her; strong).

I'm done, the words came into her head. She was thirty-two. Old enough to be done.

I need to get rid of that picnic table before Luce breaks it, she thought, picturing herself dragging it down the drive-way and leaving it on the curb where some other pair, even less lucky than the two of them, might spot value in the rotten wood and carry it off.

What would she put in its place?

What did the yard require?

No, the question was bigger and more desperate: What did her family require, what could she, Marietta, give to her family that would save them from this spiral into which they were being pulled, in slow motion, day by day drawn deeper into its centre, which she sensed was an abyss? They would be swallowed whole. Unless she, Marietta, could stop their descent.

She needed to make something. Do something. Fill the void where the rotten picnic table, once sturdy, no longer belonged, it was sending out all the wrong messages.

Whatever replaced it, Marietta would need to make it from scratch.

She needed to think.

She stood in her children's room feeling stern and deter-mined. Anything was possible! The feeling was familiar, it had been visiting her since childhood, always with hope that dwindled by invisible degrees only to be kindled anew like a little match being struck behind her eyes.

She felt it now, the spark of a tiny flame.

Marietta stepped out of her pants, pulled her top over her head, and with her uniform held lightly between her fingers stood in the quiet little house, looking at her family framed in the window outside. No picture could be sweeter, or more deceptive.

Did everyone feel like this? This powerful, this alone?

She heard a splash from the kitchen and a hissing that didn't stop. *Oh shit, the potatoes!*

The potatoes were boiling over.

⚞

Sam could hear Mom's music, her voice chanting, when Francie carried him into the warm house on her back. Sam went quiet, listening for Mom. The kitchen was darker than outside. Francie's fingers were cool on his ankles as she tried to yank off his slippers, little leather booties with holes worn in them by another baby's toes. Sam squirmed away from his sister. Dad came in behind them, smelling like fresh spring air.

Sam was fast. But Francie was faster.

She grabbed him and hauled him down to the bottom of the stairs. His slippers were covered with grass and dirt. Sam fought back. He gripped clumps of his sister's hair and pulled till tears squeezed from her eyes and she let go of him.

Dad got ahead, up the stairs. Still wearing his boots. Saying Mom's name.

Sam climbed, knee up, hands pushing, but his sister grabbed his foot, again. He kicked, again. This time she got the slipper off. He screamed. She yanked off the other and threw them by the door.

Sam crested the last step, zipped across the bumpy linoleum. Grass, dirt. Stuff. Francie was clattering plates and
forks to the table and Sam dodged her feet. Mom came out
from her room carrying fire in her hand. Sam sat down on
his bottom. He smelled the heat, the wax, the sulphur as
Mom set the fat yellow candle on the table. Now he couldn't
see it. He could hear Mom's music spilling from her open
bedroom door, spooky silver voices singing the song that
never ended.

Mom wore soft pants that Sam tried to grab. Her feet
were bare.

Sam listened to Mom's voice. Sometimes Mom was a
long way away behind her eyes and her voice came quietly
from wherever she was, and sometimes she was very here,
too much here, and her voice shot high and fast.

Which mom was this mom?

"Wash your hands."

Sam looked at his hands, he turned them in front
of his face.

Francie had something she wanted to tell Mom, she was
following her very close and her voice was very loud, but
Mom was pouring steamy water from a pot into the sink,
she was mashing, her elbow jumping up and down, she was
slamming the fridge door.

Sam clapped his hands.

Mom bent down to look. He reached up, up, up, he
tried to tell her.

"Wash his hands!" Louder voice. Full eyes. *Rat-tat-tat.*

Francie picked Sam up and he pinched her cheeks, hard.
Alone in the bathroom, Francie slapped his hands and Sam
started to cry, but she held him pressed between her body
and the cold hard sink, and she turned on the tap and let

him play in the cold water flowing out, *splash, splash!* She slicked his hair down with her fingers and lifted him up so he could see himself in the mirror.

When she turned off the water, Sam heard the sound of Mom's voice grinding away. In the mirror, Sam looked at Francie and Francie looked at Sam. Quietly, she set him down on the floor and dried them both off, and then she tried to dry the floor and the wall too. They were waiting for something to change.

Francie sang a bit of her song for him, very quietly. The same song she was singing in the backyard, when they were playing. The same song she was trying to tell Mom about in the kitchen.

Sam sat very still, listening. Listening. Till something changed.

"Supper!"

Francie opened the bathroom door and Sam crawled ahead of her. There was nothing soft about Mom, except for her voice, sometimes. Mom was made of pointy parts, not like Renee, who babysat Sam during the day. Renee was soft all over. But he was used to Mom's elbows, her chin, her knees, her ribs, he wanted them close, stabbing into him. It didn't hurt. But before Sam got to Mom in the kitchen, Dad caught him and picked him up, and tied him into the wooden high chair using a red woolly scarf. It scratched Sam's tummy where his shirt rode up over his belly, and he yelled and hammered his fists on the tray.

Mom scooped soft potatoes from the pot on the table. She walked with each plate to the stove and ladled hamburger gravy on top. The gravy had peas in it. Mom filled Sam's bowl last. His belly itched, but the tray blocked it from reach. He threw his head back and howled, feeling hot.

Mom sat on the chair beside him. "Sam," she said. She held out his spoon. Sam threw the spoon on the floor. Mom picked it up, wiped it on a napkin, set it back on the tray. Sam threw it down. Mom picked it up. She said, "This floor is already filthy, and I just swept it!"

Sam threw the spoon. Mom picked it up.

"For Christ's sake, he's just going to keep doing that, Mari."

"I'm not giving you your spoon till you stop throwing it," Mom said to Sam. She set the spoon on his tray. Sam looked at everyone looking at him and he knew exactly what to do.

He threw the spoon on the ground.

"Enough." Dad kicked the spoon across the kitchen. It clattered against the electric radiator that ran along the baseboard under the window. Sam had burned his hands on it in the winter, but only once. He didn't remember, only that he had an aversion to that part of the kitchen.

Mom took bites from her food.

Sam stuck his fists into his bowl and rubbed the food in his hair.

Mom put her face in her hands. Crying?

Francie stood up. She pushed her chair back and it crashed to the floor. "Ooo!" Sam wiggled against the woolly scarf. Mom's face was surprised. Not crying. Francie set the chair upright and climbed onto it, she stood on the seat. "Ooo!" Sam clapped and clapped. The potatoes squeezed through his fingers. Francie was singing the song again. Sam was singing too. He had two teeth on top at the front of his mouth and his tongue mashed against them.

Francie was loud and she sounded angry. Sam was louder.

Francie stopped. She stepped down off the chair and she sat and stared at her plate of food. Mostly gone. Sam stuffed his fist into his mouth and sucked off the potatoes. He stuck his fist into his bowl, sucked it.

Mom stood up. "Does anyone want seconds?"

Dad started wiping Sam's head with a paper napkin.

"Seconds, anyone?"

Dad wiped Sam's face.

"Am I talking to myself?" said Mom. Which mom was this mom?

"It was fine, Mari," said Dad.

"Everything's going to shit around here," said Mom. She picked up Sam's spoon from where it had stopped under the radiator. Dad untied the red scarf. He lifted Sam out of the chair. Clumps of potato plopped off Sam and onto the floor.

"Everything's going to shit," Mom said. Her voice was very, very quiet. But her eyes were very, very here. Sam looked at her and he didn't know what she was feeling, and he did not like that. He kicked and fishtailed as Dad carried him away from Mom to the bathroom.

Dad set Sam into the bathtub. He turned on the water and it came down on Sam like rain from up above, freezing cold and spraying them both. Dad jumped back and roared, "SHIT!" Dad left. It was Francie who came to see what was happening, Francie who turned off the taps. Mom followed behind Francie, she stood in the doorway of the bathroom and said, "Don't worry, this isn't about you, nothing is about you, don't worry."

Sam stretched out his arms, but Mom didn't see him. She wasn't in the doorway anymore.

Francie saw him.

She put the plug in and turned the water on, and it came out from the right spot. Warm water. Sam grabbed her face as she leaned over him with a washcloth. He pinched her. He didn't know why. He didn't know what was inside him, but it roared, it was itchy, it hurt.

His sister pinched him back.

That made sense, it made everything make sense, somehow.

THREE

Gun Run

Francie could hear Diego the dog barking as her legs kicked into high gear, maximum output, pedal to the metal, like Dad said when he floored it to zoom around a minivan or sedan going too slowly on a country road. "Lousy lady drivers!" he always said, even when the driver they passed wasn't.

It was true that driving with Grandma Irene was not the same as driving with Dad. Mom never drove, she didn't know how. Sally was another lady driver who Francie had driven with.

Francie didn't know why her brain was listing these facts exactly, only that it felt necessary, it had got her to the end of the alley, and now she just had to cross the street to get to the woods. Alice and Francie never crossed here, they walked down two blocks to the crosswalk because Alice's sister, Kate, told Alice that cops arrested people for jaywalking. Kate didn't always tell the truth, Francie knew, but Alice believed Kate almost all the time. It was something they argued about.

The cars kept coming, but Francie didn't have time to walk down the sidewalk and push the button and wait for the crosswalk!

A lot of things were going wrong.

The cars. The dog, barking. And when she glanced over her shoulder, fully expecting to see Diego and his big dripping mouth running after her down the alley—she saw Sally.

Never look back. Never never never.

Click, click, the picture of a cop car snapped into her brain, too late, Francie was already in the street, bolting between cars, sneakers jumping the curb, slapping the sidewalk, carrying her directly into the thicket of trees on the other side. Whatever was behind her was behind her: barking dog, hollering woman, the blip-blip of a siren, flashing lights.

If it's help you want, never trust a cop: Dad.

If it's help you want, never trust your dad, she heard clearly, as if Dad were inside her head, laughing at twisting his own words into a joke.

Francie ran, pushing through the messy brush on the other side of the street. If you walked down the sidewalk and crossed at the crosswalk, there was a paved path into the park, and you could follow it to get to the woods. Here, there was no path—just a wall of scraggly trees, and messy undergrowth, vines and dead leaves and brambles and slapping branches that grabbed for Francie's hair and scratched her face. Tiny burrs stuck to her favourite shirt and she couldn't brush them off. She was hot and sweaty and moving as fast as she could, which wasn't fast enough. Her sneaker caught on a root and the sole ripped right open.

She was pretty sure these trees belonged to the woods in the middle of the park, where she and Alice liked to play, but nothing looked familiar.

You're a horse. No one can catch you, you'll never be broken.

Grandma Irene had a prayer she prayed a lot, out loud, and Francie heard it now. It began: *Our Father who are in Heaven. Hollow be thy name. Thy kingdom come. Thy will be done. On Earth as it is in Heaven.*

What came after Heaven? Bread?

Francie couldn't remember how the words all fit together, even though Grandma Irene had been trying to teach her, urging her to memorize it: "This is something you can use any time, whenever you need it." Why would you need it? What would you need it for? Francie hadn't asked Grandma these questions.

The words started over again in her head: *Our Father who are in Heaven.*

But who was that? Our Father? Father. Like a dad. Dad.

Francie was very thirsty. She sank into a crouch in a patch of something that looked like ivy, hopefully not the poison kind, because it was too late, she'd already touched it.

Here was the gun, stuck in her hand. She looked at it. Black. Scuffed, not shiny. It looked almost like a toy. Like if it was pointed at you and went bang, you'd only pretend to be dead. But you wouldn't be dead. You'd fall down like you were dead and your eyes would be open and looking up and just pretending.

Here. Take it and go.

Francie felt a rush of panic, the way the gun was stuck to her hand, like it belonged to her now.

Dad would say—Take a deep breath, kid. Don't worry so much, it's the worry that'll kill you.

Francie could hear him saying it.

We're not going to sit here all morning waiting for some cop to come and help us, Dad was saying. Francie could see him, climbing out of the Caddy, steam rising from under its hood. They were on their way to Grandma Irene's, just the two of them, they were out in the country, somewhere Mom called "the middle of nowhere." Dad opened Francie's door and she slid out of the car and landed hard on her tailbone. That's how steep the angle was, where Dad had stopped in the gravel, like the whole car might slide down into the ditch.

"What are you so scared about?" Dad said. "Take a deep breath, kid. Don't worry so much."

The car door hung open, but Francie wasn't strong enough to push it closed. Dad was headed down into the ditch. She followed, heavy grasses soaking her jeans. A crooked stream of water flowed along the bottom of the ditch—"Isn't this something else," Dad said. He took one big step across with his long legs, and reached back for Francie.

"Give me your hands."

He swung Francie up and over the trickle of water. His limp hardly showed at all as he climbed the little hill. They walked right up to a line of cedars planted as a windbreak to protect the big green field beyond, a lush carpet of fresh green. "Winter wheat," Dad said, telling her about the windbreak, about how the farmers planted this crop in the fall so it came up before everything else. She noticed he was breathing hard, sweat broken out across his forehead.

"Wait here," he told her.

She did what he said. She didn't look around. There was a smell, like something burnt. After a while, Dad came back, his eyes soft and a bit dusty or woozy, he smiled like he was glad to see her. He said this was just what he needed, a dose of nature. He sat down in the weeds, even though the ground was wet. Look, he told her. Look at the cars going by, they don't even know we're here. Look: he showed her tiny yellow flowers growing on tough stems. None of them even know this exists. We're the only ones. This is just for us.

When he stood up, his pants were wet, but he didn't seem to notice.

It was going to rain. The sky was dark, even though it was the morning. They walked all the way across the field till they got to a long gravel lane, and they walked up the lane till they got to a tall house made of yellowing boards, with a big barn on the other side of a gravel yard and a machine shed in between.

"Hello? Anyone home?" Dad was holding her shoulder, leaning hard. They'd walked so slowly. It was starting to rain, big fat drops plopping out of the sky.

"Can I help you?" A man and his little kid came out of the machine shed.

"Overheated," Dad said, thumb to the road. "Old rad. Needs water."

"That all?"

They drove down the lane in the man's pickup. The Caddy hadn't slid into the ditch, but the door was hanging wide open. Something about the way it looked made Francie's stomach flip-flop. She was hungry. All she'd eaten this morning was a doughnut. Jelly-filled. But still.

The men shook hands after they closed the hood.

"You've done us a kindness," Dad said.

"Try it once," said the man, and Dad sank into the driver's seat and turned the key.

"That does 'er!" The man picked up his little boy. Francie climbed in through the open door, and the man walked around to her side of the car and slammed it shut. Francie waved goodbye to the little boy, but he buried his face in his dad's shoulder.

"Strangers are better than friends," Dad said, looking in the rear-view mirror.

"What about me?" said Francie.

"What's that?" Dad said. He flipped on the wipers. The rain was really starting to come down now. Francie's stomach grumbled. But she knew where they were going. They weren't far from Grandma Irene's house. And Grandma Irene always had food.

Of course, it wasn't always the best food, Francie considered, sitting in the patch of ivy (probably poison).

A lot of things were going wrong.

She shrugged off her backpack and checked the lunch box with the rainbow pony on its front. She almost cried, seeing the rainbow pony—why?—or maybe seeing the broken zipper, Mom was so mad when it broke right away, *cheap piece of garbage*, but Francie wouldn't let her take it back to the store, she loved that pony too much. She even loved the broken zipper.

It was hard to open zippers with just one hand, especially broken ones.

Squashed sandwich crusts. Carob oatmeal cookies, crumbled into bits. A bunch of twenty-dollar bills—*don't think about that!* No water bottle, she'd left it at school.

Also, she might be lost.

There were no trails in this part of the woods, no signs, no arrows spray-painted onto tree trunks, no flapping plastic ribbons knotted around branches.

Francie returned the backpack to her shoulders and stood up. It was better not to be on a trail, she thought, because she didn't want to see a stranger, and she really really didn't want to see a friend.

Throw it away. Throw it away!

But the gun was stuck in her hand.

FOUR

Gym Bag

Irene switched the wipers on high, put her powder-blue sedan into reverse, and began backing down her short driveway toward the country highway, quiet on a rainy Sunday morning in May. Irene was not looking for trouble when she checked the rear-view mirror, but she could hardly have said she was surprised when the next instant she had to stomp on the brakes, as with much honking and flashing of headlights her son Luce turned his golden boat of a Cadillac into the driveway and blocked Irene's sedan. He climbed out before she'd even pushed the gearshift into park.

Irene rolled down the window a crack. "What a wonderful surprise!" she called out. "You're just in time for church!"

Her son pretended not to hear. "House open?" he said, leaning down to her window. He wasn't even wearing a rain jacket, holding one arm over his head.

Irene dug into her purse, through the lipstick and powder and comb and roll of mints, the chequebook and coin purse, the scraps of grocery lists and reminders, and retrieved the key that unlocked the back door. You could never be too careful living alone, out here in the country. "Dare I ask?" she said, as she rolled the window down a little further and stuck out her arm. It was a simple silver key on a cheap metal ring, attached to nothing else.

"Francie can go to church with you. Hey, Francie?" Luce waved at the Cadillac, and Irene turned and saw her granddaughter sitting in the front seat. Oh dear. A child her size shouldn't be riding up front. Francie slid over and out the open driver's-side door. She was not dressed for church, her t-shirt looked inappropriate, and her jeans were too big for her, dragging in the gravel. Already half-soaked.

Where to begin?

"Hurry!" Irene said. "Get in!"

Francie obeyed, climbing in behind Irene.

"Won't you come too, Luce?"

He put one hand on the top of her car and tapped twice. "Not me, I've got work to do." He winked at Francie as if Irene wouldn't notice.

"Work? On a Sunday?"

"We had ourselves a bit of car trouble. I'm going to poke around under the hood."

The lines around her son's mouth were tight even as he smiled at her, his face streaked with rain. He was better-looking than his father had been, in some ways, superficial ways, but he was closed, even to himself, closed and foolish, she could see it.

"Thanks for the key," he said. "I'll get out of your way."

He limped back to his car, and Irene watched him in the rear-view mirror. Such a helpless fury he raised in her. "Are you strapped in?" Irene listened for the seat belt's click before putting the car into reverse. She waved at Luce through the window, but he didn't see, he didn't wave back. He was leaning sideways, looking for something in the glove compartment of his car.

"You shouldn't sit in the front seat till you're older," Irene told Francie.

She wouldn't get anything out of Francie and knew better than to try, but she kept an eye on the child in the rear-view mirror all the way to town. Sulky? Morose? Scared? Irene couldn't guess the cause, but her granddaughter did not look happy.

At a stop sign in town, someone behind Irene laid on his horn. "Oh, for heaven's sake!" she said. "I've half a mind to make him wait even longer." She earned a smile from Francie for that.

Irene parked as close as she could to the church doors, to preserve her hairdo from the rain. She hurried Francie down to the ladies' room in the basement, not the new part of the church. This bathroom was never busy. The ceiling was low, the walls a dull yellow, the stalls poorly lit and provisional. Irene used the little comb from her purse to fix her hair, which needed fluffing up, but she quickly discovered that Francie's was beyond remediation.

"When is the last time your mother brushed this?" she whispered, the comb snarled in tangles, as Francie stared grimly into her own eyes in the mirror.

"I brushed it yesterday," said Francie, which was the most she'd said to Irene all morning, and Irene gave her a quick, fierce hug from behind.

"Of course you did," she said. *Not your fault.*

Audrey Shantz came out of the furthest stall, and Irene knew she must have been there all along, *hearing everything*, and before Audrey could say a word, Irene turned and smiled. "This is my granddaughter, Francie. Luce's daughter. She's visiting for the day."

Audrey dried her hands on a paper towel and shook Francie's hand, and Irene felt that it would be okay, they were safe, for now. "Aren't you lucky?" Audrey whispered, giving Irene a little hug. Irene was quite sure that wasn't the right word for whatever she was, on this particular morning, but it was preferable that Audrey be given that impression. It made Irene herself feel better.

They sat in a pew near the front, Irene's usual spot, and Francie examined the church bulletin in detail. Behind the pulpit, the woodwork stretched to the ceiling: dusty. You'd need wings to clean it. Jean was playing the piano for today's service, rather stridently, Irene thought, then corrected herself: with force, with certainty. Irene couldn't help but inform Francie that sometimes this was her job—that she, Irene, played the piano for some services too; as if Francie were interested.

Francie fidgeted, gazing around the room, looking for children her own age, no doubt, and Irene pointed out the Bast boy on the other side of the church.

The great mystery was why Luce had come. Was it a blessing, seeing as it had given Irene this time with her only granddaughter, in this sacred space, or was it a cry for help, another cry for help? How was she to know the difference?

Oh, you will know.

She felt her spine steel itself against the hard wood of the pew.

"Go," Irene whispered to Francie when the minister called the children forward for storytime, and despite a flicker of resistance, the girl obeyed, slumping down the aisle, the bottoms of her jeans frayed from dragging on the ground.

"Hello children!" It was singsongy Mrs. Krupf, who, to be fair, spoke to all God's creatures—not just children—as if they were children. "Sit down, gather round!"

Irene held her breath as Francie plopped onto the polished wood floor, her head tilted back on her neck. From this angle, the tangles of her hair looked like spiderwebs or bird nests, something organized by nature for a purpose.

"This morning, I'm going to read you a story about welcoming visitors! And aren't we lucky! We have a visitor with us this morning! What's your name, honey?"

Oh no.

Francie's lips touched the microphone and her voice boomed through the sound system: "Francie." Of course, laughter followed. What was this, comedy hour? Give the poor child her dignity!

"Can everyone welcome our new friend Francie?"

The usual cadre of toddlers sat on their mothers' laps picking their noses, babies squirmed. The sleep-deprived mothers said, "Welcome, Francie." Where was the Bast boy? Irene spotted him sitting on the far side of the church, and her heart sank. She saw her error writ large and wondered at herself, having sent the child forward like an overgrown sacrificial lamb. Silently, she called Francie back to her.

Forgive me.

The story was not about visitors, trust Dolores Krupf to muddle the message. It was about a refugee child, on a boat, which sank, and the child was pulled from the sea, travelled for days hungry, separated from her family (mother and father and brothers), alone. Wasn't this all a bit dark? Wasn't this all a bit much, for the children's story, even if the characters appeared to be depicted as animals?

Eventually, the child emerged from the woods (when had

the woods come into it?) and knocked on a stranger's door, and the stranger spoke to the child in a strange language. But when a bowl of hot soup was placed before the child, the child sat at the stranger's table and ate till she was full.

Francie had her hand up. *Uh-oh.* "She shouldn't talk to strangers." Francie's noisy voice did not require a microphone.

"This stranger is good," said Mrs. Krupf, as if speaking to an idiot. "This is a good stranger." She turned back to the page with the soup. "Even this tiny little mouse knew he could help the refugee child." The refugee child appeared to be a cat.

Francie sat up defiantly, and the bejewelled letters on her shirt seemed to catch the light—*LOVE*. "The cat will eat the mouse," she said, not even bothering to put up her hand. She sounded satisfied, like she'd fixed whatever problem she had with the story.

An uncomfortable ripple of laughter spread through the congregation.

"Oh my! That's not a very nice way to say thank you!" Mrs. Krupf laughed and glanced at the pulpit. "Back to your seats now, and you can think about this important question: What will I feed the poor little child knocking on my door? Ask your parents!"

"Let's pray!" said the minister.

"Wasn't that nice?" Irene whispered to Francie, as Francie clambered over Irene's black stockings, treading heavily on her foot.

"I'm hungry," Francie whispered.

Irene rustled through her purse and handed over the roll of mints. Francie leafed through the bulletin and chomped on the candy. She could not seem to sit still. Rustling, shifting, crunching. Irene's father would have

said: *Spare the rod, spoil the child.* A lesson Irene had refused
to repeat with her own son.

She'd refused to treat a child to such fear.

Had she been mistaken?

It was easy for Irene to sit still. She felt like a heavy sack
of flesh and bones, sinking into inertia, even her heartbeat
seemed to slow. She'd trained herself to turn toward calm,
away from disaster, but it seemed also to turn her away from
feeling anything at all. To become a breathing body, tethered
by threads to the distant terror of her mind. That she'd done
it all wrong. That she was being rebuked for sparing the rod,
for not trusting the wisdom of her forebears. The evidence
of her error trickling down through the generations.

"Did you like the sermon?" Irene asked on the drive
home, wipers on high. "What about the scriptural passage?"

Of course, her granddaughter said nothing.

Irene wondered: Why did she demand that those she
loved most prove themselves, or reveal their deficiencies,
according to her measure? Was she of a challenging nature,
stubborn and combative, pushing, pushing, pushing everyone away?

"The scriptural passage was on the Israelites wandering
in the desert," Irene heard herself saying. "They wandered
for forty years until God showed them the Promised Land.
It's funny, Francie, but what I was thinking as the passage
was being read was, Forty years—that's not so long!" Irene
stopped, but the stream inside her head continued. Twenty
years, thirty years, forty years; a lot happened, but a lot didn't
happen, a lot repeated, and in the repetition there was comfort; if not peace, it could feel like peace. "Time is a circle,
not a line." Irene said this last bit out loud, but Francie was
looking out the window.

As inscrutable as Luce. Of him. Of me too, thought Irene. Diluted.

"Why did your dad drive out here this morning, Francie? Do you know?" But she was pulling into the driveway. She shouldn't have asked. The child had enough on her shoulders, that was clear, nests in her hair, *LOVE* on her shirt, hungry, apparently, and Irene hadn't even thought to stop in town for ice cream after the service!

"Almost home," Irene said. "We'll make something nice for lunch."

She pulled in beside Luce's car, which was parked in the grass where it shouldn't be, where it would leave tracks in the soft, saturated earth. The car was facing the wrong way, toward the road—she didn't like what that implied. But at least it meant he was still here.

"You should visit more often," Irene said to Francie as they unstrapped their seat belts. "I would like that."

Irene didn't want an argument. She wouldn't choose an argument. She wouldn't call it an argument.

Of course, Luce said he was in a hurry, couldn't stay for lunch. He didn't look like he was in a hurry.

"Did you get your car fixed?" she asked, and he said, "All good, nothing to worry about." Francie was safely in the bathroom.

Irene said, "Do you need anything? Anything I can do for you?" She resisted the urge to paw at his sleeve, hold on to him.

"It's just a visit, Ma. You always get yourself worked up over nothing."

"Well, you can't leave without something." She meant food, but he laughed and showed her the gym bag he'd found in his old bedroom—"I'm taking this."

"Oh?"

"Look." He unzipped the bag and pulled out a pair of red shorts with the tags still on, unused. "Must have been from that last cross-country season, I never had a chance to wear them," he said. High school. Last season. Interrupted season. Interrupted by—

Was Luce thinking what Irene was thinking? There was no way for her to know. He held up the shorts for her to see. They looked too small to fit him now, but he didn't seem to notice. He seemed pleased, blurry, his pupils were pinpricks, she saw, switching on the overhead light in the kitchen. It was a dark day. She tried to interpret his mood, his emotions, but in that way he was just like his father, he hid himself from her, his intentions, his plans. It was enough to send Irene around the bend, fear clapping at her heart.

From the window over the kitchen sink, she could see the farmhouse where they'd lived as a family, up the long lane, across the wide front field, planted this season in corn; their home, before the interruption, before Frank's death, before his *passing*.

You never got used to it, the fear.

"You must be hungry . . ." Irene's hands moved automatically, mashing up three boiled eggs she'd found in the fridge, stirring in mayonnaise and chopped celery and onion, and spreading the mixture onto slices of whole wheat bread. Topped with a lettuce leaf. Cut in half. Wrapped in wax paper, and tucked into a grocery bag along with a reused yogurt container of homemade cookies, which she'd pulled out of the freezer.

Francie was taking a long time in the bathroom. Luce had put the shorts back into the gym bag. He kept checking his phone.

"Are you sure you can't stay for lunch?"

"Don't worry so much, Ma, it's the worry that'll kill you." He looked up from his phone and smiled. It was such an easy smile. It looked so easy for him to let it break across his face. Why didn't she feel easy in return?

It was only later she thought to check her purse. Later, after she'd waved goodbye from the front stoop in her slippers, still wearing her church clothes, after she'd closed and carefully locked the front door and the back, after she'd walked slowly down the hallway to Luce's old bedroom, which she'd never in all these years cleared out or packed up, even though it had been his room only a brief while, that last year of high school, and a few unmoored seasons beyond that while he was finding his feet, before he'd left home for good (or for worse, Irene thought).

Irene turned the door handle, looked around the room, saw evidence of nothing in particular out of sorts: the curtains were open, the lighting dim, she let her eyes rest on the shelves of trophies catching dust, posters of bands tacked to the walls, pennants from sports teams, an empty room even when Luce had been here, like he'd been filling space, trying out whatever personality might suit to fit the void. The bed was neatly made up with a blue quilt, two pillows at the top, all a bit dusty, a rectangular dust-free spot on the floor where the gym bag had been, no doubt.

What was she missing?

She closed the door. What was this feeling? Like stone.

That was when she thought to check her purse; she'd been putting it off, she knew. She'd carried the purse to church, of course, removed several bills from her wallet and placed them into the collection plate, and when she'd gotten home, she'd hung the purse, zipped up with the wallet safely inside, on its hook beside the back door. She'd had her eye on Luce the entire time! Hadn't she?

But there it was: the bad news. Hands, heart, steady, slow, numb. All her cash was gone.

Of course, that's why he'd come.

Frank, how could you leave me here to deal with this crooked son, all alone!

Now, she knew this feeling. Fury. Its blast obscured that other feeling, lower down and underneath. Shame.

⁘

The day was a dark one. The sun hadn't managed to burn off the fog and now the clouds were rolling in and it was really raining for real. Liane's polish was taking forever to dry and Seth was going to be pissed that she'd stunk up the joint. She cracked the window over the sink for air, rain slapping in like fat, stupid tears, but the lacquer high lingered, poison gas.

Liane balanced on one of their two kitchen chairs, white moulded plastic with arms, and rested her feet on the table-top. She spread her toes and admired the job—she could have worked as an aesthetician, her hand was steady and she had an eye for colours, her stepmom always said. Purple today, rich and almost black, like plums. Silver rings on two toes. Sweatpants, stretchy tank in sparkly thread. A good day for doing fuck all.

The dog came charging out of the back room with a bone to pick. He'd heard the knock on the door. She couldn't see Seth from here, but she could see him in her mind's eye, and he wasn't getting up.

Liane slid her feet into her white flip-flops with the pretty pink straps, careful not to smear the fresh polish.

She had to haul the dog off by its collar. A tall man and a little girl were standing on the stoop, under the flapping plastic—the house wasn't finished yet; in Liane's opinion it never would be. It was nothing but a half-built skeleton on the other side, which guaranteed they'd have no neighbours and no hassle, suited Seth just fine.

"Here for Seth?" Liane said, the dog growling deep in its murderous throat. "Seth?" she hollered. "It's for you!"

As if it would be for her. She had to go out to do her work. This place isn't zoned for that, she thought, but the joke felt old, rattling around her head. She recognized this guy, he'd been around a bit too often lately, like he was thinking of moving in. You can have my half of the bed, she told him in her head.

The first time she saw this guy, she thought, Mm-hmmm, now here's a fine specimen, like her stepmom used to say, but today he was nervous as the rest of them, making him ugly as the rest of them, greedy and desperate and a chicken-shit to boot. "You brung someone," Liane said to him, and she felt angry, could he hear it in her voice? Don't go getting yourself into debt with my man Seth, she thought.

"My daughter, my kid," said the man. He was in over his head, he was using the shit himself, he was not Liane's problem—*stop trying to save everyone, Liane, you're too soft, you'll get used, used up*, her stepmother was saying inside Liane's head.

The kid had on a sparkly shirt too, with jewels that formed the shape of a cat sitting above the word *LOVE*.

'Cause that's what cats are known for.

The kid was staring at Liane's toenails. "Do you like the colour?" Liane said, and the kid's eyes turned into goggles. Liane remembered the colour was called Porno Purple, so she kept that to herself. "Seth!" Liane yelled again. "He's wearing his goddam headphones," she told them. "Pardon my French."

She dragged the dog behind her into the main room. She was worried the dog was going to shed his damn hair into her fresh polish, hoping, too, the dog wouldn't turn on her and take her arm off. She and the dog shared a mutual distrust, and rightly so, on both sides. Seth was sitting on the sofa in the near dark, television flickering. It was the kind of sofa that looked better in the near dark, looked like leather, but was actually a species of plastic that stuck to your thighs if you sweated even the tiniest bit.

"Come in," Liane invited them. "I got a good hold on Champ here. He's not gonna getcha." Full name: Champ the Killer, to match the kind of dog Seth thought the kind of person like him oughta have. The man and the girl looked like a matching set themselves, eyeing the dog. They took a step into the room. She remembered this guy had a bad limp, but maybe it'd gotten worse.

"Do you like soda pop?" Liane asked the kid, and the kid nodded.

Seth was sunk into the desiccated foam cushions, his legs splayed wide, big black headphones over his ears. He wore sweatpants that were gathered at the ankle and a white undershirt, a skinny guy, deceptively skinny. He was all wire and gristle. You don't want his hands locked around your throat, Liane thought, as a warning, a private warning, sent from her past self to her future. Seth's legs rattled and jumped and danced, he couldn't sit still.

"I hope you like orange," Liane said to the kid. She hauled the dog through the kitchen and locked him into the back room, a place she didn't like to visit or think about except when she had to go there. It smelled like a cave, an underground cave where people were taken to be buried alive. The bed was on the floor and the sheets were full of dead skin.

The kitchen was its own farce of domesticity, but Liane found it cheerful in its way, the light was natural even if the window faced the streaked siding of the house next door. On the counter were opened jars and cans with bits of food mouldering in them, dirty plates stacked in the sink, but something could be made of this room, curtains could be sewn, meals prepared, dishtowels hung on the cupboard doors.

Liane pulled a can of orange pop from a flat on the floor, and she took it to the kid, who was waiting with her dad in the front room. The pop was room temperature, but beggars can't be choosers, and the kid said, "Thank you." Liane didn't feel like saying, You're welcome. She went to sit beside Seth on the sweaty sofa. She put her hand on his leg to rouse him, have some manners, you've got customers, but he was past all that, thought he was king of the world now he'd got people working for him.

He brushed her fingers away like she was a fly, worse, less than a fly, fly turd. *You always make bad choices*, she could hear her stepmom saying. *You're never going to change and till you do, don't come crawling back here again and break all of our hearts.*

"You shouldn'ta brung the kid," Liane said. She lit one of the cigarettes she'd been storing inside her bra, and her fingers shook, which wasn't like her. Hands of a surgeon, steady hands, cold heart. She didn't like the feeling shaking her up. She ashed into an empty pop can on the floor.

"Smoke outside," said Seth, like he was so pure. At least she'd goaded him to speak.

The kid had her eyes locked on Seth, and Liane thought he wasn't going to like being studied like that, even by a kid. She looked down at his white sweat socks stuck in black plastic sandals as she stood, and Seth pinched her as she passed, hard, twisting the flesh in her tush and daring her to squeal. Like he could hurt her. Like anything he could do could hurt her.

"Come on," Liane said to the kid, and she stared daggers at the kid's dad, to warn him, damn him, but the guy just grinned like he could see right through her, down to the vanity over the toenails, inside to the hungry part of her that would fuck him for free if he asked. Shame was an animal. She loathed him, even more than she despised Seth—they disgusted her, she didn't need them.

"Shouldn'ta brung her," Liane said again, and called the kid to follow her by tilting her head toward the door. The kid looked at her dad to ask his permission.

"Go on," he said.

Liane and the girl stood on the front stoop under the flapping plastic, which kept them mostly dry. The rain was spitting now. Liane felt bad filling the little shelter with smoke, but she dragged on the cigarette till it was down to the filter, then wiped the butt end on the raw wood frame around the door and flicked it into the muddy yard.

"You live with your mom and dad?" Liane asked.

The girl nodded, making slurping sounds as she guzzled the pop.

"Your dad take you around with him lots?" Liane pulled another cigarette and her neon-green lighter from inside her sparkly tank top. Maybe she was just jealous of the kid.

"I guess," the girl said. She burped and tried to hide it with her forearm.

"Well, excuse you," said Liane.

The girl tipped her head way back to drain the can. Liane could resuscitate that feeling if she tried, that willingness to go all the way to get what you wanted, down to the very last drop.

"That your dad's car? Fancy." Liane squinted out toward the street.

The girl didn't respond. They stood in silence, Liane's smoke collecting beneath the clear plastic that framed them like tent flaps. Liane'd never been camping, not on purpose. You could have one life or another life, but not both. It got to the point where it was too late for both.

The kid stared down into the pop can, like there might be more. She ripped off the metal tab and dropped it in.

"What's your name? My name's Liane," said Liane.

But the kid kept staring into the can. She shook it. There was a railing on the stoop, and the grass around it was churned-up mud mixed with dog shit where neither she nor Seth could be bothered to pick it up.

"Oh, I get it, you don't wanna be friends, that's okay, why would you wanna be friends with the lady who gives you free pop, right?" It was wrong to say this, she knew, kids shouldn't go around trusting everyone who gave them free shit. Still, it enraged Liane to be ignored, or even feared. She hadn't asked for this—visitors on her day off, intruders, abandoned children possibly needing rescue.

"I'm a nice person, don't worry," she exhaled. "Jesus, they're taking a while." What was she, a babysitter?

The kid had started to sing, so quietly Liane thought she was imagining it. But the kid kept going, a bit louder—"Hey, it's that song." Liane knew some of the words. She hummed along for a bar or two, and then, without looking at the girl, she joined in. She could hear her grown-up voice in her ears, different from the child's voice and different from her own voice as a child—rough in patches with ridges of smoothness, like corrugated cardboard. The girl faced the street as she sang, going for it now, her head thrown back, breathing properly from the diaphragm. Someone had taught her properly.

Who taught you? Liane asked herself, but she could sing without remembering, couldn't she? She didn't have to go around remembering all the time, all the things that could actually hurt her.

She invented a harmony under the kid's melody. *Wade in the water, wade in the water, children, wade in the water. God's gonna trouble the water.*

God. Not a person of her acquaintance these days.

A man walking a German shepherd, decked out with a studded collar, glanced at them from the sidewalk.

"Whaddya think?" Liane called out to him.

He pulled his hood up over his head and walked on.

"Fuck you too!" she yelled after him, and flicked her cigarette butt in his direction. She'd forgotten she'd been smoking and it had burned itself down to the filter. "Know any other songs?"

The kid shrugged.

"What about this one, you know this one?" Liane sang: *My eyes have seen the glory of the coming of the Lord.* "I don't know the rest. Do you? Can't remember the whole thing now, just the beginning."

The kid didn't know. She opened her mouth and sang, *Laudate Dominum omnes gentes.*

Showoff.

"What's it mean, hon?"

But the kid didn't know. Liane laughed. She was starting to think the kid belonged to her, almost, like Liane had already rescued her, like the kid was a message out of the past come to frighten her to behave, just be good, *be a good girl, I know you can, Liane, we all love you so much.*

The door clicked open behind them, and the smell from the house pushed out through the rain, sweet as rot. It was harder to notice on the inside.

"Kid likes to sing," Liane told the tall guy. She wondered where he was stowing the stuff he'd come for, wondered idly what he'd taken and what he owed and how he planned to get rid of it. "We been out here just singing away." She felt something like affection, possessive affection, as she lifted the empty pop can from the kid's hand and watched her pick through the mud and dog shit and climb into that ancient pimpmobile. Still didn't know the kid's name.

"Francie!" The girl rolled down her window and yelled as the car pulled away from the curb. "My name's Francie!"

What mattered? What mattered, if not this? She was gonna cry, but she was gonna save it for later.

Liane turned and walked slowly into the house. Her feet hurt, she was shuffling, she felt older than she had half an hour ago, it was so much later in the day. She'd grown right past the point of rescue, oh, she'd passed that point so long ago she couldn't remember when it'd happened. No marker, no signpost, no stone.

She might have no one alive to go home to, but that wasn't the point. The point was, this wasn't home, never would be, never was. This was just another way station. And she had no provisions. No provisions for the road.

My eyes have seen the glory of the coming of the Lord. She sat in the kitchen and painted her fingernails Porno Purple to match her toes and the words to the song rushed into her with all their awful, magnificent prophecy. *He is trampling out the vintage where the grapes of wrath are stored, He has loosed the fateful lightning of his terrible swift sword, His truth is marching on . . .*

"I don't know what that joker is up to, but I sold him the old 9mm you never shoulda brought with you," Seth told Liane when he walked by to the toilet. He always seemed to be scratching himself, itching his parts, adjusting his crotch and his shirt at the underarms, picking away at himself.

Now what was she going to use to kill him in his sleep?

Liane's hands shook so hard, she knocked over the bottle of polish. "That was mine! That wasn't yours!" she yelled at his lazy, scrawny backside, throwing the bottle of polish at his head, missing, the rest of the polish spilling on the lino-leum, and he turned and laughed at her. He laughed. She lunged in his direction. *You always make bad choices.* And the battle hymn wouldn't be enough to take him down, she knew, as he grabbed her by the wrists and she fell under his familiar weight, gave way, his familiar hands, the truth drop-ping through the rotten floorboards, falling down under the house, under the mud, at last, underground.

"Don't touch my face! I need my face!" It was too late to cry. I never do get around to doing my crying, she thought, struck by the injustice of it. Struck.

The dog wouldn't quit barking.

There is nobody going to save you but yourself, she told the kid in her mind. There is nobody but you.

FIVE

Gun Run

BANG!

Whatever happened didn't happen in an order that made sense. A branch swatted Francie's face, the gun jumped in her hand, the noise it made was so loud it seemed to echo all around her, like voices telling her to run!

Run! Run! Run!

The gun was stuck in her hand. She was running blindly through brush and branches, stuck with this stupid gun.

Keep your seat belt on, she could hear Dad saying, *I'll be right back.*

He took the keys.

They were parked on another street not so different from the last one, where the lady with the nails like claws gave her an orange pop. It was hard to tell these streets apart, grey in the rain. Broken, strange. Broken things, in strange places. A baby stroller with three wheels toppled under a bush. A bike tire chained to a telephone pole. Black bags of trash piled on porches, ripped open by squirrels, spilling eggshells and chicken bones.

Dad was not right back.

Francie was hungry, and Grandma Irene's egg sandwich was long gone. There were cookies in the yogurt container but, like Dad said, watch out, you'll break a tooth on one of those. Francie burped a bubbly burp and it smelled like orange soda. A dog was barking from inside a house across the street. Was that the house that Dad went into? She couldn't remember.

She twisted around to look, and there was Dad's black gym bag, the one he took from Grandma's house.

Not stolen.

You can't steal it if it's already yours.

Inside the bag, Francie saw: One pair of red gym shorts, brand new, tags on. A black t-shirt. A taped-up manila envelope with something inside. Plastic bags, for sandwiches. A gun.

This gun. Same gun. The one stuck in her hand, stuck to her.

She tried to remember what she'd felt, seeing it for the first time.

It was true, she couldn't have found it without looking, it was buried at the bottom of the bag, she had to unfasten her seat belt, climb over the seat, unzip the zipper, dig around.

Don't look 'cause you're not going to like what you find.

Her hands jerked away from the gym bag like they were on fire. She was scrambling back over the seat, kicking, landing on her head, crunching sideways, flipping upright, strapping herself in, fingers woven together in her lap to show innocence, fingers that had touched a gun, had seen it, picked it up, dropped it down, in total silence. What had it felt like, in her hand? She watched rain strike the windshield, hard, then harder, and she pushed down the lock on her door and on Dad's door.

"Let me in!" Dad was banging on the window. "What're you so scared of?"

He was soaked, hair plastered to his forehead, rain dripping down his shirt collar. Dad reached behind the seat and pulled the black t-shirt out of the gym bag and dried his face and neck with it. He didn't know what Francie knew, and she was amazed that he didn't guess it, that he couldn't read her face like she could read his. He was excited, exhilarated, not angry.

"Last stop," said Dad, "and don't look at me like that." Francie didn't know what she was looking like. "Like your mother," he said. They were home, pulling into the driveway, parking.

Mom, stomping out of the house, holding Sam in her arms: "You've been gone all day. You didn't tell me you were taking Francie! Why didn't you answer your phone? I almost called the police! I had no idea where you were, no idea. This is my life now? I was scared out of my mind!" Mom, in her grey uniform: "And on top of it all, I'm going to be late for work!"

"Never call the cops, Marietta. Never. Do you hear me?"

Mom, in unlaced tennis shoes, hair pulled into a stubby ponytail at the back of her head.

"We'll drive you to work, right, Francie?"

Mom, looking at Francie, hard. Mom, not asking any questions. Mom, lugging the car seat out of the trunk, strapping Sam in beside Francie, Mom, sliding into the front seat, Mom, who never asked Dad for a ride to work or to pick her up after a shift, who took the bus, two buses because she had to transfer, and if she timed it wrong, it took twice as long, but sometimes one of the other ladies from the Lodge would give Mom a lift home.

The new place, the Lodge, where Mom only got overnight shifts.

Dad, pulling into a circular driveway, it looked like a mansion, but Mom said up close you could see things were falling apart.

"Thanks for the ride."

Mom, kissing Dad in the front seat.

The gym bag, on the floor between Sam and Francie. Francie wanting to kick it.

Mom, slipping out of the car and running to the Lodge, opening the big wooden door, ivy growing all over the stones and across some windows, shutters painted dark green, tilting on their hinges, dangling like ears torn loose from a face.

Mom, not turning around to wave goodbye.

Sam, starting to kick the back of Dad's seat.

Dad, not taking them out for ice cream, like Francie had secretly hoped.

Dad, carrying the gym bag into the house.

Francie, staying in the back seat with Sam, hoping Dad would come back out and take them for ice cream, waiting and hoping, till Sam got too fussy and Francie unbuckled him and carried him inside and she made them peanut butter on bread for supper while Dad took a very long nap with the bedroom door open. They could see him lying on his back with his boots still on, sprawled out, snoring softly.

The gym bag, under the bed, Francie saw. There it was.

BANG!

It had happened, she was running. The gun was stuck in her hand.

Throw it away! Throw it away!

The light was changing, brightening between the leafy shadows. Francie was running downhill, a gentle rolling, then the drop got steep and the trees thinned out, and she was almost falling, her legs spinning like wheels, feet skidding. There was a rushing sound that poured over the ringing in her ears, louder and louder.

Water.

She had come to a stream, the stream in the woods, water hurrying over rocks. Francie was sure this was the same stream that she and Alice had never been brave enough to cross. It looked deep.

She was almost surprised to see the sky again, opening over her head, surprised by its bright blue, streaked with white cloud. Surprised by today. This was today.

A dog began to bark, somewhere behind her.

"We have to cross the stream," Francie said, but saying it made her feel even more alone. It was just Francie, pushing the sneakers off without untying the laces. Grandma Irene would shake her head—*You're wrecking those shoes, Francie, just look at them*. Francie crouched and peeled off her socks, shoved the bottoms of her jeans up above her knees, very hard to do with just one hand.

A dog, barking.

"Hurry, come on!" she whispered, as if Alice were here too.

Alice wouldn't want to cross the stream. Alice would be scared. Francie would have to grab Alice by the arm and drag her in: "We don't have time! We have to get there before nightfall!"

Wait, where? Where are we going?

The bank was slicker than Francie had guessed. She slid into the stream, quick, a shock, arms stuck out, trying to hold on to socks, shoes, gun. Water washed above her ankles. Clean. Cold. *Not so deep after all, see, Alice? We're fine!*

But the dog was barking, louder and louder, and Francie turned—*don't turn, don't look!*—she wobbled on a loose stone, she slipped off balance, she fell. Gasping, splashing. The arm with the gun above her head, protecting it. *Why?* The other arm underwater, hand holding shoes and socks pushing off the bottom. Up, thrashing to the other side, crawling up the muddy bank, hot and stinky in the sun.

"Okay," Francie said. "It's okay, it's okay."

The gun was dry. But her shoes and socks were soaked, jeans too. Francie sat and tried to stuff her bare feet into the sneakers, but they didn't fit anymore. The laces were fat and waterlogged, fixed into place, knotted and sopping. *Just like I told you*, said Grandma Irene.

Not you! I want Alice!

The stream and its banks and the sky were too open. The dog was still barking. Francie jammed her feet partway into the sneakers.

"It's really happening," she said to Alice. "They're really after us."

She stood up, sneakers sloshing, squashed down at the back with her heels hanging out.

The other side was flatter, wetter, swampy in parts. It was hard to run with sneakers half-on, half-falling-off. It was such a stupid thing to get stuck on, such a small and stupid thing, but Francie was almost crying as she stopped, kicked off one sneaker, and tried yanking at the knotted laces with her teeth.

She was crying, almost.

Leave the shoes, there isn't time to worry about them, Alice said.

"Alice! Is that you?" But Alice didn't answer.

Francie was on the other side. She'd made it—exactly this far. Exactly this far.

SIX

Jewels

"My dad has a new job," Francie told Alice.

Alice said, "I thought your dad was sick, maybe?"

Francie frowned, she ignored Alice. "He has a new job," Francie said. "He gets jewels."

Oh!

Alice said, "What does he do with them?"

Alice knew that Francie's dad was not like her own dad—not much like a dad at all, in most ways, more like someone from one of their make-believe stories. What Alice couldn't figure out was what kind of a person he was—good or bad? Francie and Alice were always good, but everyone else was trickier to measure. A good person could be disguised as a bad person, or a bad person could be disguised as a good person. Francie's dad seemed, maybe, to be bad, but Alice knew that could mean anything.

They were walking in the park past the baseball diamonds. Men and women in red and white t-shirts threw balls at each other, shouting in a friendly way over music that pumped from a car's radio, pulled up behind the fence at home plate. Pop music. Alice didn't recognize the song.

Francie was humming, maybe she knew the song.

"What does your dad do with the jewels?" Alice persisted. In fact, she was pretty sure, almost certain, Francie's dad was bad. He scared her. Francie knew everything about Alice, but not this. Alice's fear of Francie's dad was too deep, too real to speak of. She didn't want Francie to know.

"He picks them up and drops them off," said Francie. As far as Alice could tell, Francie was not afraid of her dad.

"Does he get to keep the jewels?" Alice asked.

Francie didn't answer right away. They were walking on the paved path to get to the woods in the middle of the park. "Sometimes," she said at last, but Alice wasn't sure she believed her. Francie did not always tell the truth, according to Alice's mom. Sally wouldn't let Alice argue on Francie's behalf. "Are you saying your friend never makes things up?" *But*— "Are you saying she's always perfectly honest, and you believe everything she says?"

No, but—

no.

Are the jewels stolen? Alice wanted to know, but couldn't ask. She sensed that this story meant something different to Francie than the usual stories they played together. Were the jewels real? Was Francie talking about something real?

"Let's pretend we're refugees," said Francie. "A bomb fell on our town and we had to escape. My name is Arabella. What's your name?"

"Alice?"

"You can't say your own name."

"Alecka?" said Alice, hoping it would satisfy Francie.

"You always use Alecka. It's not even a real name."

"You always use Arabella," said Alice, risking an argument.

"Okay," said Francie. "Alecka. We're riding horses, because when we escaped from the bomb, that's all we had—two horses. You have to decide your horse's name and what it looks like. You can't say pink just because you're wearing pink."

Alice frowned. She looked down at her shirt. She thought it looked like cotton candy. "Cotton candy," she said.

"Cotton candy is not a colour," said Francie.

There were parts of the games they played that Alice could never manage to Francie's satisfaction. This was not Alice's problem to solve, as Alice saw it. Besides, Francie loved these parts—deciding who they were and where they were going and what they looked like, details that would hold firm or shift as necessary, while the game lasted, according to Francie's whim. "You do it for me," said Alice.

"Okay, you're riding a chestnut mare with a reddish mane and tail. She is just above 14.2 hands, which means she's a horse, not a pony, but she's small for a horse. Her name is Estellina."

"Estellina." Alice sighed happily.

They stopped for a moment beside the playground to look at a big kid on one of the baby swings, a teenager, his bike tipped into the sand. He wasn't sitting idly atop the swing, he was pumping his legs to go higher and higher. He seemed lost in his own world, he didn't seem to notice them.

"We'll be safe in the woods, Alecka," Francie said softly, and Alice knew the big kid must be a bad person.

"Where does your dad keep the jewels?" Alice whispered back. "Are the jewels somewhere safe?" The jewels seemed to be part of this game, she couldn't separate them out.

Francie said, "I can't tell you, it's a secret, I'm not even supposed to know."

Game, then.

"What kind of jewels?" Alice pushed. Maybe the big kid was going to steal the jewels. Maybe, when the bomb fell on their house, Francie had secretly taken the jewels along with her horse.

"Diamonds," Francie whispered. "Emeralds, rubies, also sapphires and topazes. Fool's gold, too."

"What's fool's gold?"

"It looks like real gold, except it's not."

Did that make it better than real gold? Alice wasn't sure but decided not to ask. They were in the woods now, and the paved path changed to dirt sprinkled with wood chips. They were walking downhill. Francie was thinking, her head down. "I can show you some jewels. Maybe the fool's gold," she said at last.

Better than real gold!

Was this part of the game? Alice couldn't be sure. Excitement bubbled into her throat, the excitement that came from being with Francie, who was different from anyone else Alice knew. What they shared couldn't be spoiled, not by anyone. Overhead, the leaves were thick, the late morning sun moved in thin, bright strands through the canopy, shadows and light splashing their faces.

Alice returned to the game. "What's your horse like?"

"He's golden with a jet-black mane and tail. He is a few hands taller than your horse, with a black fringe around his hooves." Francie paused. "Estellina is adorable," she said, and Alice knew Francie wanted to reassure Alice, wanted to avoid an argument about something Alice didn't really care about, one way or the other. "Estellina is also very spunky," Francie insisted, "even though she's small."

"Okay. What's your horse called?"

"Champ," said Francie. A new name in the game. "Champ is a little bit mean. He bites, but he can jump fences. He can even jump across the stream at the bottom of the hill."

They had never crossed the stream. Francie was afraid of the other side (or was that Arabella?). Either way, neither Alecka nor Alice wanted to get wet.

"Let's gallop," said Francie, and they turned their horses up a different path, away from a couple they could see walking ahead carrying a baby in a backpack, with a small spotted dog on a leash.

Alice had to gallop hard to keep up—because Francie's horse was taller, she thought, a thought interrupted by a dog barking behind them. Had the little spotted dog gotten loose from its leash? Alice wasn't scared of dogs, not like Francie, who shouted, "Faster!"

Estellina picked up her hooves.

Francie, galloping ahead, turned around, and screamed— a real scream. They were being chased, and not by the little spotted dog. Alice screamed too. She was not afraid of dogs, but this was not a dog. It was a wolf, enormous and shaggy, with giant paws and fur like a mane around its neck, its big red mouth rimmed with black lips and yellow teeth—the last thing Alice saw as she followed Francie off the path, into the brush.

"Stop! Stop!" a woman was hollering. "He's very gentle! He loves kids! Don't run!"

Alice and Francie galloped through slapping branches and old leaves and green forest ferns. What happened when a story came to life? Francie's horse was veering wildly, Alice had to save her! She ran toward a large fallen tree trunk and threw herself off Estellina. "Hurry, Arabella, hurry!" She grabbed Francie's hand, and they scooched up the trunk, safe from the wolf, which had found them.

Oh no, the horses!

"Will the horses be okay?" Alice cried. Francie looked stricken. "They'll be okay, right?" Alice begged, but Francie didn't reply.

The wolf circled and growled. It thought it had them cornered, trapped. It could hardly have been more proud to show off its catch to its owner when she caught up, purse bouncing off her thigh, breathless and homely with fright and rage. The woman's hair was grey, chopped to her shoulders.

"You shouldn't have run! He's friendly, can't you see?" The woman folded over to catch her breath. The wolf did not fool Alice, even though it wagged its tail like a dog, an enormous fringe arching over an enormous hairy back.

All teeth.

The woman righted herself, red in the face. Maybe she was Little Red Riding Hood, all grown up and turned mean because she'd married the wolf at the end of the story—Alice wanted to tell Francie.

"Why were you running? What are you doing here all by yourselves?" The woman held the wolf's collar, eyelids narrowing. "Where's your mom? Or your dad?" she added as an afterthought.

"They're playing baseball," Alice heard Francie say, as easily as if it were true.

"Let me walk you there," said the woman. Anyone could see she was only pretending to be nice—she wasn't very good at it.

Alice and Francie locked eyes. They shook their heads no. "Well!"

"We don't talk to strangers," said Francie loudly.

"What are your names? Where do you live?" But they didn't answer. The wolf was growling again, its fur standing up around its collar, and the woman couldn't control any of them, wolves or children, she couldn't make them do as she pleased, and she was angry—she thought she'd disguised herself, but she couldn't fool them!

"She's a witch!" Alice said to Francie as soon as the woman had gone, fighting every step to drag the wolf away.

Alice waited for Francie to agree, but Francie had gone very quiet. Her eyes weren't focused on anything in particular.

Alice inched up the fallen tree till she was at the end where the trunk rested on the stump that had once held it up, she leaned down to touch the splinters, soft, rotten, crumbling under her pinch. She wasn't hurting the tree; it was already dead. She was feeling a familiar disappointment that she didn't like to think about too much—she'd been so proud to recognize the witch in disguise, but Francie seemed to be somewhere else, her thoughts scattering out beyond where Alice's were able to travel. Francie sat as still as a statue, or as still as a sleeping body whose mind is dreaming of leaving her body behind.

"Where are our horses?" Alice said at last.

Francie stirred and looked around. "We can ride them home now," she said, which meant the horses must have survived the wolf attack. Alice felt relieved. It had been in Francie's power to decide otherwise, of course.

"Where is home?" said Alice, and she felt between them a shiver of delight that might also have been fear. It seemed possible that they might someday find themselves so deep inside their make-believe world they'd never escape.

"Let's go to your house," Alice said, even though she knew Francie wanted to go to Alice's house; they both liked what the other had, and didn't have. "If we go to your house," Alice said, "we can look for the jewels." An argument worth having.

"What jewels?" Francie said, and Alice felt duped, as angry as the witch had been, uncertain, now, whether she was Alecka or Alice.

"Fool's gold!" said Alice. The words were dangerous, sparkling in her mouth, hard on her tongue. Francie didn't reply. They were galloping across the field beside the baseball diamonds, where soccer nets had been erected, white chalk marking lines on the grass.

"We can go to your house first," Francie said when they'd reached the main path that took them to the cross-walk. "Your house is closest."

"After that we'll look for the jewels!" Alice squeaked.

And Francie didn't say no.

Alice and Francie sat cross-legged on Francie's front stoop in the full sun. Francie's mom and baby brother were napping, so Francie had made them lunch, Alice's favourite: peanut butter on soft white bread, the good kind of peanut butter, the kind that Alice's mom said was full of icing sugar. The stoop was made of concrete slabs and did not attach per-fectly to the house—Francie peeled off her sandwich crusts and dropped them down the gap, but Alice ate the whole sandwich, crusts and all.

Just then, Francie's mom came around the side of the house carrying Francie's little brother Sam. "I thought I heard voices," she said. She set Sam down into the grass and picked up their empty plates. Her voice was sharp, her movements quick. She frowned at Francie. "What are you wearing? Is that a wedding dress? Where on earth did you get it?"

"It's my mom's, she said it was okay, we're playing

dress-up," said Alice. Francie's mom did not like this at all, Alice saw, so she quickly added, "My mom doesn't care."

"Well, I care on her behalf, or on behalf of that beautiful dress. It looks like raw silk. Don't you dare go dragging it through the dirt, Francie."

"We can babysit Sam, Mrs. Fultz," Alice offered.

"Don't call me that, Alice, you know my name."

Alice nodded, but she couldn't bring herself to say it. Marietta was a straight-spined woman who seemed to hum and crackle with energy. She was much thinner than Alice's mom, her hair cropped into an angular frame along her jaw on one side and shorn up over her ear on the other. She had a piercing in her nose that caught the light, very tiny, like the head of a silver pin. Not gold.

Carefully, Alice negotiated the concrete steps, trying not to trip on the hem of her sister Kate's grade eight graduation gown. While it was true that Sally had given Francie permission to wear the wedding dress, Kate didn't know Alice was borrowing her gown. Kate never would have said yes.

The gown was made of slippery silver material and had spaghetti straps and a very long skirt. Alice was swimming in it.

She lifted Sam out of the grass and took a good sniff of his head as she pulled him close. He smelled like baby fluff, wet popcorn, maybe a little bit like pee, if pee smelled good. Sam grabbed Alice's cheeks in both hands and squeezed.

"No pinching!" Marietta scolded him.

"He's not pinching," Alice said, wriggling as one of the shoulder straps slipped down. She stared into Sam's black eyes, willing him not to pinch. Her own eyes began to water. "Peekaboo!" she said, and Sam giggled, the sound rumbling up from his belly.

"If you want to watch him . . ." Marietta drifted up the driveway, holding the plates. She was gone before Sam even noticed.

As soon as her mother was out of sight, Francie said, "You don't have to hold him."

"You're so lucky," Alice couldn't help saying. "I want a baby brother."

"You can have him." Francie grabbed the black metal railing that was sunk into the concrete stoop and swung through its wide bars down to the grass, the dress swishing as she landed. She dusted rust off her hands. "Let's do something."

"Let's look for the jewels!"

Francie shook her head no. "He can't come along, he's a spy." She pulled Sam out of Alice's arms and set him to stand, wobbling, on the grass. "Look, he can walk now." Balanced upright on bow legs, on fat, round feet, arms outstretched for balance, it looked like a trick, like a doll come to life, or maybe a miniature zombie, staggering away from them. He was surprisingly fast, rocketing down toward the bus stop where a man stood smoking; but the hill was too steep. Sam fell, bounced up again, fists out, like he was looking for a fight.

"Bad boy, bad Sam!" Francie caught him and snatched him up roughly, and the smoking man glanced to see what all the shrieking was about, and it seemed to Alice that people were watching all of a sudden, the invisible wall separating them from everyone else had been broken.

"I'll hold him," she offered, caught in Kate's train. The shoulder straps kept slipping down.

Francie's expression was weary. She let Alice take Sam. They no longer seemed to be refugees, the dresses had transformed them into something grander, but not princesses. They were wearing stolen gowns.

This isn't a game, Alice thought.

"Is your dad stealing the jewels?" she whispered over Sam's head. "Tell me! You have to tell me!"

"We have to be very quiet," said Francie. She looked tired, like she'd already gone on a long journey. Alice followed Francie's trudging steps up the empty driveway, her mom's wedding dress sweeping before her on the cracked pavement. Francie paused and they listened.

Someone was singing in the backyard.

Silently, Alice came up beside Francie, but she couldn't interpret what she was seeing. Marietta sat on the ground facing away from them, cross-legged on a blanket, her lower body unmoving and still, legs pasted to the ground, while her upper body turned in whirling circles. It was Marietta's voice singing, monotone. Alice shivered, but Francie looked satisfied, and grim, as she opened the side door. She moved purposefully—she knew where the jewels were!

The plates from lunch were stacked on the bottom step inside the door. They didn't take off their shoes. Alice almost tripped on Kate's skirt, scattering the plates. But she didn't drop Sam.

Alice had never been inside Francie's parents' bedroom before—dim, no window.

She held her breath as Francie swept toward the bed, knelt down, and pulled out a black gym bag, the zipper unzipped. Francie dug around, it was too dark to see, Alice could hear the crinkling of plastic. "Where is it, where is it!" Francie whispered, almost frantic.

"Fool's gold?" Alice breathed. Sam was unusually alert and quiet in her arms.

Francie pushed the bag back under the bed and hurried to the wooden dresser. Her hands fluttered across its top.

What were they looking for?

Francie yanked open a drawer, digging through soft piles of clothes, slammed it shut, opened another drawer. Alice didn't like this feeling at all, not knowing. She pressed in closer, she had to see!

"Oh!" they gasped.

At the exact same moment, Alice saw what Francie saw. Francie's hands jumped apart, jumped away from the object like she'd been burnt. "There," she whispered.

The object was not very big and not very well hidden. It lay on a bed of neatly folded socks and underwear.

Not fool's gold.

Alice had never seen a gun before. Yet she knew what it was. "Is it real?"

Francie was trying to shut the drawer, but the drawer was stuck. "The jewels are gone," she said in a strangled voice, like she wanted to say more but couldn't. The words were stuck, the pretending was stuck. "Stolen!"

"We have to find them!" Alice almost shouted, forgetting about being quiet.

Did Alice believe there were jewels? Or ever had been? Did she believe the jewels had been stolen? Yes, in the same way the dog was a wolf, and its angry owner was a witch, and the horses had carried them to safety. But the gun—that was in a different category, all its own, less believable and more real.

It had the power to destroy their story.

Francie pushed Alice, shoved her to get her moving out of the dark bedroom.

"Hey!"

"We have to hurry," said Francie. "We have to find the stolen jewels."

Alice couldn't hurry in Kate's skirt.

Anyway, it was too late. Francie's mom stood in the doorway, holding a rolled-up blanket under her armpit. She didn't say a word. She pulled Sam from Alice's arms. Time lurched. "You're not allowed in this room."

"We're very sorry," squeaked Alice.

"You're never allowed in this room. What are you doing in here?"

"Looking for jewels," said Francie. That made it sound real, after all.

"Someone stole them!" said Alice.

Marietta sighed. She almost laughed. Alice felt herself relax, she pushed up a shoulder strap. Francie's eyes darted to the drawer, slightly open, but Marietta didn't seem to notice.

"I think it's time you both got changed out of those dresses," she told them. "You're going to ruin them. Look at that train, it's already filthy."

Outside, the air was clear and everything looked bright and weird.

Alice wanted to talk to Francie about it, about what they'd seen and what it was and what it meant. But she couldn't. Francie said the jewels were buried in the front yard, and Alice wanted to help her, to make this bad feeling go away, this feeling she didn't understand—that she needed to wreck something. She was sure Francie was feeling it too. This was why they stopped and knelt beside the stoop and started digging. There wasn't much grass here, but it felt good to tear into it, rip it up, dig their fingernails into the dirt. They dug as one bus stopped and another and another.

No jewels.

No gold.

No nothing.

But of course, there wouldn't be. There never was. Alice knew it in her heart. She wanted to tell Francie, but she didn't know how. The words were plain and obvious, but impossible to speak out loud. Why?

They dug all along the front of the house, making a royal mess, efficient as killers (of grass and weeds), till Francie's dad pulled into the driveway in his big golden car, window down, elbow resting on the door frame, sticking out, a song playing loudly on the radio. The car rolled past them, parked out of sight, around the corner of the house. Alice hopped up and said they needed to go home now and get changed. "Come on, Francie!"

She didn't want Francie to know how afraid she was of her dad.

But maybe Francie guessed it anyway. "What're you so scared of?" She sounded almost mean.

Alice shook dirt off the skirt. "Kate is going to be mad about this dress," she said. But that wasn't true, not at all— Alice wasn't scared of Kate.

Oh.

So that's what it felt like to tell a lie.

It felt a little bit like playing, a little too near to playing. Alice didn't like this feeling. But Francie just said okay, and they left the mess in the yard and started walking down the sidewalk, holding up the skirts of their fancy gowns, watching everyone watching them.

≪≪

Honestly, that pair! In Marietta's opinion, Alice was too nice, too easily swayed by Francie, it wasn't good for Francie, she needed a friend with more backbone, someone who would push against her more.

Marietta noticed that one of the dresser drawers was ajar. That wouldn't do. But when she went to close it, there was some resistance, it was jammed. The room was dark, this cave in the middle of this house. Marietta shivered, she was always cold these days. She flashed to a vision of herself naked and walking through a boiling hot desert, alone, nothing to hold, nothing to drink or eat, dissolving into dust under the searing sun. It would feel so good.

Sam wriggled in her arms, waking her to her task.

She set the folded blanket on top of the dresser.

She pulled on the drawer, wrenched on it, and it slid open. Marietta's eyes had adjusted to the dim light in the room. And now she knew, she thought, seeing herself frozen in time, in this moment that had been waiting for her to arrive, gazing down at the gun. Instinctively, she covered Sam's eyes, as if he would understand. A flood of questions, and then only the one, the question that was not a question: Did he want her to find it?

With her free hand, she covered it up, nestled it into the rough, worn fabric that filled Luce's socks-and-underwear drawer. The drawer slid back into place, returned to its grooves, flush with the front of the dresser. Without thinking, she ran her fingers along the dresser's edge: no dust. There were no decorations on the plain white walls. Nothing on the floor. This house was just a house, did not belong to them, it could be left behind on a moment's notice. She could do that, it felt like it would require no effort, leaving this place behind.

It would turn to dust behind her.

The bed was as she'd made it after waking from her nap, the pillows fluffed, neat and tidy. She sat down.

Well, now she knew. Now she knew, which was better than not knowing, with knowledge came acceptance, or action. But ignorance was preferable, so much easier. Sam squirmed. In one fluid, automatic motion, Marietta pulled up her t-shirt and offered her breast to Sam, forgetting he'd been weaned, forgetting her milk had dried up. But Sam knew. He knew he'd get nothing out of her. He didn't even try.

She folded down over his body, crooked in her arms, suddenly so tired she could scarcely stand the thought of the long night that awaited, ahead—awake in the halls of the Lodge, sluicing urine off the bathroom floors, listening for the sounds of terror.

She longed for the bliss of ignorance. The blank of it.

If only she could empty out her mind.

Luce would be home soon—or should be, needed to be, if Marietta was to leave for work in a few hours.

Should I leave the children with him?

The thought washed through her body, cold at first, attacking her gut, but it changed quickly, burning from cold to hot in an instant of deep discomfort, almost pain. She sat up straight.

"I need to look you in the eye," she said as if Luce were here before her.

Marietta tugged her shirt down over her stomach. "Nap time," she said, though of course it wasn't. She washed Sam's face in the kitchen sink and set him into his crib with a sippy cup of powdered milk, closed the rattling blind against the sight of the backyard with the rotten picnic table at its centre. Sam stared at her, outraged, as she left him, pulling the door shut as she went.

She could hear him beating his sippy cup against the slats of the crib.

Now, Marietta locked herself into the bathroom, sat on cold tiles with her lower back flush against the wall. She leaned her head on the coolness of the porcelain sink; cold, cold, cold to the bone. She opened her pay-per-minute cell and began tapping in Irene's number—Mrs. Fultz, as she still thought of her. Mrs. Fultz, former school secretary, who knew a few too many of Marietta's secrets, her high school secrets, her stupid, partying, rebellious, sad little truant secrets. Mrs. Fultz who said, sitting behind her desk outside the principal's office, "You should stay away from my son." Locker doors slamming in the hallway. "You can call me Irene, I feel very fondly toward you, but you should stay away from him. You're a smart girl and I want more for you." *But we love each other!* Oh, teenaged Marietta, hair in a long braid over her shoulder, heavy black makeup around her eyes. *Only I can save him.* "My dear, you'll ruin both your lives."

Marietta snapped the phone shut. Not Irene.

She tapped in another number, hoping she'd remembered it correctly.

"Hello?"

Marietta held her breath.

"Hello?" Mikey sounded far away. "Hello, who's there?"

"It's me," breathed Marietta. "Marietta."

"Marietta! No way! How are you?"

"It's about Luce." Marietta's voice trembled, contracted. "He's got a gun, Mikey."

Something was up with Mari, Luce thought. She came out of the house as soon as he put the car into park, in their driveway. He didn't even have time to roll up the windows or turn off the radio. Country station.

"You have to help me move the picnic table," she told him. "Okay?"

He climbed out of the car. It took him a minute to get himself sorted, he needed time, she needed to give him time, and he could tell she wasn't thinking like that. She was miles ahead of him already, and not in the mood to watch him stand propped against the open door, shifting his weight from his good leg to his bad leg, trying to wake the thing up, trying to get rid of the pins and needles and the goddam pain. "Give me a minute, Mari."

She was rushing off to the backyard. She had plans.

Okay, Mari. After you.

She sat on the picnic table to show him how it shifted and tilted as she rocked its rotten frame—not safe, no longer safe, a danger to us all. *Sure, Mari, yeah, the picnic table is the problem.* She hopped off and began dragging it, she was having trouble, pulling it by inches through the grass, but she was strong, she had this, she didn't need him. She was almost to the driveway. "Mari, I'm gonna have to move my car," Luce said, she'd better not scrape his goddam paint job with that thing.

"Help me!" she yelled at him.

He got back into the car and put it into reverse, rolling down to the end of the driveway to give her room.

He climbed back up the little hill. She was on the pavement now, the wooden legs were starting to buckle. "Here"— he lifted the back end with a gut-level groan he hoped she wouldn't notice, and together they carried the table across the yard, over the sidewalk, and set it down beside the bus stop. *Jesus.* He had to sit on it for a minute. The pain was always, it was ever, but sometimes it was worse. "I can't carry shit anymore, Mari, you know that."

"I'm sorry," she said. "I feel better now, I really do."

She climbed up and sat beside him on the picnic table. *God. Mari.* He put his hand over her knee, enfolded it. "Hey, I'm glad," said Luce. *I'm glad you feel better now.*

This felt good, it felt right, the two of them, pretending no one was staring from the bus stop, traffic speeding by. It never stopped. Relentless.

He wished he had something to give her, some good news.

When Marietta called, it wasn't like Mikey hadn't thought about it happening, hadn't hoped it might happen, hadn't imagined her voice on the other end of the line. It had been a while, but it was always a possibility, as long as they'd been friends—since high school—although that would have been a land line, and in truth, Marietta only called Mikey's house to ask if he knew where Luce was, back when Luce went by Lucky. High school, not Mikey's favourite time of life. And yes, Mikey almost always knew where Luce was—Lucky—and it was never somewhere he wanted to tell Marietta about, so they'd get to talking instead, about Lucky, and how much she loved him even though he kept hurting her like this, but also about other things, whatever was going on in her head, how messed up her parents were, or how she was thinking about dropping out, what was the point, and Mikey would reassure her and talk her down and remind her that she was, like, the smartest person he knew. *If I was so smart, would I be going out with Luce?* She always called him Luce, not Lucky, like she saw the irony and wanted nothing to do with it.

When Marietta called, Mikey was in line at the drive-through, thinking about ordering the triple burger combo with a chocolate milkshake.

It had been such a long time. Almost a year, but he knew her voice instantly.

"It's me," she said, "Marietta."

She could've stopped at *It's me* and he would have known, her voice was a key, it unlocked him: *It's you.*

"Marietta! No way!" I've been thinking about you, he wanted to say, but she was already talking. She seemed rattled, she seemed off. "Hang on, I can't hear you," he said, "don't go anywhere," and he leaned out the window and asked for the chicken wrap, skip the fries, and a diet soda. Because of her. He did it for Marietta. She always made him better than he was. Wasn't that the definition of a true friend? Or had he got that muddled—was it the definition of true love?

Either way. It didn't really matter, he didn't want anything from her, just this.

"I'm back," he said, "I'm here."

She didn't reply immediately, and he couldn't get a picture settled in his head of where she was calling from. "Hey, Marietta, are you there? How are you? It's great to hear your voice."

"It's about Luce," she said again. He'd heard that the first time, but not what came after. Maybe he didn't want to hear what came after. Maybe, just once, he'd like to hear from Marietta and not have it be about Luce.

"Okay," he said. He was pulling up to the window to pay, digging for change in the ashtray so he could hand over the exact amount, down to the penny.

"Mikey, he's got a gun."

Okay. Okay, okay, okay.

"Did you hear me? Mikey?"

"Don't say it again," he said. "I heard you."

"What the fuck, Mikey? What the fuck am I supposed to do now?" Yeah, she was in a bad way, it was reminding him of that time Luce got pulled over driving from one job to another, broken taillight or something minor like that, and he decided on the spot to eat all the acid in his possession—in case he got caught with it, great solution—and he freaked out and spent the night in custody. Luce and Marietta had just had their first kid, and Luce and Mikey were working together on the same crew, early days, before they set out on their own.

Of course, Marietta had been a wreck. Of course, Mikey had sorted it out.

Of course, this was much worse.

"Hang on." Mikey counted out loonies, toonies, nickels, and dimes in his palm and passed them over to the girl waiting at the open window. The girl was wearing a headset and seemed to be taking an order even as she counted the change.

"You're short ten cents," she said.

"Impossible," said Mikey, "are you sure?"

"Yes I'm sure!" said Marietta.

"Sorry, I'm talking to . . ."

"Yes," said the girl with the headset, her hand held out for more.

Mikey gave her a quarter. "Keep the change."

"Food's at the next window," said the girl, to him, then into the headset: "Can I take your order?"

"Is this a bad time, did I catch you at a bad time?"

"I'm listening, Marietta."

"Mikey, I don't know what to do."

"Where are you right now?"

"I'm at home."

"I'll swing by," Mikey said. He stopped at the second window, another teenager in a headset handed him a bag of grub and a large cup stuck into a cardboard holder. Mikey didn't want the cardboard holder, but it was too late. He had to keep moving, that was the nature of lineups and drive-throughs, out of the parking lot and into traffic, one hand holding the phone and the other trying to organize the excess packaging across the bench seat, beside his right thigh.

"No!" Marietta was saying. "No, no, no! You can't come here. Don't come here."

"Right, right." Mikey was already in the turn lane, blinker on. He was driving kind of erratically, he realized, changing lanes without checking his mirrors, digging around in the paper sack for the chicken wrap, wishing to God he'd ordered the fries. And maybe one of those hot apple pies. And a milkshake.

"I want you to talk to him," Marietta was saying. "I can't talk to him. Someone needs to talk to him. It can't be me."

"Okay, but what do you want me to say?" Mikey took a bite of the wrap and mayo squirted out onto his dark t-shirt. Great! Now he really couldn't stop by. *C'mon man, she just told you not to come over!* Mikey chewed, swallowed, said: "We're not really talking right now, me and Luce. I told him not to come to any of the sites anymore."

"I didn't know that."

"You didn't know that?"

"Do you think he tells me anything?" Was she crying? He hoped not and he hoped so, in a way, confusion doubling his vision, twining together contradictions. "You'll know what to say, I just know you'll know, you always do," Marietta said. "You've always been so good for Luce. Like a brother."

The damn truck was driving itself directly toward her, it was like Mikey had nothing to do with it.

"Of course," he promised her. "I'll talk to him."

"Thank you! Thank you, thank you."

He was slowing now, the truck was slowing of its own accord, and his head snapped to the right as he passed by her house, where she must be, this very minute. Wait! Was that her? He was confused—could that be her, kneeling beside the driveway in a fancy dress? No, his mind was playing tricks on him. The house was behind him in the rear-view mirror, gone, out of sight, and the chicken wrap was gone, and he wiped his palm over the mayo stain, and Marietta was saying, "I have to go now. Thank you, I love you."

Wait, what?

Say that again.

"Don't even mention it," Mikey heard himself saying, cool as a goddam cucumber, a real sensitive guy, reaching for the soda, *diet*, for Pete's sake. "I'll take care of it. It's gonna be okay, Marietta." He loved her name, in his mouth, on his tongue. But what now?

She'd hung up. He was going fast in the wrong direction, and he needed a plan.

SEVEN

Gun Run

Francie was in the woods on the other side of the stream. She breathed in a giant, calming gulp of air and set the busted, soaking sneakers down, arranged them neatly on a rock sticking out of the ground. They were too small. She'd outgrown them this spring. Her toes had poked holes in the tops. She didn't need them anymore, and anyway, she still had the socks, wet, but fine: pale-blue ankle socks decorated with tiny rainbows. Mom had found them at the dollar store, three pairs for a dollar, such an amazing deal that Mom had to tell Francie, even though she'd wrapped the socks as a birthday gift.

Francie rolled them, one then the other, onto her feet.

Stood.

Her stomach dropped as she looked at her feet in socks, and at her sneakers, waiting to be left behind. She wanted to say goodbye to the shoes, but she knew she shouldn't, couldn't, wouldn't. She stepped over them and began to walk away, and she didn't turn around, not once. She said, "They're just shoes, they're not even people."

She could almost hear Alice agreeing: *The shoes are not alive.*

For a moment, Francie felt like she wasn't alone. The feeling was nice, but she had to keep moving, even if she didn't know where she was going—especially because of that. The bottoms of her feet hurt, poked by sticks and rocks. It was going to get harder. It was going to be impossible, Francie understood.

She was walking in circles. Here was the stream again. A different part, but the same. Everything looked the same: clump of weeds, clump of scrawny little trees. A swarm of fly specks hovered over her head. Something sharp tore a hole in one of the socks.

"We'll get there by nightfall," Francie said, and again, she could almost hear Alice's squeaky voice insisting: *We have to be back in time for the concert!*

The concert the concert the concert!

EIGHT

Tickets

Mrs. G's music portable was warm this morning, humid, the way it got every year during the final month of school, when the fullness of leaves on the trees met the sudden warmth that accompanied the lengthening days, all in a rush.

Mrs. G (short for Greenaway) did not go by Mrs. G anywhere but here, in the classroom that had been hers for the past seventeen springs. There was no Mr. G, hadn't been for more than a decade, and she didn't miss him, her mother had been right, they were an odd match, not to say a bad match, just downright peculiar, no one could understand it, as her mother said, but Mrs. G had kept his name, thinking of it as her professional name, her stage name, as if she were a famous musician or conductor, which pleased her, tickled her funny bone. The children— her audience—did gaze at her sometimes with greater than average attention, even mild adoration. *Our beloved Mrs. Greenaway, our magnificent Mrs. G*, she imagined the principal of the moment intoning upon the occasion of her eventual retirement . . . and there the reverie both began and ended.

She sipped at her mug of hot lemon water, perched on top of the desk in the corner, legs swinging, waiting for the bell to ring and the children most keen, most devoted, to burst through the portable's door, those willing to forgo recess for choir practice. Their scents of salami and carrot sticks and damp socks would mingle with the scents born in the portable itself—dried spit inside plastic recorders, the metallic green of tarnished music stands, musty sheets of music, and, she was certain, the persistent tang of black mould spreading behind the walls.

Grey sky pressed against the narrow, high windows. This was a cocoon, a safe, sheltered space for these hungry children, little caterpillars turning unknowingly into butterflies before her eyes. Part of her rejected the sugary sentiment, while another part reached for a spare ukulele, resting on the desktop, and strummed a chord to go along with it. Her sugariest compositions found the biggest audiences. In the past year, she'd started recording herself playing and singing, uploading the grainy digital videos. She was careful not to show her face, just her hands on the strings of her pineapple uke, beneath breasts pleasantly framed in a low-cut t-shirt.

Anonymous Maggie.

Words and melody came easily to her, almost always paired, but to no practical end. "Why aren't you the most famous singer in Canada?" Mrs. G's mother had asked with astonishment as genuine as it was innocent, the last time Mrs. G dropped in for a surprise visit, expecting disaster and finding nothing definitive. Half a store-bought pie, draped in a tea towel, gone mouldy on the counter? Dead fern on the windowsill? Unmade bed? "Why aren't you altogether famous? Maggie, you should be!"

"Oh, Mom! Good grief. I love what I do!"

"You should be rich and famous and then I would be rich and famous."

"As you deserve to be." She bent to kiss her mother's soft cheek, looking into those amber eyes, the colour fading, fading, fading away (accurate, and also a promising lyric line). How long should her mother continue to live on her own, was it safe, and how would either of them recognize when the threshold had been crossed?

Surely the fact that her mother had figured out how to watch Anonymous Maggie videos on YouTube was an argument for giving her the benefit of the doubt!

The bell had rung.

Mrs. G set down the ukulele, and hopped off the desk.

"Leave your shoes at the door!"

The children who were playing ukuleles for the concert retrieved them, and tinny, arbitrary, off-key plucking commenced.

"Clap if you can hear me." Mrs. G spoke softly. "Clap if you can hear." And the children organized themselves in record time, she should have a stopwatch to show the other teachers, the cruel ones who in the lounge discussed "bad" kids and "good" ones.

The choir sat cross-legged on the carpet before her. Together, they were a self-sustaining pod floating through space.

"Tuning time!" She blew a G through the pipe, followed by C and E and A.

This was the place to be, this was the bliss. Those who needed to drift could drift. Those who needed to sing with their heads thrown back could sing with their heads thrown back. Though collectively they were working toward the end-of-year concert, a shared project, the concert was but a destination. This could go into her new song: that in between caterpillar and butterfly was the cocoon, that there was beauty in being in-between. Not like that, she would need better phrasing.

"Let's begin with our ukes!"

Mrs. G could hear some of the children humming their parts as they waited their turn, others were almost asleep, eyes closed, relaxed. The ukuleles struggled against the tyranny of rhythm, against time itself, though she raised and lowered her baton in ever more meaningful slashes: "On the beat, one and two and three and four and—"

She was on their side, she was with them, even as she fought to give them structure—she too was struggling against time itself, struggling to control it, to hold it, as they floated together in their protective pod through the universe.

How badly she wanted everyone to be safe.

"Stand," she commanded the choir. They burst forth like flood waters released from a dam. "Soloists, step forward." There was only one soloist for this song, an African-American spiritual that Mrs. G feared might attract censure for its mention of God. She imagined herself arguing for the song's cultural value, its roots as code along the Underground Railroad, its astonishing endurance, its ability to shift and remain relevant across eras, she could play the Ramsey Lewis version and the Ella Jenkins version and a gospel choir version (which she had done for the children); but it would not help her cause that the soloist was a pasty-faced child with the voice of a weary truck-stop waitress, an arresting voice, a deep range for a child, and threaded with odd colours and textures. Not entirely in tune, but that was part of the appeal. You sing like a fallen angel after an all-night bender in a small-town bar, was not an appropriate comment to offer, so what she'd told the child was this: "You sing like an angel."

She did not fear the compliment would go to the child's head. A little sugar in the tea never hurt anyone.

Mrs. G did not get attached to the children who flowed through her portable, year layered upon year. Talent was capricious, fickle, it did not belong to the person on which it had been visited, no more than it belonged to those who wished to profit from it. But she revelled in these random visitations from a greater source. She was a diviner, looking ever for water in a parched field, and finding it, more often than you'd think.

"Ready for your close-up?"

The child nodded and opened her eyes wide, as if stapling the lids to her brow—good girl. She'd been paying attention.

Arms raised, and . . . they were off!

"*See that boy all dressed in black?*" the child sang in her rough voice.

"*God's gonna trouble the water,*" the choir replied.

"*He's come far away and he won't go back!*" the child shouted. Okay, not exactly the line, but close enough.

"*God's gonna trouble the water!*" the choir shouted back.

You don't teach this, Mrs. G knew, you can't. You can't teach a child how to throw her whole body into a performance, and you don't need to. You just need to give her a few tips, give her the stage. Give her an audience! Let her break all those hard, yearning adult hearts. This was school concert gold, this would be what everyone came looking for without knowing they'd come looking for anything at all.

The children were singing the last line together now: *"God's gonna trouble the water."*

Hold that final note, hold, hold, hold. Every eye was attached to Mrs. G's. Her arms drew circles, closing it down, and her fingers pinched shut—almost.

The last note faded out softer and softer till she could hardly hear the hum of its vibration from their lips. And—done!

"This is going to be good," said Mrs. G. "Next, let's try our version of 'Landslide.' Ukuleles step forward."

The loudspeaker crackled and she turned, frowning, her baton held aloft. "Francie Fultz please come to the office, Francie Fultz."

"Always during our choir practice!"

The child stared at the carpet.

"Are you coming back?" Mrs. G felt impatience creep into her shoulders. "I have forms for ticket sales today. Children, you need to sell tickets for the concert, it's a fund-raiser for—" But she couldn't recall which pet project the new principal had selected this spring. "They're stacked on my desk. Take one as you leave, Francie."

"Francie Fultz to the office, to the office, Francie Fultz."

"We hear you!" Mrs. G's head snapped round to address the loudspeaker. She'd spoken too harshly, even if only to an inanimate object. The choir stopped its rustling and seemed to hold its breath.

Francie hadn't moved.

"Go on!" Mrs. G barked. She could hear herself, the pressure was going up, but she couldn't stop herself. Interruption of the flow caused a breach in focus that would waste precious minutes. Choir practice was squeezed as it was, with the new principal's interest in healthful physical activity and participation in team sports (as if choir didn't tick both of those boxes!).

The child stood by the door trying to stuff her feet into her shoes without touching the laces. "Take a ticket form from my desk, Francie, the green form, take one before you go."

When the portable door opened, fresh air rushed in. The ukulele chorus couldn't settle themselves to strum in unison, and Mrs. G thought this rehearsal was over. She would have these children for eight more minutes, but it was over.

Let it be.

"Put down the instruments. We're going to do jumping jacks! Everyone! Make room, make space!"

The portable shook and the children were laughing and Mrs. G joined in too, till her anger and disappointment and worry thinned out, like her mother's hair, seen from above. She was jumping like an oversized child in a room full of actual children, and she was watching herself massage oil into her mother's scalp after helping her to wash her sparse curls in the sink, her mother sitting patiently with a towel around her neck, and everything was turned around the wrong way.

Time, it rushed. It rushed away from you.

A good day. A perfect day. Today was the day everything was going to change. Luce could hardly wait to tell Marietta, but he needed more details, she liked details, she didn't have time for pie in the sky.

Give me potatoes on the table.

Or something like that. Wow, he felt good. He was a bit high, truth be told, riding his own DIY project, a patch sectioned into a grid, scissored into doses, zipped into a plastic bag. But today, this is over! Today, it ends!

Luce reached for his phone, on the floor beside the bed, to listen to Mikey's message again.

"Luce, it's Mikey. I'm sorry, man, I know it's been a while. Listen, can you come out to the site today, the one on Highway 9? I'll be there all day." Pause. "There's something I need to talk to you about. It's important." Pause. "Okay? Okay. Hope to see you. Call me back."

Mikey! The man! Coming through for Luce just when Luce had given up on him. Like he always did.

Luce had been up and down since 5 a.m. He'd woken alert, energized, excited, like he'd been expecting Mikey's call, he thought, expecting a twist, a change, something good coming around the bend. Up at 5 a.m., turned on the shower, burned one-ninth of the patch, went out to the backyard, nowhere to sit, a sickly rectangle of yellow grass where the picnic table had been, bathroom again, burned another ninth. Took an actual shower. Back to bed before Mari got up with the kids. Stayed in bed, dozing, listening to them getting ready to leave.

Them, leaving.

Him, staying. Digging in the bag under the bed for a pill, crushing it on the dresser with the back of his phone, inhaling. Wiping the top of the dresser clean with his arm.

Dozing.

Soon, he'd have a job again, and then he could pay for this shit without having to sell it, he wouldn't owe that Seth character a goddam wooden nickel. He wouldn't owe anyone anything.

But you're quitting this shit, remember?

Funny thing—listening to the message, again, Luce thought it had gotten into his dreams. Like he'd just seen

Mikey, grinning at him, throwing his arms out wide, saying, *It's been too long, man, I really missed you. We need you around here.*

Yeah, you do.

This is the good news. Luce looked at the ceiling. Mari had closed the bedroom door and it was very dark. The good news he'd been waiting for. It was time, time to go clear, time to be a different man, he would get up early and do push-ups, crunches, he'd start those physio exercises printed on the piece of paper from that doctor at the walk-in clinic, he'd rehab himself. It wasn't too late.

This is the day. I'm back in business. With no one in the house, Luce smoked another grid of the patch freely, standing over the kitchen sink, squeezing the gel onto a little platter of foil, sweeping the flame of his lighter on its underside, breathing it in. His thoughts rolled like clear water. When he saw Mikey in person, he was going to say: I'm clean. All that trouble is over. Look at me, I'm back, Mikey, it's me. His thoughts tumbled, cutting a route through the rapids. He was the clear water, he was the tumbling, he was the motion, the action, the rush, the calm.

You need me, Mikey, you always have.

He put on a shirt that buttoned up, with a collar, splashed his face in the sink, ran a comb through his hair, decided to leave the stubble, he liked the way it made him look—tough, not trying too hard. There was nothing in the bathroom mirror to tell him that what was happening wasn't what was happening, no warning flares, no smashing on the rocks, he looked like a man who was on his way to success, of some kind or other.

He'd have good news for Mari, by dinnertime.

Imagine taking Mari out to dinner!

He went out the side door, and tossed the gym bag in behind the front seat. It was time to get rid of this shit. In the car, he noticed his stomach was none too settled. The presence of six more opportunities zipped into a sandwich bag in his shirt pocket—no comfort. Appetite and desire were unhinged, unhooked from each other, free-floating agitators pinging like electrical shocks.

He needed the kid. She steadied him. He needed her.

Francie Fultz to the office, Francie Fultz.

Thank you, ma'am.

"Come on." He grabbed the kid by the arm to hurry her up. No time to waste. The day was dissolving. "What's this?" Kid was trying to hand over a flapping piece of paper, medicine green, Luce tossed it on the dash, turned the key, the roar of the engine could be coming from his own chest. Better. Wasn't it?

The green paper threw a glare onto the windshield and Luce swatted it off as they did a U-turn, back home. He'd just remembered something important. One more tick on the to-do list, to do: get clear, get clean, get rid of. New day, new start, new life.

Kid looked a little green herself, clutching her paper to her chest. "What's your problem?" Luce said. That wasn't fair, he knew, hating himself—was he expecting a different kid than the one who'd turned up? "It's all okay, just a little housekeeping," he added. "Important to keep track of the details, right, kiddo, or the details'll track you down."

He pulled into the driveway. Left the engine running.

Wait here. Maybe he said it, maybe not, it was hard to tell what was happening inside his head and what was happening outside. The pain was creeping back. In through the side door, boots on, *fuck the mess, Mari, get your priorities straight, I'm doing the right thing, I'm about to do the right thing.*

Luce stopped in the bedroom and burned another ninth. Five left.

Okay, after that thing, I'm doing the right thing.

Smart little gun, wasn't it. Handy. Its purpose not yet clear. For protection? Maybe. That's why he'd asked Seth to hook him up. But it didn't make him feel safer. Holding it, walking out of the bedroom, it rattled him, it wanted to be used.

He had to take care of it, hide it, neutralize it, he had things to do, a whole series of right and perfect and good and simple things. Luce banged out through the front door, it opened easily enough—"See, it's not broken!"—and he stopped and eyed that gap between the stoop and the house, a little gap to solve a big problem. In one clean movement, he dropped the gun. *There!* It fell silently, and he checked over his shoulder as if someone was watching. Who would be watching? Smooth, he'd moved so smoothly, like his thoughts, like clear water, rushing.

Now shut the door.

But the door wouldn't shut. Luce wrestled with it, feeling eyes burning into him, watching, judging—*I'll fix it, Mari, I swear!*—till he got it jammed into the frame, closed. Most of the way. Almost. Enough.

He swung his bad leg down the steps, gripping the railing, starting to sweat. "Gotta fix that door," he said, and the kid looked at him. Had she been looking this hard at him her whole life, or was this new?

"It's all good news today," Luce told her.

"Okay," she said, and stared down at the green piece of paper she was holding on her lap.

His phone was buzzing, but he didn't pick up. He had everything he needed right here. A plan, a kid, a bag of shit to get rid of. He turned on the radio, punched through the stations. They were in the country now, cruising. *You can relax.*

Kid was rustling around. Humming.

"Jesus, kiddo, can't you ever be quiet? I'm trying to think." *For fuck's sake.*

"You make this much noise all the time? You're like an alarm clock with no snooze button."

He looked at the road getting eaten up by the car.

"Know where we're going?"

"Grandma's house?" No more humming.

Luce reached over and patted the kid's hand. He felt soft toward her, soft toward everything that was coming at him. Soft toward the horse and buggy trotting in gravel on the side of the road, soft toward the man in the cap holding the reins. "He's sitting on a bench seat from a car, did you notice? They use car seats in their buggies, must be heavy for the horse." *Poor horse.* The softness was melting, oozing, turning into something that felt like tears, leaking from his eyes. What was happening wasn't what was happening, but he didn't want to know.

At his mom's house, he grabbed the gym bag and dragged himself around to the back. The kid followed. Field looked great, yard looked terrible. Luce rapped on the window in the back door. "She's home, her car's here," he said to the kid.

He tried the door handle—open. "Ma! You've got company!"

A person could spend his whole life trying to get back to the one place where he remembered feeling safe, and it wouldn't be enough. It wouldn't be there anymore. Didn't exist. This house was proof.

His mom came from the kitchen wiping her hands on her apron.

"I'm making pie," she said.

She was always making something. She could be counted on for that.

What was he making?

"Say hi to Francie."

"Isn't it a school day?" She frowned.

"Francie wanted to visit. She wanted to learn how to make pie." He pushed the kid forward, and went down the hallway to his old bedroom. It smelled like sawdust and mould, mouse dirt on the carpet. He set the gym bag onto the twin bed and took a look around. The person who won all these trophies could not imagine you, he thought, even as he was overcome by the memory of running through the woods, a pack of stringy boys behind him, feeling like he was tearing all his feelings out of his body, emptying himself to nothing so he wouldn't have to feel what it felt like to belong to someone who hadn't wanted to exist anymore. *What did you do that was so bad?* The question was for his dad, the question was for himself.

He moved away from the gym bag. It wasn't even zipped up. It belonged in this room, with the rest of this shit. *Leave it, leave it behind.*

In the kitchen, his mom was tying an apron around Francie's waist.

"Stay, I'll make you a cup of coffee."

"Not now, I have an important meeting."

"Oh?"

"It's a good day, Ma. I'll have good news when I come back for a piece of pie."

"Good news?" Her voice rose and wobbled.

"Try to be happy for me, for once," he said.

She held his hand. What if she knew his hand didn't feel like a hand, it felt like a piece of wood? She might as well be holding a piece of wood. He'd leave it behind for her, she could keep it in his old bedroom, display it on a shelf till it was covered in dust too.

He'd forgotten about the kid till he was limping around the side of the house, the yard was full of weeds, needed someone to mow it once in a while. The kid was following after him, saying she wanted to come with him, please, grabbing his arm.

"Be back soon," Luce told her. He didn't need her anymore, funny how the urgency came, and went. He shook her off. Easy. *Leave it, leave it behind.* What was happening was not what was happening, and just then, he knew it. He knew it was a lie, because he knew he was a liar. But the lie felt important. It felt like love.

⚜

"Does your mom know where you are?" Irene stood with Francie in the front yard and watched her son's ridiculous Cadillac peel out and away. Where on earth was he headed with eyes like that? Pupils like pinpoints, two dots on the way to vanishing.

Irene put her hands onto Francie's shoulders and steered her into the house. "Is your mom at work today? Where does she work on Thursdays?"

But her granddaughter didn't know. The child was preoccupied, unhappy, locked as tightly as a vault. What were the right questions in this situation?

"Where was your dad going, just now?"

Francie had stuffed her backpack behind the wicker magazine rack in the front room, where she stood, hands behind her back. The apron strings had come untied. "Dad has a cellphone," she said.

"Thank you, I know that."

Francie rattled off the number anyway, following Irene to the kitchen.

Was this an emergency?

The tabletop was covered in flour. Four balls of pie dough, wrapped in wax paper, were warming past their ideal temperature. Irene put the balls back into the fridge. "It rolls out better if it's cold," she said, and she looked at the clock. "We can roll out the dough in half an hour."

Francie pulled off the apron and dropped it on the floor.

"Pick that up," Irene said, feeling agitated, not herself. When Francie didn't move (refused to move?), Irene bent down to retrieve the apron. Folded it, unfolded it, hung it on a hook beside the fridge. This was the time of day when Irene liked to take a little nap. She had the habit of brewing a cup of peppermint tea and leaving it to cool on the counter while she went and lay down on the sofa in the front room, and closed her eyes for a few minutes.

"Or maybe you don't want to make a pie," said Irene. "That's fine with me." (It wasn't!) "What you need is some quiet time. We both do."

One of life's traps was the pressure to alter one's own behaviour to meet the needs (projected, imaginary, or expressed) of other people. Back when she'd worked at the front desk of a country school, before retirement, Irene had excelled at building barriers that kept other people in line, she did not bend the rules, nor sentimentalize about human failure. People were full of excuses, and she refused to coddle that nonsense. She accepted none of it. Irene had not sat there smiling and nodding and agreeing and sympathizing. She'd wanted other people to look at what they'd done, confess it, and do better. (Was this why she'd been *encouraged* to take early retirement, an ongoing disagreement about *tone* with the school's principal?)

The truth was, Irene's skill set translated poorly to the situation before her now, and didn't Irene know it! The other person, her granddaughter, shuffled restlessly, eyes darting, the very picture of unhappiness. "I'll try calling your mom," Irene said.

There was no answer, so she dialed Luce's number, just in case, and it picked up immediately, direct to voice mail.

"Don't worry," said Irene. "There's always a logical explanation."

Yes, and it wasn't always a happy one, was it?

She put her hand on Francie's shoulder and guided her to the front room. Francie crouched beside the magazine rack and started leafing through a cooking magazine, ignoring the shelf of children's picture books that Irene had collected over several decades, purchased or salvaged on remainder from the school library.

It took a moment or two for Irene to settle herself under the crocheted blanket. "Wake me in twenty minutes," she directed Francie, but that was merely to give the child a sense of responsibility, a job, not because Irene would need to be woken, her interior clock was eerily accurate.

In fact, the child did not wake Irene. Irene surfaced of her own accord, disturbed by a soft snore snagging in her throat, an unpleasant sensation. The child was bent over the magazine rack, her posture guilty, like she was hiding something, which aroused Irene's suspicions, naturally, but also seemed likely to be ridiculous, insignificant, when measured against the probable sins of the father (and the mother!).

What have you got there? Irene could have said. But she didn't want to know everything about everything. The bliss of ignorance took effort. *Bliss. This?*

Irene sat up slowly and wrapped the blanket around her shoulders. She wished she'd woken on a different day, alone. She did not say a word to Francie, because she couldn't think of anything, reassuring or otherwise, to say, shuffling off to the bathroom, where she spent some time rearranging her hair, which had gotten squashed at the back during her insufficient nap. She should have slept till it was all over, slept through—whatever *it* was.

Surreptitiously, she dialed Luce's number again, then Marietta's. Nothing was clearer than it had been before.

Nothing was clear.

"I'll freeze the pie dough for another time," Irene called out to Francie, who had remained in the front room, apparently engrossed in the fantasy world of low-fat, full-taste cookery. "Why don't we go for a walk?"

The child seemed compliant. They walked along the road, on the wide gravel shoulder, cars and trucks whizzing by. Never the gold Cadillac. Irene knew Francie was looking for it too. A hawk on the wire overhead caught Irene's attention, still as a carving, watching them with its beady eyes. She pointed it out to Francie, and Francie waved her arms and shouted at the bird, till it roused its magnificent feathered body and rose.

"Now why'd you that?" Irene asked.

The hawk circled them and landed, just ahead, on top of a pole.

Francie ran for it, screaming, and Irene froze, watching her grandchild behave in a way both uncalled for and all too familiar. The child was "losing her shit," as Frank would have phrased it, and it was his voice in Irene's head, half-amused, goading her (he knew she hated when he used profanity), and half-regretful to be pointing out this truth, that the child was just like the father.

Weakness slip-sliding from one generation to the next. Poison in the blood.

"Francie, pull yourself together!" Irene marched over and grabbed the child by the shoulders. Shook her, shook her, shook the sense back into her.

The child went limp and yielding.

It was Irene's own fury that was unnerving.

Uncanny how the hawk followed them home, hopping behind them from pole to pole, swooping into the sky and settling again, watching them—watching Irene, Irene thought, so she'd not hurt the child again. *Is that you, Frank?*

No gold Cadillac waiting for them in the driveway.

"A bath will calm you down," Irene told Francie.

In the bathroom, Irene turned on the taps full blast and squeezed dish soap into the tub for bubbles, sprinkled purple salt crystals from a big plastic container with a handle. Lavender. Frank used to grow lavender beside their summer kitchen in a special garden he planted and tended just for her, with peonies, mint, and sage. A garden of wonderful smells. The lavender grew big and bushy, and Irene liked to stop and run her hands along its thick, furry stems, milking them of scent. She would lift her palms to her face and breathe deeply. It had a calming effect, and didn't Frank know it.

Didn't he know her.

Didn't it pain her terribly, like a secondary death, to lose the bush. First went the farmhouse and the fields—hurriedly sold (except for the small plot with the granny house at the end of the lane, severed by Frank in secret, before his death, for herself and Luce). Then the new family ripped out the lavender and peonies, and rototilled the plot into a truck patch for vegetables.

But of course. It got the best sun.

Irene lifted her hand to her face, palm open, and breathed in the scent of the purple crystals, only dimly related to the soft, bee-laden, scratchy perfume of the real thing. She did not feel calm.

"Leave the door open a crack," Irene told Francie.

But before she got to the kitchen, she heard the door slam shut. That set her teeth on edge. *What a disobedient child!*

Irene rang the numbers again, to no avail.

It was maddening how little she knew. She didn't know the name of her grandson's daycare, assuming Marietta had him in care of some sort (probably not the regulated, legal kind), she didn't know exactly where Marietta worked, nor Luce, if he worked anywhere at all anymore (doubtful!). She didn't know the names of their neighbours, their friends, except for that one who'd stuck with Luce since junior high, Mikey something.

Irene did not think well sitting down.

She paced the kitchen and the short hallway. Quiet. Too quiet? She pressed her ear to the closed bathroom door. Should the child be taken home? What decisions had she already made that she might regret?

No, Irene would wait for Luce. You have no reason not to believe what he said, she told herself, while Frank, his father, long departed, shook his head inside her head: *You have every reason not to believe him.*

Sorry, Frank! Not your business anymore! I'm the one

who had to stick it out and raise him, for both of us. You made your choice.

Oh, she was angry.

Oh, not again.

Irene found herself standing before the fridge, peering inside. Her hands moved automatically to gather ingredients to make soup: homemade low-sodium broth in a yogurt container removed from the freezer, a single frozen chicken breast, an onion, three stalks of celery, a carrot. She set the yogurt container into the sink and turned on the hot water.

She saw herself, holding a knife, hacking at the frozen chicken breast.

You want to think you are improving, but really you just stay the same. It hurt to fall into the past, but just try to stop a memory from flooding you, just try. It was like being pulled out to sea, if the sea were a field of corn, like being pulled into a field of ripening corn, leaves rustling and cutting your arms as you tried to disappear. You would not disappear, nor would you be taken further from your past, your memory of what it felt like to be pulled into the heart of despair, fear would remain a fist around the heart. What happened after Frank died? Immediately after, who could say, but in the ever-after, what happened was that you knew it could always happen, the possibility of a hole being blown in your life remained with you, and it hurt you in ways you could not protect yourself from, because it (fear, shame) looked like protection, it sealed you off behind your walls and doors, because you weren't the same. Your heart was not the same. It had been severed, cut off from the living veins and arteries. Preventing its reattachment was the cost of survival.

Never again.

Do not be ashamed for I am with you.

Hot water poured from the tap onto the lid of the yogurt container she'd set into the sink, her hands were covered in bacteria from the raw chicken, she'd made the mistake of marrying a man who would die in his pickup truck at the end of a dirt road, alone, by his own hand, and they'd never recover from it—not Frank, who couldn't shield himself from his suffering, except in this way, using the shotgun he kept for the groundhogs; not their son, who ran out the other side believing himself immune from ordinary punishment; and not herself, Irene, no matter how she petitioned God.

Irene was remembering a woman who'd come to the farmhouse after Frank died—a neighbour to whom Irene had previously spoken no more than Hello, how are you, how about this rain, this sun, this weather? The woman greeted Irene with a glass pan of lasagna, she placed the dish, cool, covered in foil, onto Irene's forearms, and said, "Bake at three-fifty for half an hour, or freeze it, it will keep till you need it, don't worry about returning the pan." A good glass pan. The kind of gesture that you keep for a lifetime, even if forgetting the woman's name, her face, the way she looked at you with lines etched around her chapped lips.

Irene stuck her hands under the hot water, knife too.

"Grandma?" Francie, wrapped in a purple towel, hair dripping puddles onto the floor.

Irene wrapped her arms around this small body, wet hair soaking Irene's plain everyday blouse.

"I want to go home," Francie said loudly.

"Let's wait a little longer for your dad," said Irene. She could hardly countenance herself, believing in him the way she did. Frank was right. She could not justify it.

Francie pulled away. Irene noticed only then that she was still holding the knife.

"Get dressed," said Irene.

She ran the knife around the ice block of broth, and the block fell into the pot with a metallic *thunk*. She moved the pot to the element, turned it on, chopped and added the onion, celery, carrot. No salt.

In the front room, Francie, dressed, was pecking at the piano keys. "Keep playing!" Irene called out. The music, if it could be called such, stopped abruptly. "Keep playing!" Irene called again, in case Francie hadn't heard the first time, but this was followed by a discordant crash.

Irene went to the doorway to look at the child. Francie stood by the piano holding a sheet of green paper, soaked hair sopping into her t-shirt. "What's that?"

"Nothing."

"Give it to me."

Francie snatched it close to her chest. "It's an order form for tickets. To my concert."

Irene's slippers were wet. She'd walked through a puddle. "I didn't know you were in a concert."

"I have a solo!"

Irene grabbed a dishtowel hanging on the fridge door and dropped it onto the floor. "Isn't that nice," she said, using her foot on the dishtowel to mop up the puddle. "Where did you leave your towel? Your hair is still wet."

"The tickets are ten dollars." Francie had not moved.

"Come here," said Irene, but Francie refused, so Irene went to her instead and used the other dishtowel hanging on the fridge door to squeeze-dry the ends of Francie's hair.

"It's a lot of money," said Francie.

"What's a lot of money?" Through the front window, the sky and fields were framed and clean, and trucks and cars sped by on the road, but not his, not Luce's.

"The tickets are a lot of money," said Francie.

"Oh?"

"But my dad says he will buy everyone a ticket!"

Irene's hands froze, a tiny alarm sounding behind her eyes, though she fought to ignore it. She did not want to know more, she wanted to know less! She said, "Go get my purse, I've got a comb in there, we'll get through these tangles." She could smell the fatty broth beginning to thaw and simmer on the stove. The chicken breast was only partially chopped, frozen on the cutting board. Irene had things to do.

"Can't you find it? It should be hanging behind the back door."

Irene took the comb from her purse (whatever had the child been doing?), and began working through the worst of Francie's tangles, starting with the ends. Francie clutched the green piece of paper to her chest like it was armour. The tangles were intractable, like these wires crossing inside Irene's mind, these flashes of terror, snarled tight.

"I would like to buy a ticket to your concert, Francie," Irene said, breaking the heavy silence between them. "I can buy my own." She felt like this was the first coherent thought she'd processed and expressed all afternoon. She felt like she was getting out of her own head for a moment, seeing the child and the child's desires, and responding in a way that was kind, generous, good.

But Francie broke free and turned around, her eyes full of tears (from the yanking of the comb or from something else? Irene had no idea). "No! My dad will buy you one."

But he wouldn't, would he. The child's dad, Irene's son, had no follow-through. He had only the idea, the spark, the belief, the con, the lurching lunge, the leap, the escape, the run. The endless run.

"Absolutely not, I insist!" Irene felt a familiar urge, to cover for him, her son. "Let me do it, it's my treat. I'll buy everyone a ticket!" She dropped the comb and dug in the purse for her wallet. She stood for a while, looking into its folds. Empty. Of course. He'd stolen from her again. The heaviness descended. Her breath slowed. She felt such an inevitability about what she was seeing that she scarcely registered disappointment. Would she never learn? When she looked up, Francie was staring with huge eyes, her yellow shirt soaked and see-through across the shoulders.

"Remind me another time," said Irene. "I seem to be all out of cash."

The phone was ringing. The phone was ringing!

Irene looked at the clock over the table: after five.

"Luce?" she said without thinking, it was as if he was there, breathing down the line, but a tiny pause was followed by a catch in the throat, and Marietta said—Irene knew her voice immediately—"Tell me you have Francie, the school said he took her out early, but they said it was just him in the car. They promised me. It was just him."

They said.

"Who said?"

"The police, Irene! The police! The cops!"

Irene gripped a kitchen chair with one hand, forgetting Francie was watching, listening, even as she promised Marietta, "Yes, Francie is here, she's here with me, Marietta, don't worry, she's fine."

Marietta was sobbing. A sound you never wanted to hear from the woman married to your son.

"Francie's here," Irene repeated, as if to block out whatever else Marietta was trying to tell her.

Slow down. You move too fast.

"Luce is in the hospital. Mikey said they arrested him, but he's in the hospital now, they said he totalled his car, he broke some bones, he was high on drugs."

Irene did not want to listen to this nonsense.

She hung up the phone. The smell of broth was overpowering, rolling to a boil, steaming up the window over the sink, and Irene stepped to the stove and turned the element to low, she began hacking at the chicken breast, raising the knife and stabbing it down.

Out the window, here was the day, still progressing, the weeds in her yard still flourishing, the fence still broken, rotten old posts splitting, wire sagging. The field was planted and green: corn, hip-high already, though not quite tall enough to disappear into. Beyond the field, the sky, beyond the sky, the thumbprint of the moon, white as a cloud, beyond the moon, unseen stars and planets and rocks floating, spinning, all of it expanding with every breath she took, so that she could be convinced, if she let herself, that she too was expanding, growing both larger in her thinking and braver in her actions, as her cells asserted their right to split, and someday to leave her.

Beyond that, God.

There. Done. Into the pot.

Her head felt very clear. The light had changed inside the kitchen, maybe a cloud crossing the sun, maybe the changing angle of the earth, but she could see the outline of every object.

Irene stirred the soup. A pinch of dried thyme. Lemon pepper.

When she turned around, she saw that Francie had left the kitchen. And there was a rectangle of light shining into the hallway, across from the bathroom: Luce's bedroom door was open.

Irene began to pray out loud as her feet in their slippers carried her toward the room, the child, the discovery that awaited, *Our father who art in Heaven*. "You can use this prayer," she said to Francie, "we'll pray it together," as she came into the room behind the child and put her hands onto her shoulders, and they looked at the black gym bag, resting on the twin bed, unzipped and full of some things that needed to be destroyed.

Evidence.

She didn't need to see more.

"We'll have a bonfire in the burn barrel before dinner," said Irene.

"I want to go home," said Francie.

The phone was ringing. "Don't answer it," said Irene. "Not yet." But the child escaped and ran down the hallway, she was in the kitchen saying hello, hello, and Irene picked up the gym bag, she did not hesitate. She carried it out to the backyard in her slippers, tossed it into the burn barrel, stuffed the barrel with nice dry twists of newspaper, and lit the match.

NINE

Gun Run

The concert the concert the concert!

Francie could hear a dog barking, again, and her heart pumped hard as she turned away from the rushing water, this different section of stream she'd found, as if she were walking in endless circles. Her legs were too tired to run, her feet, in the rainbow socks, hurt too much—and what mattered? *The concert?*

She was hungry, also thirsty.

She stopped walking for a moment and knelt, unzipped the backpack, checking the rainbow pony lunch box like there might be something she'd forgotten she'd packed this morning. She felt around: stale crusts, crumbled cookies, money, slick folded bills. Nothing good.

You're rich, you're a thief, you're a liar, you didn't need to do it.

Francie slugged the backpack over her shoulders and kept moving, away from the sound of the dog barking, away from the shushing stream.

A lot of things were going wrong, but a lot of other things already had.

Inside her mind, Francie saw Dad coming out the front door of their little house—Francie was sitting in his car, watching him from the driveway, watching through the windshield. What was he doing? No one used the front door, not since it got broken, but maybe Dad forgot, he stepped out and looked around, he leaned down, holding on to the railing, and he dropped something. She saw it fall. Whatever it was, it was gone, slipped into the crack between the house and the stoop. But Dad didn't look for it. He was trying to close the front door. *Slam, slam.*

It wasn't going to close, not all the way. Francie could see it, but maybe Dad couldn't.

"What?" Dad said when he slid into the driver's seat.

"Can you come to my concert?" Francie tried to show him the green piece of paper from Mrs. G.

"What's that?" Dad was wearing a nice shirt, also he was sweating, his forehead was wet. He rolled down his window.

Francie held on tight to the green paper so it wouldn't blow away. She said, "It's ten dollars for a ticket."

Dad blew out through his lips, his cellphone was ringing. "Bloody hell, not right now."

They were going to Grandma's house, Francie already knew, even before they got there. Dad didn't stay, he didn't say why, he wouldn't let her come along to wherever he was going next, he said he needed to go alone, he said it was good news. At Grandma's house, Grandma was making pie, but the dough needed to rest, so Grandma said they could take a little nap while they waited. Francie did not need a little nap. She dug in her backpack for the green paper, and examined it while Grandma snored on the couch. *Tickets $10 for*

adults, $5 for children. Tickets MUST be ordered in advance.
NO EXCEPTIONS.

Francie checked, Grandma was asleep with her mouth open.

Grandma's purse hung on a hook beside the back door. Grandma's wallet was full of twenty-dollar bills, Francie saw, kneeling on the floor beside her sneakers. Her heart powered up with pounding. Grandma's money smelled like her purse, perfumed and powdery, and the bills were slippery in Francie's fingers. A feeling washed through Francie, dark and frightening, breathless and exciting. She could take the money right now and hide it.

She didn't need all of Grandma's money for the tickets, only some of it.

But she wanted it all.

Smoothly, silently, Francie dropped Grandma's emptied wallet back into the purse and lifted the purse onto the hook. It seemed like her fingerprints were everywhere, on everything. It was strange how her heart now slowed to a heavy steadiness that hurt, like a drum being beaten with a fist. In the front room, Grandma was snoring softly, her arms folded over the crocheted blanket. Francie zipped the money into her lunch box, beside the sandwich she'd made herself this morning: two pieces of bread stuck together with mashed potatoes and ketchup. Mom had been too tired to brush Francie's hair, she'd been too tired to make breakfast for Francie and Sam, so Francie made them breakfast too: toast with margarine.

All this thinking about food. Even the mashed potato sandwich sounded good right now (and it wasn't).

What mattered? Earning a solo, learning all the words to her song (most of them!), practising with Alice, stealing money for tickets, not telling? She was holding a gun, hungry, also thirsty, also her underwear was wet and it rubbed and itched, and ahead of her was a fence, sagging wire the colour of dead leaves slung between thin metal posts.

Francie stopped.

On the edge of the wood, on the other side of the fence, there was a clearing.

Open.

A field of yellow grass and cattails. She could hear a faraway roaring sound that wasn't water, it was cars and trucks speeding along a highway, on the other side of the field. All that traffic going somewhere, away from her. Maybe Dad was going somewhere too, in Mikey's red pickup truck. Away from them.

Maybe Dad was escaping. Maybe she was helping.

Throw it away.

Francie sat on a chunk of concrete that was pushing out of the ground near one of the fence posts. The socks were done, wrecked, they were goners now too. She peeled them off, one then the other, with her free hand. The fabric looked grey, the rainbows smeared with dirt. She squeezed the socks into balls and threw them over the fence. Her feet were cut and scratched.

She wrapped her hands around her legs, the gun pointing straight ahead.

She was never going to get there, wherever it was, before nightfall. She was going to miss the concert—*the concert the concert the concert!*

A lot of things were going wrong.

You just need one thing to go right, Francie heard Dad say in her head.

"THIS IS ALL YOUR FAULT!" she screamed.

TEN

Interventions

What would he tell Marietta?

God, he was feeling almost faint. Like he'd had an out-of-body experience, not in a good way, like he'd been abducted by aliens and spat out onto this unfinished gravel driveway, splayed on his back, had he hit his head? The sun flickered bright through his eyelids, red and orange, and he heard one of his men, the new hire, coming closer at a clip, calling his name: "Mikey! Mikey! Shit, man, you should call the cops on that guy. I thought he was gonna kill you."

From this position it was hard to determine precisely what had gone wrong.

Everything?

One miscalculation after another.

Mikey did not want to make another call, probably the wrong one. He thought about moving, but seemed unable to decide to. "Mikey, who was that guy? Mikey? Mikey?" Mikey heard himself grunt in reply, his eyes sealed shut of their own accord. Better that way. Give him time to think. *Think. Think.*

All day he'd been nervous, sure, he'd been on the look-out, checking his phone for a return call every two minutes, reminding himself he was doing a good thing. He was going to tell Luce to get rid of the gun. He didn't know the words he'd use yet, but the goal was clear. Marietta trusted him. Right, Marietta? He was doing a good thing. For Marietta. For those kids. Even for Luce, Luce wasn't such a bad guy, he was just—messed up.

The new hire tapped Mikey's shoulder with his boot. "Boss, you awake?"

I'm awake. Mikey tried to speak, but nothing came out.

"Hey, boss, you okay? Boss!" There was a pause, and Mikey could hear the new guy debating his next move: "What the fuck should I do?" Don't start shaking me, Mikey thought, regretting the bat signal he'd just sent out.

The guy started shaking him.

Mikey didn't need someone else freaking out, losing their shit, not after that shouting match turned into a shoving match. Of course, Luce landed the better punch (or punches, for accuracy's sake), he had better hands than Mikey, quicker.

It's all good, Mikey tried to say. His eyes popped open.

"Jesus, boss, your eyes just popped open!"

Yeah, help me up here, I guess. Mikey's head weighed a ton, it wasn't going anywhere.

His rested his eyes.

He could see Luce pulling in, hard to miss that fat gold Cadillac, looked like he'd cleaned it for the occasion, it was shining, and when he stepped out, Mikey thought Luce looked pretty good, for all his troubles. What would it take to take this guy down? he thought, and immediately retracted the thought, buried it, because he wanted the best for Luce, his old friend, that's what he kept telling himself.

"Mikey!" Luce waved, striding over to where Mikey stood, near the front door of this palace Mikey was building (without Luce), and Mikey couldn't help noticing that Luce was wearing a nice shirt that buttoned up. In retrospect, an ominous detail. Mikey himself was in a schlubby t-shirt that was doing no one any favours, self or viewers, ha ha. Luce swung his leg like a golf club, like he was getting used to carrying it around, like he could make it work for him now. That's when Mikey twigged to the possibility that Luce had come here thinking that Mikey had good news, thinking that Mikey might give him his job back.

This was not going to go as planned. If there was a plan. Mikey's plan, Mikey realized in that moment, began and ended with the idea that Luce would come here, to the place where Mikey felt most powerful, not exactly neutral territory, and Mikey would hit him with some bad news. But the bad news was that Mikey didn't feel as powerful as he'd hoped, Luce's presence had a way of reminding Mikey who he really was (a fat kid who'd do anything to keep a friend), and this place, this location, was sending up all the wrong flares.

Of course Luce was thinking of this as a business meeting.

Everything was a business meeting to Luce. He was simultaneously the least professional and most entrepreneurial person Mikey had ever met. Luce was fast cash, easy money. Flash and burn.

"Hey, man, how you doing?" Mikey's voice came out about an octave too high.

"What's up? What's this all about? I'm ready for anything, I hope you know that, brother."

They were not brothers. But what Mikey wouldn't have done to have a brother like Luce, way back when. Grade seven. New school. Bad times, good friend.

Shit, shit, shit.

"Let's walk," said Mikey, "I'll show you around." The sweat was puddling down his neck, gluing his shirt to his shoulders and chest.

"Looks good," said Luce, of the palace, the fresh lumber frame, towering sky-high, the circular driveway with the roughed-in fountain in the middle (not yet operable), the five-car garage. Up close, Mikey noticed Luce's leg didn't move as well as it had appeared from a distance, and he thought he was a genius, for all of half a minute, suggesting the walk. He thought, idiot that he was, that he'd leveraged an advantage.

"Who's the new guy? With the white hard hat?" Luce said, stopping.

And Mikey had no good answer.

"Is he supposed to be me? You're hiring me back as a labourer? What the fuck, man?"

"I'm not hiring you back," Mikey said, surprised at how it felt to speak so clearly. Like a clean breeze through his system. Head full of fresh air.

Luce's eyes looked hollow, the pupils were pricks of black in a green sea. He'd gone very still. His hands heavy at his sides.

"I need to talk to you." Mikey forged onward, sailing on adrenalin, the words leaving his mouth before he could reflect on the consequences. "Marietta says you've got a gun. You need to get rid of it."

Marietta.

That was the switch that flipped the breaker in Luce's brain. Why'd Mikey have to go and bring her into it?

"You've been talking to Marietta."

"She called me, I didn't call her, trust me, man."

"Yeah, I might have a gun. A person can have a gun, can't he, Mikey?"

"I suppose so, but I think she was worried, um, about the kids, or maybe . . ."

"This sounds like none of your fucking business, my friend."

"And the drugs, you've got to stop using."

"Is that all? All you've got for me? I put on a nice shirt for this?"

Mikey searched the recesses of his brain, which were distressingly empty, echoing as he pawed around for what might come next. Apparently, all the words had been blown clean out, leaving behind sawdust and pap.

He stood before Luce, half as tall and twice as wide. It was clear who would eat whom if they met in the wild. One was predator, the other was prey.

"You and Marietta," Luce said, but he left it at that, because, Mikey saw, not even Luce could believe it.

"She just wanted help, she wanted you to get help. You need help."

"You telling me what I need? I needed a job, man."

"I gave you a job and you screwed it up, Luce, I'm sorry, but you screwed it up!"

"We were partners. Who put you in charge?"

"You're going to have to go now, or I'll call the cops."

Luce laughed at that, "Hey, you invited me, man," and Mikey knew he'd lost, at least in the short term, the term that would be most acutely painful. Luce knocked Mikey's flip phone out of his hand, kicked it away. Mikey tried, he'd been working out with a trainer three times a week, but that was a gym, that was weights and crunches, not jabs and punches.

"If you go near Mari, I'll kill you."

"She doesn't belong to you," Mikey said, he was losing the plot, he saw the fist, heard it connect from the inside out, a plushy, rattling thump, he fell backward. The sound of tires on freshly graded gravel, *that'll leave ruts*, that was too bad.

The new hire was muttering, "I should call 911. Should I call 911?"

Mikey sat up sharply, blood rushing behind his eyes. "Don't call anyone, I'm fine, I'll be fine."

What was he going to tell Marietta?

It's me everyone wants to hear from, but I'm not saying a word, said Luce. I know my rights.

Look, I didn't know I still had pills in the glove compartment, and I wouldn't have taken them if Mikey had brought me back on board like he promised, after I covered his ass last summer, I lied for him, for us, and now I get no disability, and he cuts me loose, and he owes me, the fat fucking bastard, he owes me more than he'll ever be able to pay back, and no, do I look suicidal? I'm homicidal, okay, is that better, so I took a few pills, okay, so I took what I found, all at once, and I drove off the road, according to you, and I'm not in pain, no, and I don't have a problem, I'm clean now, I'm clean, and it's not like I killed anyone, this was just a stupid mistake that anyone would make if they'd just been stabbed in the back by a friend.

You can't arrest me for that.

Be a pal, give me those last couple of doses you found in my pocket. I'll take care of it. Then it's all gone.

Who's my next of kin? Call Mikey, his number's on the card. In my wallet. Back pocket. Funny thing, I can't move my arm. Funny thing. My number's on the card too. Funny thing, we used to be partners. Call him, tell him I'm dead and he's next.

⟞⟞⟞

Even at the best of times, David didn't like driving at dusk, and this was not the best of anything—shadowy country road, destination unknown, and a blaze of headlights tracking toward him, splintering off the windshield in distracting patterns, symmetry, even here.

David blinked.

He'd been on this straight, flat road for a while and he lacked confidence in the GPS device suctioned to the tiny dashboard, and more specifically in the coordinates given to him by his wife, Sally, who tended to operate out of a flurry of goodwill that trumped basic competence. The coordinates had come from Sally's friend Marietta, a woman David knew on sight, he could have picked her out of a lineup, he supposed, stalling on the inappropriate thought—funny how the brain made connections, though it was her husband who'd been arrested, not Marietta herself, at least according to Sally. Forget the lineup. What he meant was that if he were to see this woman (Marietta) in a grocery store (unlikely—Sally did the shopping), David would have recognized something familiar about her, even if he couldn't have placed who she was, exactly, in relation to him, nor known her name. David did not, as a general rule, remember names. This was a quality he was comfortable not possessing, a forgivable deficiency, reflective of the inconsistent nature of names themselves.

A name was an arbitrary abstraction. Or, not arbitrary, no, because a parent bestowed a particular name on a child,

reflective of their spoken language, family history, what mattered to them most, or even just the collection of phonemes
that sounded most pleasant to their ears, given their era. But
an abstraction, yes. Because "David" could be attached to a
boy born in urban Argentina in 1964 and no outward char-
acteristics would reveal him to be particularly David-like,
nor link him to the multitude of other Davids inhabiting
planet Earth.

Also, Sally remembered everyone's name. So there was that.

A fresh set of headlights flared across the bug-spackled
windshield. Focus on the road, David told himself, even as
the GPS voice (a woman's) announced that he would arrive
at his destination in eight hundred metres. "Where? Where?"
David saw nothing at which to arrive emerging from the
near night. The dark was darker here, outside the city.

"Your destination is on the left." And the voice continued unperturbed, "You have arrived at your destination."

David whizzed past the faint glow from a window, the
shadow of a mailbox. The little car shuddered as he yanked
on the steering wheel, pumped the brakes. Tires touched
gravel, stones battered the undercarriage. The car shimmied
as if David had lost control, but that, he considered, would
suggest David had at some point been in control. And that
wasn't how David saw it. None of this was his idea.

Why had this man (Marietta's husband) been arrested?
How bad was this guy? What had happened, exactly?

Nobody seemed to have the story straight, least of all
Sally, who'd insisted that he, David, behave like some knight
in shining armour and gallop out to the countryside in his
Smart car to rescue the child of this wretched pair. A child
who just happened to be his own daughter's best friend. Yes,
Sally, I understand.

Francie. He had no trouble remembering her name. Funny kid.

As David executed a U-turn with more composure than he was feeling (it was like driving a tin can), it occurred to him that the man, Francie's father, was someone he truly couldn't have picked out of a lineup. *Ouch*. He kept putting these people into lineups. He must stop. He was about to see Francie, who was just a child, and he must under no circumstances cause her distress. David hated when children were distressed.

Sally said his heart was too soft.

But it isn't my heart, Sally, it's my brain.

A short driveway appeared on his right, popping out from behind a row of shrubbery, and David turned in. Tucked the tiny car behind a sedan. He'd delayed thinking about what he would do or say upon arrival—do and say— and now, here he was. David switched off the headlights. It really was dark outside the city. Soft lamplight, an orange glow through the window, no curtains. He'd come to drive Francie home to her mother. As Sally had said, we would want someone to do this for Alice, were the tables turned.

But the tables wouldn't be turned, David thought. Impossible.

When he opened the car door and unfolded himself, he noticed the air smelled like smoke.

The grass was high. He stumbled through the weeds, up some steps, and knocked on the front door. Knocked again.

"Who's there? What do you want?" The woman wouldn't open the door all the way. Her voice was accusatory.

"It's me, David. I'm here to pick up Francie." Weren't they expecting him?

"David? David who?" The woman was trying to push

the door closed, and David instinctively pushed back, calling through the crack.

"My name's David, my wife's name is Sally. Marietta asked us to drive Francie home. My wife gave me directions. She said Marietta called and asked for help . . ." He trailed off, impressed by the multiple connections he'd been able to supply off the cuff, the names he'd remembered (okay, half belonged to immediate family members, including himself). "My daughter Alice is Francie's friend," he added, but the description seemed inadequate. The girl practically lived at their house. She had an enormous appetite, David had observed, polishing off three bowls of cereal in one sitting. Impressive! Francie rarely spoke to David when she was in their house, but he took no offence. He rarely spoke to her either! Adults lived in a separate orbit of existence—why couldn't Sally see it? Adults were rooted in place, in thought, in behaviour, grown wooden and rigid with age, while a child was rootless and free, a child could think in wild patterns to which adults had lost access.

David should know. He remembered with an almost sacred grief (saccharine, nostalgic, mistaken?) the fluidity of his own youthful mind, its seemingly limitless capacity to incorporate and expand on mathematical concepts; the adult stiffness seemed disabling, crippling. He could expound, he could teach, he could even learn more, but he could not roam the universe. (Not that he wanted Sally to guess at or to see his inevitable diminished potential; not that he could have said any of this to her, in any words that made any sense to either of them.)

David knew it was mildly pathetic—how he soothed his sadness with habits that Sally considered wasteful, selfish . . . the occasional all-night gaming session, the fondness for soda pop and vile salty snacks, the afternoon naps. Even his running Sally misunderstood—for him it was escape into physical lightness, freedom, adventure, but she thought he did it for his health; she approved of the running.

Never to see the world again with such vast curiosity and openness: the kids know more than us, Sally, the kids are wiser than you, or I, leave them be.

"The girls are good friends," said David. He gave up pushing on the door.

"I see." The woman did not fling open the door in welcome, but she stepped around it, holding on to the door handle, coming up close to David. Too close. Her head tilted back to look him in the eye, which had the unexpected effect of making David feel smaller than he was, like a child being disciplined. "I believe there's been a misunderstanding," the woman said. "As I told Marietta, it does no good to disturb the child tonight. I told her. You shouldn't have driven all the way out here. It was a foolish thing to do."

David wasn't the best at reading faces and tone, but he didn't need Sally here to tell him that this woman was livid.

"Uh, my wife said Francie needed to come home, because of, you know, the thing that happened, and my wife said Marietta doesn't have a car . . ."

"I'm afraid you've been sent on a wild goose chase. Francie is asleep, and I won't wake her on account of someone's hare-brained idea. All this disruption! I told Marietta, everything will be clearer tomorrow."

On the whole, David agreed. But he could not disappoint Sally, he could not return to town without the girl. The mission's goal superseded its obstacles.

"Grandma? What's happening?" The voice was loud, husky, familiar.

"You've woken her," the woman snapped.

David was very tired. He'd risen at five thirty this morning to run twelve kilometres, as scheduled into his training regimen, which Sally supported even if she did not understand. This summed up their marriage: they supported without understanding each other's impulses and needs. It explained how David found himself standing on a stranger's doorstep on a humid June evening, the errant fool on a rescue mission gone awry.

"I'll just wait here," David said.

The woman closed the door, emphatically.

From the porch, David could see through the uncurtained window into a front room, it reminded him of a computer screen shedding brightness, and he was encouraged by the activity signified by an overhead light coming on, and the top of the child's head moving toward a wall of bookshelves.

It was like a scene in a role-playing game, where your avatar knocks on a door and awaits instructions. What would happen next? It wasn't exactly up to him, he heard himself explaining to Sally.

The door opened. "She wants to go home," the woman spoke quietly, "but if she goes, I go. I will drive my own car, and Francie will ride with me. She is getting ready now." The woman gazed up at him with an authority he recognized and respected.

"Wonderful," said David. "We can drive together." Relief flooded his system. The task would be complete. Was this how other people felt all the time? Awash with unsupportable certainty?

The woman stepped back, inviting him inside. "Do you know"—her voice dropped to a whisper—"do you know my son, then, do you know him well?"

What was this? The pleasure of certainty evaporated. David neither recognized the tone nor understood the question.

"You didn't know Luce was my son?"

"I'm sorry . . ." He barely stopped himself from asking, *Who's Luce?* If Sally were here, Sally would be putting the pieces to this puzzle together without even trying, the arbitrary, the nonsensical, Sally'd be making leaps to unforeseen conclusions, but David couldn't process the unexpected so efficiently (and, frankly, lackadaisically). David needed to step from one proven equation to the next.

Thankfully, the woman didn't seem to fathom the depths of David's ignorance. "Francie's in the bathroom," she said. "I don't know what her mother told her over the phone, but it would be best not to speak about any of this with her in the room."

Here came Francie, though David struggled to recognize her. She looked different to him. Out of the context of his own house, in the absence of his daughter, she seemed a stranger. Her hair floated around her head, staticky, like fur, and her shoulders slumped, her eyes seemed vacant and dull. He began to worry, or, more accurately, to experience distress, which manifested as confusion. He'd never worried about Francie before, she'd seemed self-sufficient, boisterous, pluckier than their own daughter.

He'd never understood why Sally didn't like the girl.

"Hurry, this nice man has been waiting long enough," said the woman—Francie's grandmother, of course, earlier she'd addressed the woman as "Grandma," David remembered. He tried stacking the connections, one atop the next.

"Hurry!" the woman said again.

She picked up and folded a blanket and set it back on

the sofa. She dithered out loud over whether to bring along some soup she'd made earlier in the day.

Francie was wearing a backpack and sneakers. She stood near David, observing her grandmother's frenzied activities; they stood in silence. At last the woman was ready, pushing them before her out the front door, clad in a bulky sweater, carrying the blanket she'd folded, her purse, a large bag crafted out of what looked like juice boxes (intriguing), a pair of fuzzy slippers poking out the top. She was also juggling the soup in an ice cream container and two sets of keys. She wouldn't let David help, not even with the soup.

David was parked behind her car, so he led the way— they didn't discuss the arrangement. A procession of two departed into darkness. The house, with one lamp left on, vanished behind them.

David tried to adjust his speed to hers. He didn't want to lose them. The interior of his car was quiet.

Lonely.

Such a venture was better made in the company of friends, companions, allies. He could tell himself that the two of them, behind him, were fellow seekers on the same journey, but their fates were quite separate from his own. And there was nothing David could do about it. He'd dragged them out into the night, urged them from their relative safety into the unknown, and that was his role; soon they would part ways. David looked at the stars fixed behind fast-moving clouds, the tips of trees and wires cutting the sky. When they glided inside city limits, and the street lights took over, he felt something akin to disappointment. On the whole, it was safer, on the whole, more boring.

The GPS voice announced his destination. David didn't know what he'd been expecting. Not this. He gunned the tiny box up a steep driveway and parked, wondering how he'd get out, with Francie's grandmother blocking him in.

The house looked like a stick drawing of a house: inverted V roof, door, window.

He unpacked himself from his Smart car (silly car, foolish car?), came around to the rear door of Francie's grandmother's sedan and opened it. Francie had been asleep, the blanket bunched around her. Seat belt on. She looked up at him, her face full of complicated emotions and tones, and he wondered, How could anyone claim to know what anyone else was feeling or thinking? Ever?

Yet people did, all the time.

Baffling.

David wanted to help her, but he didn't know how. He reached to fix a twisted strap on the backpack over Francie's shoulders and handed her the blanket, which had fallen on the ground.

The house was lit in a blaze of electric light, the only house on the block sending out a distress signal. Francie's grandmother walked away from them up the driveway, her arms laden with the things she'd brought along, just as Marietta—that must be her—burst from the side door, light spilling out. "Thank you, oh, thank you, David! How can I repay you?" She waved for him to come closer.

David obeyed.

Marietta held a baby on her hip. The baby looked very awake, gnawing on a banana, cheeks shining with saliva and mashed fruit. David had forgotten there were other children involved, if he'd ever known. It was entirely possible he'd never known. He was learning so much tonight! And what use was any of it? He tried to store away facts that Sally would appreciate hearing, to please her.

"Come in and have a drink!" Marietta said rather wildly, and David understood she was still talking to him. Come in, David, and have a drink! A drink of what, he could not fathom. It would be no ordinary drink: maybe something like *mate*, the warm infusion his parents so enjoyed, which Sally said tasted bitter, and anyway wasn't it unhygienic, to pass the gourd from person to person, everyone sipping through the same metal straw? It wasn't a drink to be taken alone, and just now David felt the loss of that ritual, a terrible sinking gape which he pushed back against. *It's just a drink.*

Seeing Marietta up close, David questioned whether he would, in fact, have recognized her in a grocery store. She seemed quite out of control, almost out of her head, her voice sharp and dangerous, calling attention to whatever was going on here. In short, this encounter was enticing and awkward, it put a person off balance. How to engage?

David didn't know where to look.

But his eyes, his attention, kept being drawn to her, to Marietta.

"He's exhausted, poor man," said Francie's grandmother. "Don't be silly, Marietta, this isn't an occasion for drinks. Thank you for your help, and go on home to your bed," she directed David, who accepted that he didn't know how to ask the woman to move her car. It felt right not to ask. He would walk home. It was a perfectly reasonable solution that he would take care not to mention to Sally.

David lifted one hand and waved a formal goodbye. He could come back in the morning to get the car, or the next day, or whenever, really. Or even never. He didn't particularly need the car. People were always looking at it, pointing at it, asking him questions about it. In this moment, David could believe that the car was one of many things—possessions, material and immaterial—that he did not truly need, or desire, or want. Never wanted.

All the things I never wanted, David said to himself, as if he were composing a list. But instead, he thought of the opposite: how he wished he'd said yes to the drink. He imagined it as fortification against his own complicated emotions, which rose in him unbidden, impossible to arrange into order.

He paused at the end of the driveway and watched Francie walk into the house, dragging the blanket on the ground.

One of the women closed the door.

All the things I never knew I wanted: David started a new list, beginning with Marietta's offer, but that was as far as he got, his mind turning to the exploration of the unknown and appealing interior landscape that her offer had sparked.

Best not to mention this part to Sally, either.

ELEVEN

Gun Run

Francie looked at the balled-up socks on the other side of the fence. The dog was barking, it would find her. Dogs were smart, smarter than people, dogs knew things. Smelled things. Like fear. "Dogs can smell fear," Dad said. Which made sense to Francie, that fear would be a scent, sharp but also rotten, a real stink. If fear had a colour, it would roll off your skin streaked with yellow. But fear was invisible. It was inside you, and it came out and dogs could smell it. Which made the other thing Dad said make no sense at all: "Don't let them know you're afraid."

But what if I am afraid?

Francie looked at her socks in the tangled weeds on the other side of the fence.

All you need is just one thing.

There.

There it was, waiting for Francie as she looked up from her socks: a tree. Taller than all the other trees in the woods,

maybe the tallest tree in the whole wide world. It was standing apart from the other trees in the woods, on the edge of
the field, on the other side of the fence. She looked up at its
dark-green branches spreading thick and heavy against the
clear blue sky.

Just one thing.

She got herself over the fence, balled up and squeezed
out like the socks. The wires bent and swayed as she let go
and fell into the weeds on the other side. Rust on the hand
that wasn't holding the gun, rust on her jeans, on her favourite cat t-shirt.

One thing.

She was done with running. The tree seemed to invite
her to come and hide, its lowest branches brushing the
ground. She crawled under on her belly, onto a carpet of
dead needles that was thick and soft, softly orange, and
smelled so good. Not like fear at all. Like the opposite of
fear. She rested her cheek against the soft needles and she
looked at the gun, and it wasn't stuck in her hand anymore.
She squeezed right against the tree's trunk, sat up between
the branches, and pulled off her backpack. After a moment
she unzipped it, and slid the gun in beside the rainbow pony
lunch box.

With the sandwich crusts and sawdust cookies.

With Grandma's money, too.

Now, Francie had Grandma's money in her lunch box,
and a gun.

One problem had become another problem, a bigger
problem, which was the way it went, Dad said: "You fix one
thing, and the bastard grows another head."

But what if you didn't fix anything? What if everything
you did just made everything worse, and worse and worse?

The morning after Dad crashed his car, Mom said Francie didn't have to go to school today. Francie didn't even know she'd slept late. When she came into the kitchen in her t-shirt (nightgown!), Grandma and Mom were there drinking coffee, and Mom smiled at Francie and she said: "I'm taking the day off and so are you." Mom never smiled like that, like someone was watching, it made Francie feel strange, like they were both standing on a stage, performing.

Grandma stood up and put her purse over her shoulder. She said she would go to the hospital.

Mom said she wasn't going to start arguing now.

A little while later, after Grandma drove away in her car, Mom left too. She was going out for a walk, is what she told Francie, except Francie saw Mom climb into a red pickup truck waiting in the street at the end of the driveway, and the truck reminded her of Dad's friend Mikey. The windows were up even though it was hot, and she couldn't see through them. Mom didn't notice Francie watching, maybe, even though Francie was standing in the driveway holding Sam.

Francie didn't want to stay home from school. She wanted to give the stolen money to Mrs. G and buy the tickets and then it would all be fixed.

Too late now. Francie went inside to get herself dressed; Sam, too.

How Francie wished she'd never shown Grandma the order form for the tickets. When Grandma got an idea in her head, she wouldn't let it go, she was like a pit bull, Mom said—and Grandma had gotten an idea in her head. Like how she'd gone to the hospital, even though Mom said don't go! And later, when Grandma got back from the hospital, as soon as she'd parked and stepped out of her car, she called over to where Francie and Sam were digging in the dirt, and said she'd stopped at a bank machine to get cash to buy tickets to Francie's concert!

"How many should we buy? Where's the order form?"

Francie shaded her eyes against the sun, looking up at Grandma.

She and Sam were digging in the dirt where the gold and the jewels were buried. Grandma locked her car with her key, and frowned, as if she was seeing the two of them for the first time.

"Where's your mom?"

Well, not here. Francie shrugged.

"This is unacceptable, your mother leaving you two home alone!" said Grandma. She was fumbling around in her purse, frowning. She found a packet of tissues and handed it to Francie, told her to wipe Sam's mouth, he looked like he'd been eating dirt (he had been).

"Where's my dad?" said Francie. "Did you see my dad?"

Grandma didn't answer. She slid her purse over her shoulder, and tried to go inside through the front door, and for some reason Francie didn't stop her or warn her, she just watched. Grandma turned the handle and pushed, and the door made an awful grating sound.

Francie and Sam stayed where they were, beside the stoop, watching Grandma inspect the half-open door.

Grandma said: "What's wrong with this door?"

"Nothing," said Francie, and then: "Maybe you broke it."

"Come inside!"

"We're playing," said Francie. She spat on a tissue and she wiped Sam's face till he howled.

Grandma's lips pinched thin.

But she didn't forget about the tickets! She made Francie take the order form out of her backpack and sit with her at the kitchen table while Sam took his nap, and together they filled out the form, purchasing three (3) adult tickets, and one (1) for children. Thirty-five dollars. Grandma counted out a twenty, a ten, and a five, and attached the bills to the order form with a paper clip (from her purse), and she watched while Francie put everything into her backpack.

Three tickets for adults: Mom, Grandma, and Dad.

Did that mean Dad was okay, Dad was coming home?

It was the middle of suppertime, and they were eating Grandma's soup, when Mom came walking in through the side door. Mom said, "Why is the front door hanging open?"

"It's broken!" said Grandma. "Apparently I broke it."

Mom laughed.

Grandma stood and came up close to Mom's face. "Have you been drinking? Are you drinking alcohol?"

Mom untied Sam from his chair. "Alcohol would be a good idea right now, but that's not my thing. I don't have a thing, Irene."

Grandma tried to wrench Sam from Mom's arms, or maybe the two of them were arguing about something else and Sam was just the object in between, Francie couldn't tell.

Grandma won. But only temporarily.

Mom went to the front door and began slamming her shoulder against the wood, to try to close it.

Grandma said: "Is there someone we can call? Marietta? Someone you could call for help?"

Mom crashed against the door. She said: "Things are going to be just fine around here. It's all under control!"

Sam stuck his fingers into Grandma's mouth. Grandma slapped them away, and Sam burst out crying, which made sense. It's what Francie wanted to do too.

"Keep your hands off my babies!" Mom said, and other things. Francie was sitting at the table, her arm frozen in the middle of lifting a spoon full of soup toward her mouth, and she started to giggle, helpless rolling giggles spilling out of her, shaking the soup off the spoon, making her pee her pants a little bit.

Everything else stopped. Mom stopped yelling. Sam stopped crying.

Grandma stared, then said, "Don't laugh at your mother!" and Mom turned on Grandma, "Don't tell her what to do. Look at me, I'm pathetic, Irene, I'm a madwoman. Look at my hands, I can't stop them."

They all looked at Mom's hands trembling, trembling.

Grandma said: "Marietta. You need to calm down."

"I think I'll feel better when you leave, Irene."

"But what about the door? You can't stay here alone with the door broken like that."

The door had sprung back open.

"You didn't break the door, Irene, Luce did. Luce did. Luce broke everything."

Grandma said, softly: "Like I told you that he would."

"Go!" Mom grabbed Sam back.

Grandma's juice-box bag was beside the sofa, where she'd spent the night. She moved like a bird, fluttering and hopping, gathering up the things she had brought with her the night before (forgetting the blanket, which was on Francie's bed now), and she walked out the broken front door without saying goodbye. Her eyes were staring and bright and wide. Francie followed and stood on the stoop. The air outside smelled like cigarette smoke and diesel. Two cars were parked in the driveway, but not Dad's. A bus rattled to the stop where strangers waited, strangers who knew nothing about what was happening inside this house. Francie wanted to be a stranger, but also she wanted to know—to know what was happening.

As soon as Grandma's car was gone, Francie said: "Where's my dad?"

Mom had set Sam down, she was examining the door. She sighed deeply. "I think if we do this together, we can get it jammed shut again. And then I'll prop a chair under the handle."

Mom was hiding something. But Francie was hiding something too. So was Grandma, definitely Dad. They were all hiding things except for Sam, Francie thought, and then she thought, Maybe he's hiding something too.

Mom said: "Come inside. Your dad is safe in the hospital, where the doctors are going to make him better. I promise."

It was quiet under here with the soft pine needles cushioning Francie's body, shushing branches low and heavy overhead. Francie laid her cheek against the tree's trunk like she was touching skin. She pulled the backpack onto her shoulders, and Francie began to climb.

There was only one way to go. It was a relief.

Up.

TWELVE

Race Day

When Marietta climbed into the cab of Mikey's pickup truck, it was like a choir of angels started singing. "Whoa, you've got a real shiner," she said. She gave him a hug.

He said, "Where do you want to go?"

Just drive around, she told him. She played with the radio, found a station playing eighties pop, not his personal favourite, but when she closed her eyes and started singing along to Tiffany, the remnants of yesterday's headache flew out the window.

"I need to go see Luce," Marietta said.

Right, Luce. That guy.

Mikey took them through a drive-through, ordered Marietta a fish fillet with fries and a Diet Coke, and she said, "God, I haven't had this since high school." She didn't seem to twig to the fact that, after all this time, Mikey remembered her order. Maybe that was for the best? He got himself the same, even though he didn't like fish. He didn't want to think too hard on why, or what he was doing, what this all meant.

I'm going for a drive with Marietta.

Marietta licked her fingers. She said, "You know Irene? Luce's mom? She went down to the hospital this morning. She's there now. I don't know why. It's none of her business."

Mikey didn't reply. He didn't necessarily agree, but agreement was inconsequential. It wasn't a prerequisite to friendship for Mikey, never had been.

Marietta wanted to talk. The more she talked, the more Mikey realized she didn't know the whole story—he thought back over what he'd told her when he called yesterday. Luce had been in a car accident, he'd been taken to the hospital with injuries, the police said he'd be charged, he was driving under the influence.

So she didn't know about the fight.

She didn't know that Mikey had called Luce to arrange a meeting—*about the gun, about getting rid of the gun, like you'd asked me to, Marietta*—and that Luce had misunderstood (or, as accurately, Mikey had muddled it up), that they'd fought.

Long story short, she didn't know Mikey had precipitated it all. Maybe she'd never find out?

Mikey'd told the new hire not to call the cops; the man wasn't happy about it, kept saying how that guy was a total psycho; but he'd volunteered to drive Mikey to the nearest clinic in the town nearby, waited with him, nice guy, good hire, and everything had checked out. The doctor shone a little beam of light into Mikey's pupils and he was good to go. Take it easy tomorrow, the doctor had said. And she'd given him an ice pack for the eye. Mikey was back at the site to pick up his truck, home by dinnertime.

With that call from the cops about Luce in between. Followed by his own call to Marietta. He'd pulled over on the side of the road before dialing her number, hands shaking, squinting through his swollen eyelid.

And he'd confessed nothing. Didn't say he'd so much as seen Luce that afternoon. Never would, if he could help it.

"Luce, he's not an easy person to live with," said Marietta. "But I knew that when I chose him, you know?"

Mikey turned up the radio. Belinda Carlisle.

"Do you like this song?" Marietta asked him.

"Sure," said Mikey. Mostly he just didn't want to hear more about Luce.

"I think I went roller-skating to this song?" Marietta said.

"Yeah?" Mikey laughed. You could say it was a song about heaven, but it wasn't, was it? It was a song about love, like all the songs on the radio. *Watch it, Mikey.*

Marietta said, "Remember that roller rink out by where the police station is now? Shit, I have to find out what's going to happen to Luce once they let him out of the hospital. Do you know?"

"Not my area of expertise."

"Where'd you get that black eye, by the way?" She shook the ice in her cup of soda. For a second he thought— she knows.

"Walked into a wall," he said.

"What? I don't believe you."

"Construction sites are dangerous places," he said, and stopped abruptly. Like she needed to be reminded.

They were both silent. Then she asked him, "What really happened last summer?" She was shaking her ice, looking out the window. He was driving them into the countryside, he didn't know where, exactly, they were going. Maybe he wanted to show her the palace he was building. *Look what I can do, without Luce.*

"Luce didn't follow the rules and he got hurt," Mikey said. "Simple as that."

"He said you owed him. He said it was your fault."

"I don't think that's true," Mikey said, "but everyone's entitled to believe what they want to. We don't have to agree all the time."

Marietta was quiet. She breathed deeply. She drew her feet in thin canvas shoes up onto the seat, pulling her knees into her chest, she was wearing a plain dress of some sort, Mikey didn't know much about fashion, black, and the skirt was narrow, it came to mid-thigh when she sat like that. He could see how skinny her legs were, how they were nothing but muscle and bone, and her arms too, wrapped around her shins, swishing the waxed paper cup, twirling the ice, her chin resting on her knees.

He double-checked she was wearing her seat belt.

What if it had all been different? What if this was his life, what if she were riding in his truck not because she needed to escape but because they were going somewhere together? It was strange how the same arrangement of two people, inside a place or a space, could mean entirely different things, depending on the past that led up to a particular moment in time. They could have been brother and sister, for example. Or she could have been a hitchhiker. Or his girlfriend, or his wife, or his lover.

But no matter how he tried, he couldn't even pretend. Because she wasn't in on it too. She saw him how she saw him, how she'd always seen him, and that wasn't going to change.

"I need to go see Luce. When we get back to town, can you drop me at the hospital?"

"For sure," said Mikey. He turned down a road that would take them away from the palace, this wasn't the moment, there never would be a moment.

Stay away from Mari.

His bowels felt a bit watery, the headache was returning. He wanted to help Marietta, he wanted to be a good friend, but only if Luce never found out.

She left her cup in the cupholder when she got out of his truck. He wondered how long he'd keep it, ice cubes melted, sloshing around, to remind him of what wasn't there. "Thanks for the ride."

When Marietta called later on, Mikey let it ring through.

He didn't listen to the message till around 3 a.m. She was talking very fast. She said that she didn't get to see Luce at the hospital, he'd been admitted to the psych ward on a Form 1 for talking some crazy shit, but they wouldn't keep him long, he'd be released soon, he'd be home in a couple of days, and he'd have a court date in, like, six weeks or so? "I guess he broke his arm? But they've set it, they won't keep him in for that. They're going to try him on some medication? I can't find the gun, Mikey, so I think he got rid of it? But I don't know, and he's coming home, and—" She said she needed his help, she'd had a fight with her mother-in-law, she was in tough, could Mikey please please babysit the kids tomorrow, she had to work a double shift starting early in the morning, to cover for the co-worker who'd covered for her. She was stuck for a few days till Luce got out, and what about after that, couldn't he help?

"You're not answering your phone. Please call back."

Mikey lay awake looking at the clock, tossing his body back and forth, the whole bed rocking as he tried to find a comfortable spot. He was too warm, he kicked the blankets off, he was too cold. His headache was back. He got up for a glass of water and some Tylenol.

At around four thirty in the morning, Mikey worked up his courage to dial her number. He figured she'd be asleep, and wouldn't pick up, but she did. She sounded hyper-awake.

"I'm sorry, I was going to leave a message," Mikey said.

"I don't have voice mail."

Oh.

"The thing is, the thing is, Marietta, I can't . . . I'm sorry I can't . . ."

"Really? You can't. Okay, whatever."

"Listen, Marietta, you probably shouldn't call me again. I mean, especially once Luce gets released. I'm sorry, maybe things will blow over, maybe things will change."

And she hung up on him somewhere in the middle of that speech. Which was exactly what he deserved, Mikey figured.

❦

When the phone rings before 5 a.m., you know it's not good news—unless it happens to be the Nobel Committee calling from—wherever they call from! Norway? Helsinki?

"*Guten Morgen?*" Sally was breathless from throwing off the bedsheets and hurtling into the kitchen in the dark, in her linen pyjamas. Just in case it was the Nobel Committee. Calling from . . . Germany? Would the Nobel Committee spokesperson be crying (for joy, presumably) while notifying David Sosa that he'd been awarded his well-deserved Nobel Prize in Mathematics? "Who is this, please?" Sally reverted to English, because she knew—not the Nobel Committee.

But perhaps almost as exciting, a call for help, with Sally to the rescue again.

"Don't you dare apologize," Sally said, "I'm thrilled to take your kids for the day—and overnight too? of course!—they'll just muck in with us, it's David's first half-marathon of the season, and we're all going along to cheer him on, I'm sure your kids won't mind, oh! but we're leaving around seven, yes, 7 a.m., can I come pick them up? It's no trouble at all! Don't even mention it, Marietta, this is what I'm here for!"

That's not how the Nobel Prize works, David told her, when Sally related her version of the conversational arc to him. They give out prizes in the fall, not the spring. And the Nobel Committee is in Stockholm. That's in Sweden, David told her. Not Germany. Also, you know I'm never going to win one, right?

"I'm an assistant professor of mathematical physics, I teach first-years, I haven't published in a decade."

Sally waved one hand. "Yes, yes. So I said we could take Francie and the baby with us to your race," Sally finished her story. She flung on the overhead light and began digging through the closet for extra sun hats.

"What?" David lay on his back, arm over eyes. "What are you looking for?"

"I said we'd bring the Fultz kids to your race. I explained it was a big day around here, but I don't think Marietta would have cared if I'd said we were going to the moon. She must be desperate."

"I don't need to get up for another half an hour." David squinted as he put on then took off his glasses.

"She said Luce is in the hospital on a Form 1, and when he's released, he'll just come home, and his court date will be in about six weeks."

David sat up. He looked interested, for a change. "What's a Form 1?"

"I don't know! It sounded bad. She was crying."

"Marietta was crying?"

Sally turned from a bin of winter accessories and examined her husband. Too interested? And he'd remembered the woman's name. "I'll let you sleep," Sally said, switching off the light, abandoning the sun hat search.

At least the dog was thrilled to see her. Sally released Diego from his crate under the table, and he bowed and scuttled and pranced. She made herself a cup of camomile tea while he wolfed down a bowl of the leftovers she'd put away for him: chicken and rice. He was practically human, her closest confidant, if a bit of a fool. "Shall we go for our walkies?" Outside, it was getting light, wonderfully early, as it did at this time of the year, and the lovely tall grass in the backyard sloughed wet and heavy against her flowing pyjama trousers. The smells were at once earthy and heavenly. No one in the alley. Her Birkenstocks slapped, her breasts free under the sleeveless pyjama top, an old grey sweater of David's unzipped and flapping as Diego pulled, pulled, pulled. Such a sensitive animal, reading her mind, leading them not on their regular route to the park but in the opposite direction, along well-canopied, quiet streets to the busy four-lane roadway bisecting their neighbourhood. A road designed for commuters, not people. Barren of trees, littered with power lines, street light poles, bus stops.

"We're going to be early, Diego!"

But she couldn't wait either. If David had seemed unusually interested in that woman, Marietta, Sally understood, because she felt it herself, something magnetic drawing her curiosity, unexpected, coming from this exhausted scrap of a woman. Even the way Marietta asked for Sally's help—never before, and then twice in one week!—seemed cool, detached, calculating. Like she was protecting herself, hiding

secrets. Sally was more than eager to roll up and examine
Marietta for scarring.

A crooked little house.

Something was off in there, Sally was sure, something un-
healthy that resisted Sally's interference. An inscrutable family
living their dangerous lives, attached to Sally's own through her
daughter Alice, who couldn't go a day without seeing Marietta's
daughter Francie, no matter Sally's attempts at disruption.

Sally saw it all so clearly: Francie was a sly creature leech-
ing off Alice's shy charm, devoted to Alice, yes, but like a
junkyard dog, fierce and jealous and chasing everyone else
away. It was too late to nip that friendship in the bud; but
nothing in this world was fixed, all was fluid.

Diego sat down on the sidewalk. The slabs were littered
with cigarette butts. He and Sally considered the little house
that squatted on top of the steep, grassy incline.

Francie's house.

Marietta's house.

Luce's house, too. Infamous man. Not currently on the
premises. Sally associated his presence with his car—the first
time their paths had crossed, he was sitting behind the
wheel, he was climbing out, he was leaning on the hood
waiting for Francie to come out of Sally's house. Oh my,
who's that? That's my dad. Oh! The kind of man you'd look
at twice. Tall, plenty of hair, glittering eyes, muscular but
not thick, his hand shaking hers, calloused and rough. And
now: arrested, and according to Marietta, he'd totalled that
flashy car of his. Did this add to the attraction? Only in
Sally's fantasy world. But Sally's fantasy world was impulsive,
it was insistent, it could almost replace the real one, or lie
overtop of it, opaque and veined, pulsing like the real thing.

Sally knocked.

It was as if the inside of the house were broadcasting to her ears like a radio, and the radio had fallen suddenly silent.

Sally knocked, again. She tried the handle. Not locked. She pushed and the door opened with a metallic grating as it shifted and twisted off its hinges. There was a crash—a chair fell to the ground?

"Hello?" Sally stepped inside.

"Oh. My. God. We don't use this door." Marietta was wound up, keyed up, Sally saw, feeling mild perturbation as the smaller woman began throwing her body against the door, grunting with her efforts. The woman's energy was like a tap opened full blast. "We don't use this door! It's broken!"

"Maybe you should put up a sign," Sally suggested.

"No one ever comes here!" said Marietta.

"Let me help." Sally dropped Diego's leash and heaved her shoulder against the wood. It gave way beneath her heft, it pressed into the frame like a sandwich sliding into an undersized lunch container. But there wasn't time to appreciate the effect, a child was screaming. Marietta flashed furiously past Sally, who followed, sandals tracking blades of wet grass onto a thin carpet that had been bunched up and thrown out of order.

Sally had a feeling Diego was the cause.

Oh dear. Marietta's scream sounded angrier than Francie's. A healthy, open-throated roar.

The hallway was short, and Diego bounded from a bedroom to greet Sally, as if to say: I found them for you!

"Thank you, Diego, yes, here we are—Francie and the baby, I'm sorry, I've completely forgotten his name! What a doll! Hello, Francie, are you ready to go?"

Diego made a second foray into Francie's bed, depositing fresh paw prints, while Sally reached for his leash. "He's thrilled to see you, Francie! Look, he knows who you are!" But Francie curled dramatically into a protective ball, legs drawn into her stomach, arms wrapped around shins, knees tucked under a long t-shirt, stretching out the fabric. "He's harmless, he's friendly," Sally insisted, while Marietta lifted the baby from the crib jammed right next to Francie's bed. Sally noticed several white plastic laundry baskets stacked on the floor, filled with folded clothes. The room was cramped, no space for a dresser.

The baby's nighttime diaper sagged.

"I'll dress the baby while you shower." Sally reached out her arms. Babies loved her. Sally never passed up a chance to cuddle and snuggle one. But Marietta held the baby out of reach, her skin sallow, sunken and dark beneath her eyes.

"I already showered," she said.

"Diego can always sense tension in the air," said Sally, as the dog grabbed a pair of socks from one of the baskets and ran out of the room.

Marietta's posture was of someone preparing to engage in hand-to-hand combat. "Those are Francie's favourite socks."

Francie cried: "My rainbow socks?"

Sally said: "He'll give them back. He always does. He's a very good listener."

Francie hopped off the bed and followed Sally, and they found Diego in the kitchen looking contrite and wise. "Drop them!" Sally pointed. He obliged, and Francie darted in and snatched the socks off the linoleum.

Of course. "I'll make breakfast!"

No protests from Marietta could stop Sally—she was already checking the cupboards and the fridge, bare but not empty. One can of tomato paste. One tin of tomatoes. One sleeve of pasta. A half bag of oats! Francie was watching her. "Go get dressed," Sally told the child. But she was back all too quickly, wearing jeans and a jewel-encrusted shirt, inspecting Sally's every move, as the pot of oatmeal stirred up like grey glue, sticking to the spoon, a substance that could have been used to patch holes in plaster, or to fix, say, a door. *Ha ha.*

Francie watched Diego's tail knock a plant to the floor. "That's my mom's favourite spider fern," she said in her loud voice, which always took Sally by surprise. Everything was someone's favourite something, Sally thought, trying to clean up the dirt using a dishrag she found folded neatly over the side of the sink, even while the unattended oatmeal crawled up and over the side of the pot. Sally tossed the cloth into the sink as Marietta and the baby, dressed for the day, came into the kitchen. Francie ran behind her mother's legs, regressing, no doubt, under these challenging circumstances.

Diego smothered them all with love.

Marietta brushed the front of her uniform, but the paw prints stayed, best not to mention it. A dog was such good medicine, in Sally's opinion. "Breakfast is ready!"

"I'm not hungry," Francie said.

The women's eyes fell on the pot of porridge at the same time. "Oh well," Sally said. "You can always eat it later."

"*Mm-hm,*" said Marietta, and Sally looked around the room as if through Marietta's gaze, spotting smudges of dirt on the linoleum, the plant repotted on an obviously wonky angle, porridge under the burner. The faint smell of scorched dishcloth in the air. The cloth itself, begrimed and balled up in the sink.

This house was too clean! That's what the problem was.

Perhaps there were fewer secrets here than Sally had assumed. Who could keep a secret with nowhere to hide it?

"Here's their bag." Marietta held out a plastic grocery bag. For some reason, Francie was putting on her backpack too. "You have my number? It's a double shift, overnight, I'll try to come by as soon as I can tomorrow morning."

"The kids can stay as long as you want!" Sally wasn't 100 percent sure she meant it, but she was 100 percent sure that she wanted to mean it.

"Thanks." Marietta's tone was flat, but Sally did not take offence, she never took offence! For a beat, everyone stood passively, not sure what the next move might be, and then Marietta said: "Don't use the front door." A flicker of a smile flashed across her face, her entire face, and Sally swooned—they were bonding! Over a shared moment! An inside joke. Ha ha! Even Diego was laughing and panting as Marietta pointed out the alternative exit, down a few steps, behind where Sally stood. The umbrella stroller was propped there too, for the baby. What was his name?

Sally noticed a Smart car in the driveway, how strange. Just like David's.

Though only a few blocks separated their two houses, it proved a difficult journey, beset by crooked stroller wheels, tempting squirrels, and Sally's own doubts about how much this particular baby loved her—instead of returning her squeeze with a snuggle, when she leaned down to fasten him into the stroller, he pinched her neck, and it hurt. "Ow!" Sally almost pinched the baby in return, but Francie was still watching her every move. For that matter, so was Diego.

They were nearly home when Sally realized the car in the Fultzes' driveway was actually David's. This dovetailed with the cold comprehension that she was still wearing her pyjamas.

Diego rubbed his head against her hip, as if to reassure her that no one would take her less seriously for it.

Oh, I don't want anyone taking me too seriously, Sally proclaimed. But it was hard to know whether she meant it.

She lifted the stroller, baby still strapped in, and muscled it up the front steps and into the house. Francie looked impressed. Maybe. "That's not how my mom does it."

"Well, I do things differently around here."

Did Sally want to be taken seriously, or did she want to keep matters light? Was it a choice between being a ruler or a clown? Diego understood the dilemma. He wanted to please, to flop around, to frolic, but not being taken seriously could hurt, sometimes, especially when the ones you loved most, trusted most, looked at you with disdain, baffled or perplexed, or told you what not to do. *Ew, is he eating trash? Stop jumping, you're scaring that poor child!*

"We're home! Where is everyone? *Eee-oh-eet!*"

Oh my god, do you have to be so loud, Mom? Did you go outside in your pyjamas? Why are you talking to the dog?

Because he understands me.

Oh my god, Mom, what does that even mean?

⊱⊰

Signing up for the race wasn't Kate's idea. Sally said it would help her bond with her dad if they trained together, and also, she said, Kate was getting sedentary and secretive, lying around all the time doodling in her notebook or talking to her friends on the phone or going for mysterious "walks" with people whose names Sally didn't even know half the time—or their parents' names, or where they lived! "Mom, they're just friends from school. We go to the park." (And one friend sometimes brings a water bottle with some vodka poured into it, and her parents are totally okay with it, which is either really cool or kind of weird. But you don't need to know that extra detail.)

Clap-clap! "Get dressed, Kate! It's race day!"

"Oh my god, Mom, *you're* still wearing pyjamas."

"Eat a banana with peanut butter! That's your dad's favourite pre-race meal."

"Ugh, I'm not hungry."

"You don't want to bonk in your race."

"Mom? Please don't ever ever ever say that again."

"It's a real thing, it's when you run out of energy because you didn't eat enough before your race."

"Mom, it's a fun run. I'm not doing a marathon."

"Don't forget your vitamins, for your skin. They're on the kitchen table, in your pill box."

"Mom!"

In the bathroom, Kate splashed her face in the sink, brushed her teeth. Over the running water, she could hear voices downstairs, and maybe a baby, crying? Saturday morning, and it wasn't even seven o'clock. Sometimes Kate wondered why she ever tried to be nice and agreed to do things, when it meant suffering consequences like this. The light above the sink was too bright, and in the mirror she saw a pimple rising under the dark, smooth hairs of her right eyebrow. She stopped her fingers from pinching the pimple—just barely!

Instead, she combed the knots from her long, heavy hair, drew it into a high ponytail, applied mascara.

Don't pick it, don't pick!

Okay—definitely a baby. Definitely crying. Make that screaming. *Do I even want to know?*

So apparently, and this was weird, Mom had invited Alice's annoying friend Francie *and* her baby brother to come along with them to Dad's race.

"Kate's racing too!"

"Mom, it's a fun run."

"That counts, doesn't it, David?"

But Kate's dad did not look good, hunched in the passenger seat of the minivan. Kate was sitting on the bench seat in the middle of the van beside Francie, Alice on the other side. Also, Kate was holding the baby, because apparently, and this was weird too, no one had thought about the baby needing a car seat.

"Back when I was born, they let babies roll around loose. Like watermelons!"

Oh, Mom.

Max was in the wayback with Diego. "Hey, there's a police car."

"Duck!"

Mom locked eyes with Kate in the rear-view mirror, and Kate unbuckled her seat belt and slid herself and the baby—whose name she hadn't bothered to learn—down behind Mom's seat.

"The police arrested my dad," Francie said in a very loud voice.

Kate stared at the kid. "Really? What did he do?"

Francie shrugged. "He's in the hospital," she said.

"Weird," said Kate.

"Pull over," said Dad. "I need a bathroom. This can't wait!"

"Hang on, we're in the middle of nowhere. This doesn't look promising!" Mom turned sharply and jammed on the brakes, and Kate said, "Mom! The baby!" But really, the baby was fine. He seemed sleepy. He'd stopped screaming as soon as Mom had told Kate to pick him up. But he smelled like pee.

Kate was feeling a bit sick. All she could see out the window, from her vantage point on the floor, was the upper half of what looked like a mini-mall and, above it, the sky.

They waited for Dad to come out of whatever shop had let him in.

No one said anything when he returned, bringing with him the scent of floral hand soap. Diego whined from the back seat.

The baby put his fat, round hands on Kate's cheeks and pinched. "Ouch!"

"He always does that," Francie told her.

"Ouch! Why? What should I do?"

"I'll hold him!" said Alice.

"Almost there, no one move," said Mom, another sharp turn, and then a whole lot of bumping. Kate felt a bit sicker. She lay down flat on the floor and closed her eyes, and let the baby sit on top of her. He seemed to like that.

When Mom stopped and opened the sliding door, Kate said, "I'm going to throw up now," and crawled out into the fresh air. They were in a grassy field that had been turned into a parking lot, muddy ruts, cars on haphazard angles. Mom took the baby, and Kate limped around to the back of the van. She almost wished she'd eaten something this morning, but she didn't want Mom to know she'd been right.

"Race nerves," said Dad. "Ten experience points if you barf."

"Carsickness," said Kate, "Mom's bad driving." But she knew it was nerves. Nervous for a fun run! *C'mon, Kate, pull yourself together!* She bent forward, hands on knees, staring at her long ponytail swishing the grass, but she did not barf, she didn't even gag. Diego romped over and licked her face.

"Someone grab the dog's leash, and let's get going!" Mom locked the van.

Kate met the baby's eyes, strapped into the stroller. Awake again. They were both equally trapped.

Mom had parked nowhere near the start line. After walking for ages, Kate began to feel hopeful again. "It's okay if we're late," she said. But they weren't. Mom found the registration tent, and Dad picked up their numbers.

"I want to run in the race too!" Kate heard Francie whisper to Alice, while Sally tried to pin Kate's number to the front of her shirt.

"Oh my god, Mom, you poked me!"

"I'm sorry! You moved! And this shirt is so tight—"

Kate grabbed the pins and the number.

"I can't help you if you just WALK AWAY!"

Okay, Mom. Okay, Sally. Kate followed the tide of people heading for the start line. She was looking for someone, of course. There was a reason she'd agreed to sign up for the race, and it wasn't just to get to spend more quality time with Dad (they had run together maybe three times, and even though Kate didn't want to feel this way, she was embarrassed by his long, skinny calves in these very tight socks he wore that went all the way up to his knees). The reason was that two of Kate's friends (from school, from "walks" in the park) had signed up too, they did it every year, and they said it was actually fun. "You get a swag bag," said the friend whose parents let her drink their vodka. "And there's free food."

It didn't sound all that special, honestly, but one of the two friends was the girl from drama class. *Emma.* So Kate said yes.

"Hey, Kate! Kate, over here!"

Kate scanned the forest of neon-clad legs. "Oh my god, Peter? What're you doing here?" (Neither of the two friends was Peter.)

"My mom's running in the half-marathon. What're you doing?"

"Racing, of course." Kate rolled her eyes. "Fun run. Here, help me pin my number on."

"Have you been training?"

"It's a fun run, Peter. I have not."

"You're going to die."

"What? I am not!"

"There's only one way to build endurance, that's what my mom says. You can't cheat at running."

"Peter, can you focus on the pins, please?"

"I don't want to scratch you . . ."

Rock music pounded from raised speakers, a man was shouting through a bullhorn. The number was on crooked, and Peter had only managed to get two pins fastened. Kate was starting to feel worse than before, tight, light-headed, like her guts were tying themselves in knots, cutting off oxygen to her brain. Peter seemed to guess, or understand, about Kate's nerves, and he walked with her toward the starting line, where the competition was gathering, milling about. You'd hardly say they were lining up. It was kind of a pathetic mob of characters, moms and dads pushing jogging strollers, old people, people who looked pretty out of shape, a bunch of little kids.

And she didn't see Emma from drama class anywhere.

Peter said, "When the gun goes off, don't think, just start running. That's my advice."

Kate didn't even reply, forgot to say thank you, she was feeling so sick and distracted as she pushed her way up toward the front—and there was Francie, that annoying kid! She was wearing a number pinned to her shirt (with all four pins), and she looked dead serious. One glance at Kate, and then back to focusing on the start line. The kid was intense.

When the gun went off, Francie jumped like a rabbit

out in front of everybody. Like someone was chasing her. Kate also jumped, but more vertically than horizontally, it sounded like a real gunshot, it didn't help with the whole guts-of-water situation going on down there. But she started to run. The first kilometre is the hardest part, Dad had told her. After that, you'll be warmed up, you'll feel better.

Wait, how long was this race?

They were running across a field, and it seemed hot. Then they were running in a little patch of trees, that was better, cooler, but Kate got stuck behind a dad pushing a double stroller and creating a mega-bottleneck. They passed a sign that read "1." The guy pushing the double stroller shouted out, "One kilometre down, two to go, folks!" Was that supposed to be encouraging?

Out of the trees was a hill, which didn't look like much till you tried to run up it, and Kate was beginning to wish she'd done a little more training, Dad kept telling her, if only she'd come running with him, the race would be easier.

But Dad, your socks! I'm sorry!

Don't go out too fast, you'll burn yourself out, Dad had said. Check, Kate thought, as a man with an enormous belly somehow passed her on the hill. Don't let your feet slap the ground, it wastes energy. Tell that to this guy! Feet slapping like great big baloney sandwiches. Kate felt the spark of something—she wanted to pass this guy back. At the top of the hill was another hill—no way! And the guy was slowing down.

Once you're cruising, pick it up a bit, see what you've got. *Okay, let's see. Let's see what you've got, Kate Sosa!*

She passed another sign that read "2."

Up ahead, Kate saw the kid, Francie, who was wearing a black t-shirt and jeans, hard to miss. Kate had the feeling that if she really tried, she'd be able to catch her. The kid was pumping her arms hard and she looked a bit wild, she was skinny and not that big, and her jeans were too long.

When you see the finish line, sprint, Dad said, run all the way through, most people slow down on the last few steps and you'll beat them if you keep running hard.

They were going downhill now, at last, turning into the same field where they'd started. The start line had been repurposed as a finish line. Kate sprinted, the kid sprinted, together they sprinted past another dad with a stroller, a lady dressed head to toe in leopard-print spandex ("You rock!" Kate shouted, maybe that was the oxygen deprivation talking, but she heard the lady calling back, "You go, girls!"), and together (almost) she and Francie crossed the finish line. Francie first.

Three whole kilometres!

Kate took three steps and threw herself onto the ground, but a volunteer in a safety vest told her to get up and keep moving. "No thanks," said Kate. She was feeling something special, something she'd never felt before, or quite this intensely. She was looking at the sky and the clouds, and feeling the sun on her face, and she was thinking how she could have beat the kid, she could have run faster than her, she could have passed her right at the end; but she didn't.

And it felt weird. It felt good.

Peter was standing over her, blocking the view of the sky. "Great race. You almost beat that tiny little kid."

"That's my sister's friend Francie. Her dad just got arrested."

"Whoa, seriously?" Peter was impressed, as she knew he would be. "What did he do?"

"I think I like racing," said Kate. "It's more fun than you'd think, Peter. You should try it sometime."

But then her mom showed up, pushing the baby in the stroller, followed by Max with the dog, who was licking her face, and Dad who was saying, "Great race! Did you follow my tips?"; and Alice, and Francie, who kept leaping up and down shouting, "I won! I won!" Which wasn't exactly accurate.

"You beat me, okay?" said Kate, standing up and brushing herself off. "That's not the same thing."

But she could see that Francie thought it was. And Kate had that weird feeling again, like she was going to cry or explode, or both.

"Who's your friend?" Mom asked, and Kate almost felt bad for her, she looked so excited. She knew so little.

"This is Peter."

"My mom's running the half-marathon," Peter offered.

"Oh, wonderful! Just like David!" Sally almost jumped for joy. Why did she have to be so dramatic?

Dad said he needed one more stop at the porta-potties (too much information!), and at the exact same moment someone shouted, "Boo!" and Kate turned around, and there were her friends, especially Emma. "Where were you? Why didn't you run with us?"

And that's when she noticed—her stomach felt fine. She wasn't sick anymore. It was all over. It was all beginning. "I hear there's free food?" she said.

"Are you hungry, I made sandwiches!" Sally offered, but Kate and her friends, including Peter, were already heading for the food tent.

"Later, Mom!" Kate turned around and shouted, in case Sally was worried, but it didn't appear that she was. She was adjusting a bag that was hanging over the stroller handles, and then she stood up very straight in her long, shapeless dress that looked exactly like a burlap sack with armholes, her hair in one long braid down her back, staring ahead at something Kate couldn't see, and probably didn't want to know about at all.

~~~

Sam was stuck in the stroller. The lady stopped pushing, the stroller stopped, and all he could see was a bush. The action was happening behind him. Loud music, loud voices, loud colours, loud people. *Go!* He rocked his head and chest and legs and got the stroller shaking a bit, but it didn't move. He twisted his head back on his neck and screeched.

But the lady didn't notice. She let go of the handles, Sam snapped his body backward, and the whole stroller crashed to the grass.

"Goodness! What's all this fuss!"

Sam was hot, wet, thirsty. Through teary eyelids, he saw the lady's giant legs under a swishing skirt and her head, far away, looking down at him. The dog ran up and licked Sam's face. The boy pulled the dog away.

"He's a bit red," the lady said to the boy with the dog. "Run to the van. Bring the juice boxes. And a sun hat!"

The lady unstrapped Sam, freed him from the toppled stroller, just in time for a loud BANG! Sam saw people running away. He pushed to his feet and staggered after them. There was his sister. She was digging around in the grass, looking for something, with her friend Alice. "AAA-SH," Sam said. "AAA-SH."

"He's saying my name!" said Alice.

"No he's not," said Francie. "He can't talk."

There was a loud noise: *Eee-oh-eet!* The lady was making it. Alice jumped up and grabbed the lady's arm.

"Where's Kate?" the lady said. "Has anyone seen Kate?"

"Mom!"

The dog was back, knocking Sam onto his bottom, licking Sam's mouth. Sam grabbed one of the hairy ears and pulled. The lady unpeeled his fingers, poked a straw into a juice box, and put it into his hands. *Ooooo!*

Francie said, "He's too little to hold that." But the lady didn't listen.

Sam squeezed, juice squirted out of the straw down his chin, neck, shirt, front, he was wet, sticky. He sat down hard. His sister came over and said, "Not like that, Sam!" She tried to put the straw into his mouth and he screeched. She squeezed and juice squirted onto his tongue, and it tasted sweet and he wanted more. *More!*

They were moving now, the lady in the dress was moving them, she tried to put Sam into the stroller, but Sam arched his back and screamed till she gave up. She picked him up and squashed him under one arm, the stroller under the other. Her arm was strong and meaty, but Sam kept fighting. All the way up a hill.

"What's the matter now?" The lady was talking in a whispery hiss. She hissed, "Babies love me."

The lady stopped at a picnic table beside a tree.

"AAA-SH!"

Alice took Sam into her arms. He thrashed with excitement. Alice turned in circles till Sam spit up some juice. Purple. Nobody saw but Alice. She wiped his mouth on the bottom part of her shirt.

The lady held out a sandwich and Sam took it and threw it on the ground.

"Bad Sam!"

The dog was eating the sandwich very fast, one two three gulps. Sam was hungry. He plopped over, face down, and smacked his forehead on the ground. *Smack, smack, smack.*

"What is he doing? Stop him!" the lady said.

Francie said, "He hits his head on things when he's mad. He likes it."

Alice stroked a squishy bit of bread across Sam's ear, his cheek. He stopped smacking his head and looked at her. She gave him the squishy bit of bread. And more. He sat up. She gave Sam a bit of salty meat. She gave Sam warm cheese. A whole slice of bread. But the dog got it.

"Bad dog!"

Alice tried to hug Sam and Sam pinched her face, he pulled her hair.

"There's something wrong with that baby," said the lady.

"He's not a baby!" Francie said very loudly. She threw a slice of tomato and some lettuce onto the ground. The dog did not eat either.

The lady lay down on a blanket on the grass, on her back. She folded her hands over her chest. She said it was nap time.

Sam knew all about nap time, and he was not interested!

"Quiet! I need quiet!" said the lady.

Alice and Francie were calling Sam like he was a dog: "Come, Sam, come, Sam!" He crawled after them like a dog. Then they walked faster. "Come, Sam, come!"

"Don't go far!" the lady shouted. "I'll *eee-oh-eet* you!"

"Okay, Mom!"

Sam bobbled to standing and teetered along, trying to catch Alice and Francie. When he lost balance, he had to sit down, hard, but he always got up again. They were ahead of him, sliding on their bellies under a big bush. "Come, Sam!" Sam plopped forward and crawled under too.

Alice peeled an orange. She bit each slice in half, half for her, half for Sam.

It was shady under the branches, cool. Sam was not thirsty, not hungry, still sticky.

He lay on his belly. Sighed. Ear on dirt. He fought against nap time. He felt full, round, heavy.

The girls were talking in quiet, excited voices. Alice had a watch on her wrist with buttons on it. They looked through the branches. He could hear their voices, soothing. Sam liked hearing their voices, quiet, excited.

"Here they come!"

"Do you see your dad?"

"There he is!" The watch made a beeping sound. It was the beeping sound that pushed Sam over the precipice of sleep.

When he woke up, the shadows were different, and he was alone.

"*Eee-oh-eet!*" he heard. "*Eee-oh-eet!*"

And then, oh! His sister was crawling in beside him. She was curling up beside him. She was whispering to him and he lay quietly with his ear in the dirt, and neither of them were alone.

And he knew—they were hiding. They didn't want to be found.

﹏

What Sally remembered about that day was that she lost everyone. Everyone! It was a failure at a profound level, failure of attention, failure of control, failure of responsibility. And none of it was her fault!

She'd been woken from her nap by Francie's incoherent shrieks. "What's happening?" Sally sat up too quickly and blood rushed away, leaving spots behind her eyes. "What have you done! Where's Alice?!"

So that was Alice, lost.

Sally leapt to her feet: "*Eee-oh-eet!*"

"David! David!" Francie gasped and pointed. Something terrible had happened to David, but Francie couldn't explain. David fell down, David was dead? Sally hurtled across the grass, her sandals flew off, first one and then the other, and the ground shook under her feet. David wasn't at the finish line, he wasn't in the food tent, or the lineups for the porta-potties, so that was David lost, which was when Sally lost herself, at least temporarily.

"*Eee-oh-eet!*"

Sally lost Diego when Max couldn't hold on to his leash, the wolfhound moved to feats of strength by the vision of Sally up and running madly off. Of course, Diego should, by rights, have found Sally, but he became distracted by a family barbecuing meat at their picnic site, and that was that. Diego lost.

(Sally had already lost Kate, though she didn't know it yet: Kate had caught a ride home with a friend from school whose parents said they'd buy the girls ice cream, a plan Kate had relayed to her brother Max, which Max had either forgotten or not registered in the first place.)

And Max wasn't lost, exactly, he'd just gotten bored waiting at the picnic table for people to come back. When nobody did, he remembered he still had the keys to the minivan from when he'd fetched the juice boxes for his mom earlier, so he walked all the way out through the field of parked cars and stuck the key in the ignition and turned on the radio and scrolled through the stations, till he got bored of that too, and walked back.

By then, Sally had discovered she'd lost the Fultz kids. "I can't believe it, I've lost a baby! He's not even mine!"

⋘

Although David briefly and avidly believed otherwise, he was not dead, he was not even dying. It was a simple case of heat exhaustion, the paramedic was saying, but this was as David was surfacing to a very bad smell, his throat making gruesome noises that approximated language, and he did not know where he was or who was speaking to him. His head was pounding and he was covered in goosebumps. He assumed it was the very bad smell that had both knocked him out and then roused him. That was his first conscious thought.

He was not dead, but part of him believed that he had been.

He couldn't remember much past the finish line. Big black dots blurring his vision, a closing down, like a lens clicking shut.

A commotion sounded over the loudspeakers, somewhere outside.

The paramedic said: "Once you're cooled and rehydrated, you'll be good to go." David noticed his daughter, Alice, pressed against the wall of the tent, as the paramedic helped him sit up, propped a wedge of foam behind his shoulders.

"Sip this." The liquid in the paper cup tasted like plain old yellow Gatorade. Not exactly the elixir of life David was expecting. There was a frozen towel wrapping the back of his neck.

David smiled at Alice.

Alice burst into tears, and ducked out between the flaps. The paramedic was setting up a flimsy divider. "We're going to get you cleaned up and out of these shorts." He held up a pair of scissors.

Oh. That was the smell.

⋘

What Alice remembered about that day was that she found everyone; and also, that not everyone wanted to be found.

First, Alice found her dad. Alive. In the medical tent. Talking in Spanish, which he spoke sometimes if Alice asked him to, especially. "*Hija.*" Dad sat up and smiled at Alice, and she didn't know the right words to say back to him.

Dad! You're not dead!—

She had to go, to run fast—"He's not dead! He's not dead!" Alice found her mom, barefoot, pacing blindly near the finish line, a volunteer holding her back from entering the course. "Mom! I found Dad! He's not dead!"

On the way to the medical tent, Alice found Diego, gnawing a splintered chicken bone. She wasn't afraid to yank it out of his mouth. "Bad dog! You'll choke!"

She found Max sitting on the picnic table.

She didn't find Kate, but then, no one had even noticed Kate was lost.

The real trouble started when Sally said it was high time to get home. The stroller looked abandoned beside the picnic table. "Where are the Fultz kids?"

And nobody knew.

"I can't believe it, I've lost a baby!"

Nobody knew, except for Alice. Alice had found Francie and Sam under the bush, and Francie had told her not to tell anyone. They were running away.

"But where are you going? What will you eat?"

"That's not important."

Alice did not understand. Was this a game?

"Don't tell anyone, Alecka. It's about the jewels."

Shivers ran up Alice's spine. *Fool's gold.* "Can I come too?"

When Francie said no, "We have to save our dad," Alice felt it in her heart. Something was wrong, but she couldn't make it right.

The hardest part was not telling anyone that she'd found Francie and Sam when she went back to the picnic table. Her mom was trying to describe Francie and Sam to a policeman who was wearing shorts. Alice noticed the gun holstered to his waist; she didn't take her eyes off it.

"We're just babysitting! The kids aren't even ours! Tell him, Alice."

"Francie is my best friend," Alice whispered.

"We need the best description you can provide."

"Sam has black hair," said Alice.

"He's wearing something sticky!" Sally broke in.

"A white shirt and blue shorts," said Alice, "and Francie has jeans and a cat t-shirt. It's her favourite." Should she even be giving these details? To the police? Was it betrayal?

"Her hair is quite dirty," said Sally.

"She's still wearing her race number!" said Alice. "From the race."

"Fun run," said Sally. "She ran with our older daughter."

"She won!" said Alice.

"Technically, she did not," said Sally.

"How mobile is the baby? Crawling, walking, could he have wandered off on his own? Maybe his sister went looking for him?"

"Walking," said Alice.

"Don't worry, we'll find them." The officer's right hand rested on his gun.

"What am I going to tell their poor mother?" Sally wailed.

There was an announcement over the loudspeakers with a description of two lost children.

Alice's heart felt like it was sitting in her stomach. She poked around in the picnic lunch her mom had packed and found a bag of trail mix, and one juice box. Sneaking around felt like the worst kind of pretend, the kind Alice was no good at. She was too much herself, too much Alice, not enough Alecka, too aware that her body was her own, her movements her own, her mind her own. She could not separate from herself.

When she was sure no one was watching, Alice crawled under the bush, again. Francie and Sam were still there. She almost cried with relief, to see them. "I brought food," she said. "For the journey." But she choked on the words. "Don't go!" she begged Francie.

"Sam can't eat nuts and stuff." Francie rejected the trail mix, holding on to the juice box. "You can't keep coming back. You're going to give away our hiding spot!"

"Francie, the police are looking for you now."

Sam was sitting up, fussing for the juice box. Francie's face went stiff and serious. "Who called the cops?"

"Um. My mom is really worried about you guys," said Alice. She was feeling more and more like she might have to cry.

And Sam agreed. He was fussing and grunting. He rocked on his bottom and grabbed for the juice box, and Alice's nose told her that something was going on in Sam's diaper—didn't Francie smell it too? Dirty diapers were real, not pretend, and you couldn't imagine them away.

"The policeman has a gun, Francie. I saw it. He has a gun." It was clear to Alice that someone would find them soon enough. Sam was about to blow up, and with him would go their hiding spot. "I'll say that I found you," Alice said quietly. She glanced into Francie's eyes, and was surprised to see Francie wavering, almost afraid.

Francie didn't say no.

"It's a miracle! You're a wonder!" Mom hugged Alice over and over.

"Can we go home now?" said Max.

"I've always said she's special," Mom told the police officer. "Sensitive to anyone in need." Alice stood quietly, not looking at his face, keeping an eye on his gun instead.

The loudspeakers announced the good news, but the cheers were muted, almost everyone had already gone home. The race was over. The grass was littered with trash, the reek from the row of porta-potties thick in the air as they walked past on their way to the field where the van was parked. Mom carried Sam in her arms, and even she didn't seem to notice that his diaper was full.

He fussed and screamed, "AAA-SH," and Alice was sure he wanted her instead, but she felt too tired to fight for him. She felt too tired to fight. Dad leaned on Max. A volunteer had found him a pair of shorts in the lost and found ("Don't think about that too hard!" Mom said), but he didn't smell great. Francie pushed the stroller with the bunched-up picnic blanket plunked into its seat, and Alice held on to Diego's leash. Kate's absence had gone unobserved and would remain so till they got home and Alice ran inside ahead of everyone else and found Kate already there, reclined on the good couch, writing in her notebook, with a paper sack of empty containers on the floor beside her, from a fast-food restaurant the family never went to.

But Alice didn't care.

A change was coming, or had already arrived. She was trying, but Alice couldn't see what Francie was seeing; she couldn't feel what Francie was feeling. There was something happening inside Francie that Alice couldn't understand, something Francie was trying to show her, unable to, and Alice didn't know what to do about it.

She had the feeling that Francie didn't know either. Or worse: that Francie might not even know anything was happening inside her, yet.

"I am done with this day," Mom announced, carrying in Sam. "We must never speak of this day again!"

"I think it's been a good day," said Dad. "A great day. A wonderful day!"

"Dad, you broke your record, it's on my watch," Alice remembered. She tried to push the buttons to show him, but instead the numbers disappeared. Dad patted her head and said it didn't matter.

It really didn't, he said, don't worry about it, honey, it's not important.

"Oh, there you are, Kate, what on earth happened to you?"

"I told Max to tell you . . ."

"There are several people here who require baths immediately!" Mom said. "Starting with you." And she wrinkled her nose and held Sam away from her body, like she'd just noticed his diaper was full.

Francie was last to come inside. Alice had been waiting for her, almost holding her breath, wondering if Francie would take this chance to run away, to escape from the real world into the pretend world where she would save her dad. But Francie did not do anything special or strange or scary or exciting. Alice found her sitting in the front hall, pushing off her sneakers without undoing the laces. "I want to go home," she whispered to Alice, and Alice thought she'd never seen Francie look like this before: sad, or lost, or both.

Where's home?

Francie was thinking it too, Alice was sure. It was too dangerous to say the words out loud, in the real world.

There was nothing to do, nothing to say. Alice crouched down in the pile of shoes and sandals in the front hall, and sat next to Francie, doing and saying nothing at all.

THIRTEEN

Gun Run

Francie had begun to climb. Alone. Patiently. Her feet bare and scratched. A good climbing tree had branches that weren't too far apart, so you could step with ease from one to the next, but also not too close together, crowding you out, scratching and scraping.

Francie recognized a good climbing tree when she saw it.

This tree, standing alone at the edge of the field, right beside the woods, was a good climbing tree.

Francie liked going up. She climbed methodically, like she was working on a math problem at school. She didn't have to think about anything else, here. If the wind rustled the branches, if the tree swayed, it didn't mean anything, it wasn't the tree talking to her or trying to hurt her or warn her, it was just things happening as they happened.

Francie heard her own heart, beating.

She heard wind in the branches. She heard insects humming like voices rising and falling, calling her name. Maybe the voices were just the cicadas. "Cicadas"— Francie said the word out loud, a soft-hard word, and she remembered when she and Alice had found a strange empty shell, orange and almost see-through, in Alice's backyard. They'd run into the house carrying it carefully, they were so sure it was from the fairies, but Sally had said no. Sally said the shell had come from an insect, shed like old skin. Sally had stopped stirring a bubbling pot of strawberry rhubarb jam on the stove, and she'd looked up pictures of cicadas on the desktop computer in the living room, to show them. Sally found and played them recordings of the sounds of cicadas singing, different songs in different places.

"They're speaking different languages," Sally said. "Isn't it WONDERFUL? Isn't it AMAZING?"

Was it better to know the facts or to believe in fairies?

"Just because the shell belongs to a cicada doesn't mean fairies aren't real," Sally had said, like she could read Francie's mind.

Did this make Francie trust Sally more, or less?

Francie didn't want to be thinking of Sally right now—what if she was thinking about Sally because Sally was thinking about her?

In Francie's mind, she could hear Alice saying: *Climb, higher! Higher! Right to the tip of the top.*

The branches were sticky with sap and Francie's palms and the bottoms of her feet were sticky and stained brown. Sap smelled sweet, but also golden and dark.

She was up in the sky now. *Don't look down!*

Far away, were sirens.

There were different kinds of sirens. A siren from a police car. A siren from an ambulance.

An ambulance siren would come for Mikey, a police car siren would come for Dad.

What siren would come for Francie?

"*Eee-oh-eet!*"

Uh-oh.

Sally. Was Sally down there, looking for Francie, even though she knew—Sally knew!—that Francie did not want to be found?

"*Eee-oh-eet!*"

Francie rested, listening, her ear pressed against the tree's trunk, but all she could hear was her own heart beating. A tree was alive, but the good thing about a tree was that it didn't have a heart. A heart could stop beating, but Dad said a tree could grow forever. Even a tree that looked dead could send up suckers, and its roots could reach far away underground to start other trees, and find other ways to go on living.

It seemed a long time ago Francie was standing on the risers in the gym and her mind was empty, her face hot, and only a moment after that she was walking with Dad along a strange street, like both of them were asleep. Dad was always saying goodbye in her dreams. He was always taking her somewhere only to leave her there.

But in real life, Dad never said goodbye.

He just got into Mikey's truck and turned the key—and Francie ran. She ran in the opposite direction.

"*Eee-oh-eet!*"

Sally couldn't do anything. Sally didn't know anything. Sally couldn't help!

If Dad was here, Dad could—

Francie turned a corner sharply and at speed in her mind. She started climbing again, up, up, up, pulling herself as quickly as she could from branch to branch, not patient, not methodical, her breath rushing like the wind. She didn't feel scared, she felt mad, and it helped, anger rushing through her arms and legs like fire. Her legs were so tired.

Now, Francie flew to an imaginary moment in time—maybe happening right now?—and she saw Mrs. G standing in the gym, her hair pulled high in a tight bun, stabbing her baton straight at Francie: *Francie, this is not acceptable, don't you dare miss our concert!*

Francie was saying, Someone else can sing instead. It might as well be someone else.

It might as well be you. Mrs. G turned and looked directly at Francie inside Francie's head—they locked eyes, and Francie closed hers tight. The gym smelled like wet sneakers and plastic mats, but as soon as she shut her eyes, all she could smell was pine gum, sharp and fresh.

FOURTEEN

Labyrinth

Marietta saw the labyrinth when she got off the elevator.

It was early Sunday morning, the lobby was almost empty, and the pattern on the floor stood out clearly, marked in cream-coloured tiles against the institutional grey, a series of loops that looked like the folds of a brain.

Labyrinth.

The word opened in her mind, like she'd been keeping it for a reason. She didn't know how to spell it immediately—*labrinth, labrynth?*

She'd noticed it because she was in it, she thought. She, Marietta, was walking a long, looping path away from herself, and where exactly was the exit?

The psych nurse she'd spoken to said Luce would be released to police custody, first thing tomorrow morning.

"What then?"

"They've probably got some paperwork for him at the station, and then he can go home."

What if I don't want him to come home? "Is it safe for him to come home?" she asked instead.

"Do you have concerns?" The woman looked up from her clipboard. Her hair was braided into a neat, glossy circle that crowned her head. They were speaking through a glass barrier.

"Not exactly," said Marietta, thinking of the gun. "Can I see him?" If only Marietta could see Luce, she would know—she would know! It was all going to be fine. She could see that he was himself, and she was herself, orbiting around him. She could see if that's what she wanted after all.

"I'm sorry, I can't let you in, you can come back during visiting hours."

"I can't," said Marietta. "This is my only chance, I was hoping to talk to someone."

"You're talking to someone now."

Marietta nodded. The armpits of her uniform reeked, her feet hurt, she'd spent the night sloshing through urine and hallucinations.

"A lot of families feel this way, they don't want their person to come home, they'll say, I'm not ready, he's not ready—you know?" The nurse moved over to a section of countertop where there was no glass and leaned across. "But everyone has to go home sometime. Life goes on."

"I know that," said Marietta. *Does it have to be so soon, is all?*

A labyrinth was different from a maze. A maze was a puzzle, a place where a person could get lost, passageways with blind entries and dead ends. But a labyrinth was a path. There was only one route, in or out. Once on the path, you followed it to its conclusion. Of course, you could cheat, like here on the hospital floor—you could start walking the loops, then step over the tiles and out. You could quit. But not Marietta. That was not how she wanted to see herself, as a quitter. Once in, she was in.

Deeper and deeper.

Marietta came across the lobby floor to where the labyrinth began, and she entered at its opening. Her tennis shoes squeaked on the polished floor. Freshly polished. A volunteer sitting on a stool near the revolving doors, a young woman wearing a pretty blue-and-white hijab, rested her eyes on Marietta. Not much going on at this hour. The women in hairnets behind the counter of the small Tim Hortons outlet were watching too. Marietta stepped carefully, deliberately, around and around the circular path. Slower and slower and slower. As if she were alone.

She felt alone. She was alone.

She couldn't see herself, couldn't be herself, it was the worst feeling of all.

As she neared the centre, she thought: I need out.

In the centre, Marietta came to a stop, her arms wrapped around her body as if she were cold, hands clasping elbows, every muscle tight and tensed, teeth gritted, she collapsed into a crouch, closed her eyes. What did it feel like to be invited in, to be offered something small and strange and long-lost—access to your own body? What happened when a tree was planted? Sometimes, it died, but sometimes, it grew. *Welcome!* In Marietta's memory, a plump, pink-cheeked woman wearing a white turban sat cross-legged on a blanket, her wrists encircled with strings of shiny wooden beads, painted turquoise and amber, clinking softly as she waved a greeting—to Marietta. It was Marietta she was welcoming. Marietta she was pulling into the room.

"Come in! Join us!" The woman had smiled at Marietta like she'd been expecting her.

Marietta had only ducked into the library because it was raining and she'd missed her connection; the next bus wouldn't come for nearly half an hour. This branch was aging poorly, squat to the ground, built of chunky concrete blocks showing rusted veins of metal, the ceilings low for a public space. "Come in!" It was a boxy room with a row of windows overlooking a patch of bare concrete, dark with wet just now. The walls were made of what looked like couch cushions, textured woolly fabric that absorbed sound, like she was walking into a lunatic asylum.

Here I come, then.

"I don't have a blanket," Marietta heard herself say, her voice spoiling the spell for the other women seated on the floor, they blinked and turned, a few of them, with gazes that seemed not to take her in. Several wore turbans too, though most were dressed in ordinary exercise gear: yoga pants and t-shirts. Marietta became aware of soft chanting in a language she didn't recognize, coming from a CD player plugged in beside the woman.

The turbans, the chanting, the blank eyes. Was this some sort of cult?

"Have mine." The woman at the front stood and brought her blanket to Marietta. And Marietta knew she'd have to stay now. The gesture was too much for her, it took her down, as pure as an arrow to the heart. Her nose tingled and the backs of her eyes filled up with tears. If she missed the next bus, she'd be extra late to pick up Sam. But she dropped these thoughts along with the bag she'd been carrying, which was mostly empty: a line of bus tickets, a neatly folded ten-dollar bill she could give to the babysitter as a thank you, an extra cloth bag for groceries, and a discarded plastic water bottle—not hers. She'd seen it on the bus floor, rolling back and forth, and she'd picked it up to dispose of later. Marietta hated litter.

It spoiled—everything.

It spoiled spring, it spoiled the morning shadows, it spoiled the green things pushing through the cracks, everything beautiful that deserved to be untouched.

Marietta sat on the blanket and thought about litter, about the people who tossed their trash thoughtlessly, as if they weren't responsible for what fell on the ground behind them. As if, once it fell from their hands, it didn't belong to them anymore, had never belonged to them. You could confront them, yell at them, point at the thing they'd just been holding and ask them why they'd done it, and they'd look at you like you were the nutcase, the lunatic, the psycho, waving your arms and blasting them for what was nothing, after all—just a paper cup, a cigarette butt, a pop can, a plastic bag of dog shit. *What's your problem, lady?*

"I invite you to take your hands to your knees, facing up or facing down, your choice. I invite you to close your eyes and go inward. Follow the sound of my voice. Trust the sound of my voice."

Definitely a cult.

Marietta kept her eyes open.

She focused on the woman in white, sitting in seeming serenity on the gritty library carpet while the others in the group followed her directions, how to breathe, where to put their hands, how to move. The woman met Marietta's eyes and the strange thing was that she offered no challenge to Marietta. She offered no fight, no apparent judgment. Marietta had to look away. She stared down at her hands, which lay loosely in her lap, facing up, one atop the other as if begging for something—a coin, a match—and tears spilled out and ran down her cheeks. She did not move to wipe them away.

Now Marietta closed her eyes—and what was she so afraid of, what was so hard for her to look at, behind her eyelids, here in the dark, here inside her own skull?

Her mind.

Her looping, splintering mind, racing off in a million directions, trying to hold it all together, keep it all together, all of them together, and so very, very tired.

Her tears dried up. She listened to the instructions, feeling cold all over and then hot, as she joined with the others and they rubbed their palms till the woman told them to stop. Now they stretched out their arms and rotated them backward, on an impossible angle. It was like an exercise class, Marietta thought, if the exercise targeted the tiniest muscles in the most unused parts of your body. She began to feel a quiver in the creases of her hips, a spasm and catch between her ribs, and her shoulder blades pinched together, forcing open her throat in a way that felt too exposed. She could not go there.

She let her arms lower and fall into her lap. She sat, feeling weak.

But she was not weak. She opened her eyes and the woman was watching over them. And some were sitting, like Marietta, like Marietta some had surrendered to their discomfort, while others continued the movement, their arms wide and high, thumbs out, fingers in.

"Whatever you're bringing today, let it out," said the woman.

Oh, you do not want me to do that, thought Marietta.

"Take breaks, and come back," the woman said.

The hands of the clock seemed to spin faster than Marietta knew, and an hour was nearly past when she opened her eyes again to check, from this final position lying flat on her back on the floor, in repose. She'd been asleep, she thought. She'd been dreaming. Twitching. Her brain sending out irrational images not worth chasing and catching.

"Stay here as long as you'd like. This is corpse pose."

Marietta sat straight up.

She was dizzy. The others looked so quiet, lying there like the dead, past sleep, past dream, past vulnerability. A thought came to Marietta then, clear and crisp, along with a memory: If you were dead, a corpse, nothing could hurt you. The only one who would be hurt would be the one who dared disturb or defile your rest. She thought of her father, what it felt like to see her father invulnerable at his end. Luce had not seen his father, at his end. Maybe that was what was missing from Luce. But she didn't know. She didn't know what was missing, only that something was. It was a hard thing to think.

Marietta stood.

The woman, overseeing them all from her cross-legged position, lifted her hands to her forehead, pressed together like she was praying. She was very solemn, like someone who took life too seriously—like me! Marietta thought—but then she smiled at Marietta, her face broke open, and Marietta saw her completely differently, this stranger, as if she were dancing after midnight at a club, as if she were the one in the centre of the circle drawing all eyes to her outlandishly free dance moves.

Marietta could see this woman spinning on her shoulders, leaping to her feet with a deep back bend. Beads flashing.

Like me?

"Here's your blanket." Marietta wished she hadn't spoken. The others stirred from their deaths.

"May your path be your path," the woman said. The words troubled Marietta even then. She couldn't stop thinking about them, the cruelty of them, the hardness, running them through her hands. Through the wall of windows, she could see the bus approaching down the street and she picked up her bag and ran out the side exit, setting off a fire alarm, shouting at the driver, who was going to blow right past the stop.

"Stop!"

Thanks, she said breathlessly, and the driver accepted the transfer even though it had expired. Behind them, people were leaving the building, not as quickly as they would if they'd smelled smoke or seen fire, but with confusion, irritation. Looking for the source of their disruption.

It's me! Marietta! I'm the one you're looking for.

The feeling was novel—she saw herself as invisible, on the edges, slipping like a shadow through the fingers of other people. Almost always, she had a feeling she could disappear without a ripple.

The air was cool, heavy when she got off and walked to the babysitter's front door. Sam was the last child there. His stroller folded and wet on the uncovered porch. "I'm so sorry." Marietta fished out the folded ten-dollar bill. "I went to a yoga class at the library," Marietta heard herself explaining. She was hearing an echo of someone she recognized but had not met for a very long time. The girl at the back of the class, declaring her wit. Smoking with the burnouts behind the gym. Running through the woods after him, lungs aching, trying to catch up. Making choices, doing things (brave, rash, selfish).

"Oh?" said the babysitter. She said, "You forgot to pack extra diapers, he's kinda wet."

It was really strange, actually, Marietta said, not like yoga at all. The teacher, or whatever she was, gave me her blanket, and we sat for so long my foot fell asleep, and at the end, at the end—I basically died, it felt like.

But she was telling this story not to the babysitter but to the top of Sam's head, pushing him to the nearest bus stop.

At the end—I wanted more.

"Miss? Are you okay?"

A hand lightly touched Marietta's shoulder, squeezed. Marietta opened her eyes. The volunteer in the hijab offered her hand to Marietta, helped her to standing.

"I have to walk out the way I walked in," Marietta said. She was stuck in the centre of the hospital's labyrinth, nothing but tiles on the floor, and she was terrified of being pulled through the wrong way, skipping any steps, not meeting her fate.

"Of course," the volunteer said. "Can I get you something? A glass of water?"

"Coffee? On the house?" one of the women at the Tim's counter offered, calling over.

Marietta's hand went from her lips to her heart. She was afraid—she was afraid of all the paths, even the one most familiar, the one she'd followed all this way, chasing after him, catching him, throwing her body against his, a warm wall against which she beat herself, willingly.

The volunteer held her elbow, as if Marietta might topple over.

Was she about to fall? Or fly? Or float away like dust?

Just then, Marietta saw herself in the centre, rippling with energy, tense with nerves, half-starved. But it didn't

suck to be her. *This is my body! This is what's holding me up!*
Just then, Marietta tried to step back through the labyrinth,
but just then, she wished it were a maze, a maze would make
more sense. She couldn't keep walking the same damn path.

Marietta said to the volunteer holding her arm, "It's
okay, thank you. I'm going to be fine."

The young woman let go of Marietta's arm, even if she
didn't believe her, and just then, without even thinking,
Marietta moved across the tiles and broke out.

"Coffee would be fucking amazing," Marietta said to the
woman behind the counter.

"We're making you a toasted raisin bagel with cream
cheese, too, hon."

What mattered?

Only that Irene had been invited back into the picture, invited to help her son. A long prayer answered, no
matter the unforeseen consequences. God, give me back
my son, give him back to me. And God answered: yes. It
was very important not to ask what payment God might
require in return.

Marietta's voice, strangely steady: "Can you come stay
here for a bit, Irene?"

Irene was just home from church, she would have driven
directly to the little house, as soon as she'd hung up the
phone. Her daughter-in-law hadn't apologized, but what
mattered? Irene expected neither grace nor gracefulness from
Marietta. "I'll come right away!"

"No! Please don't."

Oh! Well.

"You'll need me tomorrow morning, then? To pick Luce up at the police station? Is that what they said?"

"If you don't mind."

"I don't mind. But what time?"

"Like, I literally don't know, Irene. I have no fucking idea."

Oh dear. Okay.

"I'll call the police station and find out what to do."

"Thank you. Thanks, Irene. I really mean it. Thank you."

Oh.

"You're welcome, Marietta."

The police station told Irene to call the hospital. The hospital transferred her to a nurse, the nurse said she didn't know, a doctor would call back, and the long and short of it was that Irene could collect Luce at the hospital first thing tomorrow morning, and drive him to the station herself for the paperwork. "What paperwork, exactly?"

No one had an answer to that, it was like it was insignificant to them, a small administrative detail, a box to be ticked, not the end of the world, descent into shame, her son on the six o'clock news and ladies from church clogging the phone line with their unsolicited sympathy.

There he was, *there he is!* Coming out through the hospital's revolving doors, limping, of course, and a cast on his arm.

"What are you being charged with?" Oh dear, that was not how she'd meant to begin.

"I don't know, Mom. Where's Marietta?"

"She couldn't come, she had to work. But I'm here!"

Her son slid into the passenger seat of her sedan, and Irene couldn't help but feel that something was off, and not what she'd expected. He looked okay, which was strange, she thought he'd look worse. He had an air about him of distraction, troubling intentions bubbling under the surface. They didn't talk much on the drive to the police station; Irene asked about his arm—it was fractured, didn't need surgery, he said. "What about your head? Marietta said you have a concussion." And he just shrugged.

There was no right thing to say, Irene began to feel ever more strongly. Only a selection of wrong things, slightly wrong to altogether wrong, all bound to irritate and estrange him further.

Still, after she'd parked at the police station, she said: "Should I come in?"

"This won't take long," he said.

How on earth would he know? "But what's the plan, Luce? What will you do after this?"

"Go home."

Irene decided to accompany her son into the station. But she could see, as soon as she was inside the bland, air-conditioned foyer, that she didn't belong and wasn't prepared in the way that Luce was, he stood cool and detached while she dug through her purse, her mind racing and fluttering. She'd forgotten to tell him and suddenly had the urge to whisper that she'd burnt all those things in his bedroom—the evidence! She tugged on the sleeve of his shirt. But he didn't even acknowledge her. He was already miles ahead.

The charge was driving while under the influence of an illegal substance. Luce signed the paperwork (shouldn't he talk to a lawyer?) which stated that he promised to appear at his court date, some weeks from today, and the following conditions applied: no drug or alcohol use, no drug paraphernalia, no weapons, no driving (licence suspended), and he had to stay at his own residence, he could not move around.

"House arrest?" Irene wondered out loud.

"Not like that, ma'am. We just need to know where to find him." Now the officer behind the desk, a nice, round young woman who looked healthy as a horse, turned and addressed Luce: "You're advised to get counselling, get yourself into a treatment programme."

"Already taken care of," said Luce. Was he flirting with this young woman? His posture was amiable, persuasive.

"Okay, then, you are good to go."

"Thank you, ma'am."

He was flirting alright. What was wrong with this man, her son? Did he have to be so forward and bright, did he have to snooker everyone, make everyone fall for him? What was his problem, and was it her fault?

"What about Marietta?" she asked him in the car. But he didn't reply.

"You were flirting with that police officer back there! I saw it with my own eyes!"

He said, *Ha!* and rolled down the window. "You drive like an old lady, Ma."

"Because I am."

But she wasn't that old—she was fifty-nine, only twenty-six years older than him.

"I'm glad you're getting counselling," she said.

"Group therapy bullshit."

"Is that what they call it?"

Irene was surprised to get a real laugh out of him, some warmth. Maybe he was coming closer. He said, "I'm going to need you to drive me out to your house."

She said, "But I burned everything, Luce. In the burn barrel."

And she lost him again.

"You did what?"

"Luce, didn't they give you something at the hospital? For pain?"

"Where'd you say Marietta is today? I want to say hello."

But Irene didn't know. The Haven? The Grave? The Heavenly Home? The name of a place where nobody wanted to end up.

"Luce, you'll see her when she's done work. We can surprise her, pick her up! We'll go out for dinner, my treat. Anywhere special you'd like to go?"

"Let me out. I need some air. I'll walk the rest of the way."

"But your concussion, your arm!" And that older injury, from before—his leg, which she stopped herself from mentioning, just barely.

"Ma! Stop the car."

And she didn't know how to keep him, so she pulled over and let him go.

❦

Liane knew the guy as soon as he walked through the diner's front door, the little bell tinkling its welcoming chime. The bell was the reason she'd wanted to work here, that and the big front windows on which it would be her job to write the daily specials. Liane liked the cheeriness of the windows, a blank slate just for her, and she liked the bell's warning; she didn't think Seth would come looking for her, particularly, but just in case. You could hear the bell chime through the whole diner. Depending on where she was, she could hustle to the back and peek out from the kitchen before showing herself.

Liane was in the kitchen, talking to the cook. Slow day. She moved to the order counter and looked to see who'd come in.

A family, including a baby, that would mean a mess to clean up—and the man, he looked familiar, the way he was swinging his leg.

Shit.

Not this guy. This asshole. But she wasn't afraid of him. This guy had more reasons to avoid Seth than she did.

Of course, he had her gun. Or he'd had it, at one point, not so long ago. Right before she'd picked up and left Seth, after shit went down, it went down. She left while Seth was on the toilet. Never said goodbye, neither. The ladies behind the makeup counter at the mall got down to business when you turned up with a black eye, looking to cover it up: "It's an art, honey, and someone needs to know how to do it right. It's all about the blending." Liane knew all about the blending, and the art, it was the kindness she came for—kind hands, hands that knew, that understood. Purposeful, direct.

The eye was healed, now.

Liane'd kept the makeup and added a wig, a form of disguise she'd refined, even if it looked a bit slapped together, even if she wasn't completely committed to it. She figured if Seth wanted to find her, he'd find her. If he wanted to kill her, he'd kill her. But also, if he wanted to have her killed, he wouldn't send this guy.

Liane picked up an armful of menus, adjusted the wig, and sailed out. The guy with the bum leg had brought the whole fam-damily: little girl, baby, wife, older woman—maybe his mother. Nothing looked particularly wrong about them, but nothing looked particularly right. The guy had a fresh cast on one arm, for example. The grandmother's purse was unzipped, wide open, swinging from her wrist. The girl's ponytail was a mess, hair picked loose, hiding half her face.

Liane showed them to a booth near the front. A bit early for supper. "Can I get anyone a drink?"

But these people weren't ready to make decisions, Liane saw, so she carried out a pitcher of water and glasses for everyone. A plastic cup for the baby, which the wife appreciated. She was holding the baby on her lap. "Do you have a high chair we could use . . . Diane?" The wife squinted and read the name written in flowery script on the tag pinned to Liane's bright-yellow shirt, yellow for sunshine, Liane assumed, like the name of this place, Sunshine Grill. The uniform's shade clashed with the purples and reds of Liane's wig and nails, but the fit was alright for earning tips, tight and low across the chest. Truth was, Liane didn't much feel like dragging out that damn high chair from the back, a plastic monstrosity that weighed half a ton, but it was nice to be addressed by name, even if the name was not exactly your own.

"Let me tell you the specials, and I'll be back with the high chair."

Snarled with cobwebs, sticky from some other kid's lunch, flecks of mouse dirt in the grooves of the seat. Liane flicked at the chair with the cloth she used to wipe down the tables.

"Good luck with it," she said to the wife. The woman was wearing a uniform too, no name tag, just an iron-on patch that read *Komfort Kare*. Liane found herself looking a little too long at her, curious to know how much she knew about this man she'd shackled herself to. Dark circles under her eyes, no makeup, no adornments, but she kept herself skinny alright, and her hair was punk rock, Liane liked it. With a bit of mascara, some colour on her cheeks, a lipstick that popped—and Liane could take care of those nails—the woman would stop traffic.

The little girl was looking at her. *Uh-oh.* Liane recognized that look—*I know you.*

Liane hooded her eyes, she did not return the familiarity of the girl's gaze, she knew how to make a person uncertain, shut them down. *Do I know you from somewhere?*

Do you?

But she met the man's eyes, dead-on. Did he know who she was?

Where's my gun, you prick, I want it back.

She watched the family from the order window, leaning on the counter in the kitchen. Her eyes were sharp as an eagle's, she'd never needed glasses, and she could see them reflected in the long mirror hanging on the wall opposite the booths—the back of the wife's head, the baby in the filthy chair, and the man; the girl and the older lady were hidden by the wooden divider that separated the booths along the wall. Liane felt a bad feeling rising, same one she used to get almost every damn day, from the time she was just a little kid.

She'd never outrun it.

Might as well invite it closer, welcome it in.

She sipped from a glass of Coke, no ice, and looked at the man. His face was as small as a baby's fingernail, but she could see from the way he was moving, he was in need of something, and nothing was going to stop him from taking it.

"Platters up!"

Liane carried out the food, this was a dance she excelled at, plates piled up to her chin. It was a quiet table. Not a one of them said thank you. When she got back to the kitchen, Liane turned up the radio, all-day non-stop classic rock, whatever that meant—pasty-faced music for pasty-faced food. The cook was from Hong Kong, and at the end of their shifts he'd cook up a meal worth eating, fried rice spiced sweet and hot, with flecks of mushroom, or a soup with greens thickened with egg, or noodles with tiny, salty shrimp and eggplant. Nothing you'd find on the menu.

Here came trouble.

This guy, leaning his elbows on the counter, ducking his head to find her through the order window. "Problem with the food?" she asked him.

"Not a bit," he said. "Kudos to the chef."

The cook gave him a nod.

"Just looking for a little something extra."

"Oh?"

"Thought you might be able to help . . . Diane."

Liane debated. He didn't know her name, that was for sure. But he knew who she was, he'd sniffed her out, sensed weakness. She chose not to look at the cook, and the cook chose not to look at her.

Liane came out the swinging door, and this guy followed her to the end of the little hall, where they stored crap like that high chair. There was a door here, under an unlit Exit sign, blocked by a stack of boxes and a footstool, but it was operable, when she pushed the bar the door opened, and she squeezed past the boxes, down one big step into the alley, blinking in the bright sunshine. The actual sunshine.

"What do you want?" Liane said. She lit a cigarette. The guy was struggling to get around the boxes. His leg was giving him pain, and he was wearing that cast on his arm, and she didn't feel like helping him, not a bit. "Don't let it close or we'll be locked out," she said. Not that she cared— she wanted to know if he did.

He stepped carefully into the alley and held on to the door, propping it open with his shoulder. Oh, he cared. He didn't want his family to know what he was up to.

"Want one?" she offered.

"Not my drug of choice." He smiled. Well. Fuck him and his fucking green eyes. Smiling at her like she'd give him whatever he asked for. "I think you know what I want."

Liane shrugged, her mouth pulling itself against her will into a grin. She adjusted the wig without thinking, ash falling like fairy dust.

With some effort, he reached his left hand, the unbroken one, into his back pocket and showed her some cash. He checked his shoulder. "Help a man out, Diane?"

As it happened, Liane didn't need what Seth sold, that stuff didn't relieve the kind of pain she happened to feel, but she'd dumped a bottle of pills, loose, into the bottom of her purse on her way out the door. Insurance. "What's that all about?" Liane gestured with her chin at the cast.

"Lost a bet," he said.

I'll bet you did. I'll bet you've lost a few.

"I don't want your money," said Liane. As if she didn't know where that cash had come from. This guy. She moved to move past him, crushing the cigarette against the side of the building, mashing it into the bricks. She pushed herself against him, her chest against his stomach, her rear pressing the door open just wide enough to step up and inside, her heart racing as she struggled to catch her breath. One step up, and see how she could hardly breathe? It's those cigarettes, honey, can't you quit while you're ahead, her stepmother had begged and begged her.

But I never seem to be ahead, do I?

Liane went into the kitchen, she didn't look at the cook, she scraped her fingers around the bottom of her purse till she had a handful, and she took them to the man waiting for her like a hunger in the dim hallway. Their hands met.

"If I see you in here again"—Liane's breath came shallow—"I'll be the first to call the cops."

"Sure you will."

This fucker. He'd be back.

Liane felt nothing but tired. Maybe she'd have to find another job, a different wig.

But she wasn't leaving town. No one could scare her away from the place she came from, the closest thing to home. Who else would plant flowers in the spring by her stepmother's stone, who else would pick the weeds, who would visit? Even the dead deserve company. You don't give up on the one who never gave up on you.

He was holding out the cash.

"Give it back to your mother," said Liane. "I don't want it."

FIFTEEN

Gun Run

Francie heard a lady's voice in her head, the waitress from the diner. *You don't fix a man like that.*

But he's my dad!

Watch out for yourself, that's your number one job, but don't take my advice—who am I to tell anyone how to live her best life?

Francie could see she was almost at the tip of the top of the tree. The air was becoming brighter, even as the branches grew closer and closer together, smaller, thinner, weaker. Their needles felt soft, brushing Francie's face and arms and neck, and she wanted to close her eyes, to feel the softness and to shut out whatever was happening in the field down below.

She saw a hawk floating lazy circles in the sky.

She saw the highway.

She saw a line of cars that looked like toys, with lights flashing white and red and blue. She saw what looked like action figures moving through the field.

Dollhouse people, and other toys that barked like dogs. Coming closer, getting bigger. She couldn't pinch them between her fingers and make them do what she wanted.

Soon Francie would be out of options. She wasn't going to get any higher. She wasn't a bird, she'd never wanted to pretend to be one, she wasn't going to fly.

Holding the tree's trunk with one hand, Francie shifted her backpack around to her front and unzipped it. The first thing she felt was the rainbow pony lunch box, and she pulled it out. It was like an old friend. She dumped out Grandma's cookies and the sandwich crusts, for the birds, if they wanted them.

But she put Grandma's money into the pocket of her jeans. Just in case. "Money is money, you don't ask it any questions," Dad said.

The only thing left was the gun.

Get rid of it.

Okay, Dad, I'll try.

They had all waved when they saw Mom come out through the front doors of the Lodge. Mom slid in beside Francie, in the back seat, wearing her uniform and dirty tennis shoes. "What's going on here?"

"Surprise!" said Grandma.

"We're going out to eat!" said Francie. She was holding Sam on her lap. Grandma Irene was driving—of course she was, it was her car—and Dad was sitting in the passenger seat beside her. This looked wrong; everything was wrong, but it should have been right, because Dad was home from the hospital! He'd been sitting on the couch when Francie came in the side door, after school. She'd walked by Grandma's car in the driveway, and sure enough, there was

Grandma, bouncing Sam around the living room. Francie
saw her juice-box bag beside the couch.

"Does Mom know you're here?" Francie had said, but
she couldn't stop looking past Grandma at Dad, one arm
locked in a heavy-looking cast, resting in his lap. Slowly
his head came up, and he saw her too. His eyes focused on
Francie so slowly, it was like he wasn't exactly there; or
Francie wasn't.

"Of course your Mom knows!" said Grandma. "I'm
staying for a little while."

"They're going to be watching me." Dad's mouth moved
the words slowly, like he was feeling his teeth with his
tongue. "Don't you start watching me too," said Dad, and
he winked at Francie.

Grandma herded Francie back toward the kitchen, away
from Dad. "Did you get those tickets, honey? For your
concert?"

Francie nodded. Her hands gripped the backpack straps.

Grandma said, "No after-school snack! It's a special day.
I'm taking us out for dinner! We're going to pick your mom
up from work and surprise her, so change out of that ratty
t-shirt and put on something nice," said Grandma Irene,
"and let me brush your hair."

"You better not be talking to me, Ma!" Dad had joked
from where he'd stayed resting on the couch.

And everything was still all wrong.

Mom frowned as she took Sam from Francie. "This isn't
safe, Irene! We don't have a car seat!"

Sam slapped at Mom's chest. He was dressed in a fresh
outfit, Grandma had changed his diaper just before they'd
left, and Francie had slicked his hair. Her own hair was
pulled into a ponytail—Grandma had given up on combing

it out—but stray strands were caught in the elastic, pinching Francie's scalp. It hurt. She picked away at it.

"Well, I do agree, but I'm a careful driver, and it's a special day, Marietta," said Grandma Irene, looking in the rear-view mirror.

"Is it?" muttered Mom. She stared out the window. Her hair was also in a ponytail, a very short one that poked out stiffly from the back of her head. Her neck looked thin and exposed. Francie felt a bit strange looking at it. They'd never sat together in Grandma's car like this. Mom squeezed Sam tightly.

Sam's car seat had been in the trunk of Dad's car when Dad crashed it into the ditch and broke his arm, and now there was no car seat because there was no car.

"Turn here, Ma, turn left," Dad said.

"A boy in my class broke his arm," said Francie. "On a trampoline."

Dad said: "Bones heal fast." He looked at Francie, then looked ahead again. "You missed the turn, Ma. Take the next right and circle back around."

"Oh, for heaven's sake!"

Grandma parked behind the main strip, in a lot Dad said was free for two hours. Francie walked behind Dad so he couldn't see her watching him. He moved stiffly, carefully, like he might slide out of his body. The breeze that blew between the tall buildings seemed to blow through him. He looked like he was made of broken bits, stuck together with glue.

Was it only Francie who could see he wasn't the same as before? She needed to keep him in her sight. She needed to be careful with him.

The air inside the restaurant was thick, dim. Grandma admired the painted tin ceiling. They sat in a booth near the front, near the windows, Francie between Grandma and Dad on a puffy purple-red bench, Mom across from Grandma, with Sam strapped into a plastic high chair that the waitress brought. Her nails were long and pointy, a bright blood-red strawberry colour.

Oh!

Francie knew those nails. But the hair was different, like a purple nest perched on top of her head. The waitress's eyes flicked around the room, seeing everything. She held on to the back of Mom's chair and recited the specials. Grandma Irene said, "Liver and onions!"

"You can't go wrong," said the waitress. She was wearing a name tag, but it was a different name. Diane.

"I need a moment, Diane," said Mom, like they were friends.

"You need a moment, you take a moment."

"Irene, this looks expensive." Mom leaned across the table as if the waitress wasn't standing right there.

"No one leaves hungry, honey," the lady said, but Mom didn't acknowledge her. Not friends anymore.

"Get exactly what you want," said Grandma. "This is my treat!"

Francie wanted the fried chicken platter.

"Let her have it, Mari," said Dad. "I'll have the same. Two fried chicken platters."

"And a strawberry milkshake," Francie said quickly, before anyone could stop her. The waitress reached into her apron pocket and set down a handful of crayons that rolled across the table. The placemats were made of plain white paper. Francie started drawing a horse, but she wasn't very good at drawing, especially horses. Something always went wrong with the legs.

Grandma Irene was talking about the weather. Sam sucked on a crayon.

Dad's bad leg trembled, shaking up and down next to Francie's. Mom was biting her lips, pinching them into her mouth. She looked angry, maybe, but then she picked up a crayon and started drawing something too. Francie watched as the lines turned into a horse, its legs lifted and folded in the air beneath its belly.

"I didn't know you liked to draw, Marietta," said Grandma. Mom set down her crayon.

Mom's horse was galloping.

Francie scribbled out her horse's legs and tried again.

The smell of cigarette smoke floated in the air, and Grandma did not like that one bit. But soon the table was covered with platters and plates and side dishes, glasses and cups. Now no one needed to say anything at all. Francie ate steadily, bravely, she stuffed herself so full that her stomach puffed out under her hands. A small groan bubbled up.

The table was covered in platters and bones.

Dad crumpled his paper napkin and stood.

"Where are you going?" Grandma said.

Francie watched Dad in the mirror on the wall opposite. He was going to the washroom, she decided. Should she follow him, to make sure? She could see another customer sitting in a booth, reflected in the mirror. If you saw someone, they could see you too—that's the way mirrors worked.

"Is everything okay?" Grandma Irene half stood as Francie slid out of the booth. "Don't you want dessert?"

Everything was not okay. Francie hurried to the back, past the kitchen, along a short, narrow hallway where, behind a pile of cardboard boxes, a door was cracked open— and she saw him, or part of him, her dad, standing in the sunshine, outside, behind the restaurant. He was laughing, and a woman's voice (Francie couldn't see her) laughed in return (maybe the waitress?). Francie stopped, very still.

What if Dad saw Francie, found her following him, watching him?

A box teetered and fell with a thump, and Francie darted into the ladies' room, as Grandma would call it. The door creaked on its hinges and slammed shut behind her. What if Dad heard? Inside, two tiny stalls were separated by a wooden divider painted green. The walls were yellowish, and the lighting looked furry, a dusty bulb screwed into the wall over the sink.

Francie hid inside a stall, waiting till it seemed safe to come out.

At the sink, the hot water tap was broken. Francie took her time, washing her hands with a bar of soap that was melted onto the sink, till her fingers were cold.

At last, she pulled the door open; it slammed behind her, sprung shut.

"Did you eat too much?" asked the waitress.

Francie jumped—she swivelled her head all around to look. The door that had been open before, sun shining in, was closed, and the hall was dark. Francie could just see the waitress sitting on a box against the wall, she could hear her breathing, raspy and thick.

"Who you looking for?" asked the waitress.

Francie shrugged. "No one."

"That so? Well, your daddy's gone back to sit down."

"I know who you are," Francie told her.

"Oh, you do, do you?" Francie saw, slowly, that the waitress wasn't wearing her hair, she was holding it in her lap like a baby, cradled on her knees. "And who do you think I am?"

"You know my dad," said Francie.

"Hush, honey, your dad don't want anyone to know that." But she leaned forward and sang these words: *wade in the water*. Just the one line. Francie shivered.

The waitress stood.

"My concert is on Thursday," said Francie all in a rush, "but you have to have a ticket."

"That so? You selling tickets?"

Francie nodded.

"Well, I'll sell you something for free. You don't fix a man like him. You watch out for yourself. Look out for yourself. Look out for your mama too, you only get the one." The waitress placed the baby of hair back onto her head, and gave Francie a little push. "Go on."

"Your name's not Diane," said Francie.

"Oh yeah? You remember my name?"

Francie shook her head. She did remember, but she didn't want to say it out loud.

"Doesn't matter," said the waitress. "My name's not that other name neither. Some people never get a real name, did you know that? Did you know how lucky you are? Now get back before Mama worries herself to death."

At the booth, Dad sat sunken into the bench seat, resting his head. Sure enough, Grandma and Mom were watching him. It was warm, almost hot, sunshine slanting through the big front windows. Grandma said, "I dropped my purse, Francie, can you pick it up?" Francie crawled under the table and peeled the purse off the sticky floor, but the zipper was open, and everything had spilled everywhere.

Here came the waitress, bringing the bill clipped onto a small black tray with mints, crinkle-covered in individual packages. Grandma was digging in her purse. "Can you check

under the table again, Francie, make sure you got everything?"
But Francie only found a crumpled tissue, maybe not even
from Grandma's purse. Grandma looked around the room
slowly, her eyes finally landing on Dad's empty face, then she
said loudly that she would pay by credit instead of cash. Her
hands were shaking.

Dad woke up from wherever he'd been, he slammed the
table with his hands, too hard. Everything jumped. Everyone.
"Time to go!"

The little bell on top of the front door tinkled. Dad was
gone. Again.

"Sorry for the mess, so sorry, Diane, I really am, I know
what it's like . . ." Mom was wrestling with the tray, unbuck-
ling Sam, wiping his screeching face with a used paper
napkin.

Francie saw the waitress adjust her hair in the mirror,
while Grandma stood to get her attention. "Now, where do
I pay?"

And Francie ran out after Dad.

Tinkle went the fairy bell over the door. The air was
cooler outside.

"Dad!" Francie called, running after him, but that
didn't work, so she hollered his name: "LUCE!" And he
turned, off balance, surprised to see her. He hadn't gotten
very far at all, and he swayed a little, then dug in his pants
pocket with his good hand and showed her a bunch of
crinkly wrapped mints, more than the waitress had delivered
on the bill, and tiny jams and peanut butters and coffee
creamers encased in plastic. He winked.

The bell tinkled again, and Grandma came outside. She
held the door open for Mom, Mom was pushing Sam in
the stroller, Sam in full meltdown, but that didn't seem like

the worst thing ever—people looking would think Sam was the problem, they wouldn't guess at the real trouble. The real trouble kept walking, shuffling along, swinging his leg. Too real to be pretend. To be changed by pretending.

Francie rested in the treetop for a moment, holding the gun.

The thing about climbing as high up as possible was that there really was nothing more she could do. It was a disappointment. It was a relief. Whatever choices she'd made, this was where she was. There was only one thing left to do.

Get rid of it.

Right, Dad?

SIXTEEN

Seeds

Luce was not flat, he was not two-dimensional, but tell that to the women in the room. He could see it in the way they watched him, kept him close even while holding themselves separate, at a safe distance. His mother, studying him like a problem to be solved. Why'd she have to be here anyway, in his house, sleeping on his couch, fussing around? She wanted to reduce him, boil him down to some essence she imagined he was made of, make him make sense.

A failing proposition, Ma.

Did the women think it was easy being the wreck around which everyone else's pain was arranged? Did they think it was pleasurable, in any way desirable to be the prob-lem—everyone's problem—the source of hard times, and the picture of it too, the asshole in the room?

Luce kept reliving the lovely and terrible sequence of events that had led up to this moment of unholy stasis and inertia, this crap-load of waiting that was only getting worse by the minute, this tiresome contest of wills, if that's what this was—a contest Luce wasn't about to lose. He could bide his time, wait for the sign. Wait for the proof. Did they think he wasn't watching them in return—his mother's blinkered optimism, Mari's chill?

Mari didn't want to meet his eyes, could barely look at him, lest he guess what he already fucking knew: she wanted something different. Someone different. *Not me.*

But Mikey? Mikey, for fuck's sake, Mari?

A muscle beside his left eye twitched and clenched.

Remember, remember the way the Caddy drove like a dream to its own destruction? A car had a kind of intelligence, a way of knowing, especially that one. It tried to warn him in the hours before not to hope so freely, not to play the patsy, the fool, but Luce wasn't listening. He was watching himself like he was watching the movie version. And there was Mikey, waiting for him, on cue.

Waiting outside his monument to himself. Fuck him.

What a perfect waste, the most ostentatious of monstrosities, Mikey's specialty, a shitstorm of half-constructed columns, turrets, wings, vast plains of future asphalt. Luce parked for a quick getaway, out of habit—or was that the Caddy's doing? Luce sat behind the wheel for a minute, counting out the future, pretending he could count on a friend. He fumbled for a patch of grid and chewed it open, spat the packaging out the window, let the gel dissolve on his tongue.

Climbed out of the Caddy.

Never mind the next part, skip it. Except for the feeling of his own hand, pumped into a fist, meeting Mikey's left eye, the crunch and swell of it. The heat in his own knuckles, not quite pain. From behind the frame of a fifteen-car garage, or whatever it was, a man running, shouting, white hard hat, stranger, Mikey's new brother, his new best bud. Mikey wouldn't call the cops, but this guy would, and now Luce was swinging back into the Caddy, his one true friend, and smooth as promises they were gliding off the premises, and Luce dipped into the glove compartment for something, anything, leaving it swinging open.

Windows down. Wind rushing in.

Luce let the car drive itself. Powerful engine, all-knowing, it knew what Luce wanted, it ripped up the gravel and fish-tailed onto Highway 9. There was time, but it wasn't enough. A few turns in, they were on a sideroad, headed for that little bridge, a slow-moving tractor pulling a load of dripping fertilizer and a minivan speeding from the opposite direction, and he had no intent—he just wanted to see where this part of the story would lead. Didn't everyone feel like that sometimes? It just so happened that he, Luce, had the balls to follow through, no looking back, no hesitation, no fear.

What a headache he had, it was really sticking around.

Remember, remember the way his own foot pumped the gas, he pinned it, the Caddy hit the gravel shoulder like an oil slick. He saw their faces, heard the wail of horns, sliding away, dim and far off, and saw the bridgework sink the Caddy's door, the ravine, the little gully, the creek, and they were rolling, spinning, flipping over and over.

Was it strange how much he enjoyed this part?

Luce closed his eyes and it kept happening, the tape was stuck here, rolling on repeat, he could see himself flung out of the car, and wide. *You're lucky you weren't crushed.* Lucky? Luck had nothing to do with it. Fate was a shell game, and he'd picked the right shell.

The flaw in the plan was to hang his luck on anyone else; if you have to ask for something, you might as well kiss it goodbye. That's not how you get what you want, what you need, what's yours by rights. You take it. Take it, man, take it, take it, take it and run with it, and everyone will think it was yours all along.

Don't go around begging for shit.

The Caddy knew the cure. It dropped Luce right to the bottom and left him there, to climb back out. The best place to start: with nothing. Blank slate. Wipe it clean. Burn the place down.

The women were hovering like he was next to useless. They expected the worst, as they should. He was a bomb they'd installed in the front room of this house, with their own hands, and they were scurrying around waiting for a switch to be flipped—as if they didn't know, they didn't guess, who was going to flip it.

Mari—that's you.

Don't flip it, Mari. Look at me.

He said to her, "I know where it is, but it might as well be gone, so you can stop watching me all the time, you can stop already." His hands twitched in his lap, his eyes watered, salt water, leaking like a pipe was broken somewhere inside.

Not real tears.

"Hey," Luce said, "look at this"—he pointed at his face—"the doc said this would happen on the new meds. Funny, huh."

Mari looked away. She wasn't even trying to find a way to lift him back up to where he was when she loved him, when she loved him like a sickness. Her sickness was going away. She was getting better, and where did that leave him?

It was you who wanted me, Mari, you pulled me into this mess, I didn't know any better.

His mother came at him with a tissue.

He snapped his hand around her wrist. Stop.

She stopped.

The women were afraid, he could see it on their faces. They should really know better than to show it.

Look at him, look at Luce, his mask worn right into his skin, curving into a smile as he saw his kid, Francie, come into the room. She wasn't afraid of him. What a kid. Take her anywhere.

Breathe, dammit, breathe, man. It was cold under here. A kind of void. An abandoned well: the cover's rotten, someone's going to fall in.

His hands shook as he placed them carefully onto his knees. He was wearing a pair of jeans. The fingers poking out from the cast moved like they didn't belong to him. The kid was watching.

"A boy in my class got a concussion," she said. "Playing soccer."

"What's a little headache?" Luce told her. "They call everything a concussion these days."

Kid had her hands behind her back. "What you got back there?" Luce said. "What're you hiding?"

"Luce, leave her alone!"

"Marietta, it's probably better if—"

"Leave her alone?" Luce pushed himself to standing. The kid was holding out her hands to show him. Nothing. Hair over her eyes. Nothing at all.

The problem with the new meds was that they let you feel things, the wrong things, they left you sliced and hanging wide open with the wind rushing through your ribs, feeling colours and light in all the wrong hues. A nasty green that ate at your guts. A ribbon of red slashing behind your eyes. Piss-yellow claustrophobia, *get me the fuck out of here.*

Mari said she had to get ready for her shift.

"I'll be fine here, we'll be fine," said Irene. She put her hands on Francie's shoulders, but Francie ducked them. Good kid. Behind them, the front door. Luce noticed the rotten hinge, splinters where it attached to the frame. He got close up, inspected the hinge, ran his thumb along the rough, broken wood. He yanked on the handle and it opened, scraping the floor. Hardly seemed broken at all.

"Where are you going?" his mother fluttered.

Luce looked down, checked the gap. He steadied himself on the railing. It was down there, but he couldn't see it! He needed to know it would be there when he needed it.

He was going to need it. It was all coming at him.

Pain was not what they thought it was. It would eat him like an animal eating its own heart. Nothing mattered but shutting it up, stomping it, crushing it, whatever it took. He was here at the bottom, fighting himself. What would it take to climb out?

He limped down the steps, holding tight to the railing. It wobbled. He moved into the yard like a bear. Suckers growing on the little trees. "I told you they're not dead!" He felt excited—yes, he could feel that too, but at the wrong level, ill-calibrated, like an engine running hot, burning oil.

People, waiting for the bus, people, standing at the bottom of the hill, people, looking at Luce.

"What the fuck do you want?"

"Come back inside, Luce," his mother was calling.

"I told you that door wasn't broken," Luce told her. "Where's Mari? I told her the trees weren't dead!"

"Get out of the garden, Luce, come inside."

"I'm going for a walk," Luce said, forgetting he wasn't wearing shoes. Feeling the grass under his feet. Remembering.

The grass felt good, it felt like good news, someone shouting out good news. His mother came down and took his arm. "Hey, little Mom," he said fondly. What was this awful feeling clutching at his heart? A smear of purple, a loss felt in reverse?

His mother wasn't small.

But Luce was much taller.

But she was much bigger. She held him by the arm.

He dug into his pocket and pulled out a crinkly-covered mint. Was it heavy enough to make a sound when it fell? At the doorstep, just before, Luce dropped it down the gap, and listened—did it make a noise? He looked up and the kid was watching. Mari wasn't, she wasn't even in the room—if only. What he wanted, what he needed, was Mari's eyes on him, just hers. She could save him, she could pull him out, haul him back to the top, she could stop this. She could see him how she'd seen him, and he would be who he was.

But she wouldn't. He knew it.

Luce stepped over the threshold. The door didn't close. He pushed on it, pushed on it. No one was saying anything. Fuck them. No one was pointing out how broken the door was. How fucked the door was. Love spilled from his spine pure as silver, but not for any of them—for this door. This stupid broken door. This door was the worst. It would never be fixed.

And everyone watching. Like they'd known all along, and here he was, just figuring it out.

Sam was eating dirt.

The dirt was tender, damp, it squeezed and squished between his fingers. He rubbed his fist inside his mouth.

Grit stuck to his gums. They ached, swollen and hot with very sharp teeth trying to cut through. He already had four at the front of his mouth, and two further back.

Sam rubbed and rubbed. The dirt separated into bits, a mush of grit, dry on his tongue. He couldn't swallow it. He howled, dirt mixed with saliva oozing down his chin. Dirt up his nose, in his hair, in his ears.

His big sister Francie didn't even look. Sam was sitting on the squashing mess of his diaper, and Francie was on her hands and knees like a baby. Her elbow disappeared into the gap behind the stoop. The sun was behind the house, it was almost suppertime, they were in the shadows. Ants ran out from under the stoop, and up over Francie's shirt, arms, neck, but she didn't move.

Sam rocked and grunted as ants climbed his bare feet. His soft grey pants were rolled at the bottom and wet in the creases where the diaper was split and leaking.

Francie turned to look at him. *Shhhh*, she said. She was very serious. He hiccuped. His fist carried another handful of dirt to his mouth, he couldn't stop himself. His tongue worked on it, his teeth crunched down.

His sister had found something. She pulled it out and sat back onto her heels. She dropped it in the dirt, between them. But she was pulled to it, as was Sam, he tipped forward and rocked onto hands and knees.

Sam did not recognize the thing.

He watched Francie touch the thing, pinch it between thumb and finger. She threw it back where she'd found it, back where the ants had found it first.

Gone.

His sister was ripping open the packet Grandma had given her, from inside Grandma's big purse. Tiny dots rained down from the packet into the dirt as Francie swung her arm, shaking and shaking it. Seeds. Seeds stuck to her skin, to his pants, seeds in his hair. Sam forgot what she'd found, what she'd hidden, what scared her, the solid shape of it. He forgot she was scared.

He clapped his hands. "Move." She pushed him into the grass, away from her seeds. Mom came around the corner, and Sam began to cry. He lifted his arms.

"Look at your face!" Mom said. She said to Francie, "You were supposed to be watching him."

Wrong way round. Sam had been watching her. He knew more about Francie than Francie knew about him, like always.

"Grandma's going to be so upset," said Mom. "You are a mess, Sam, you are a mess!" Mom said, "I can't get my uniform dirty, I have to leave for work."

Sam held out his arms, and Grandma came clucking to pick him up. Sam rubbed his nose hard on Grandma's shoulder. She patted his back, *thump thump thump*, but he didn't feel settled, under her hand. He shuddered and rumbled.

Here came the bus. Sam lifted his head. Mom ran to meet it, she turned and waved.

"Say bye-bye, Sam. Say bye-bye to Mommy," Grandma said.

"BABA MAA-MAA!"

"Oh, he said it! He said it! Did you hear him, Marietta? He said bye-bye!" Grandma grabbed Sam's arm and flapped it, and Sam's hand flopped at the wrist like it didn't belong to him. The bus was moving. Sam could see Mom through the big windows, walking as if she was walking toward him, even while the bus was taking her away.

"You need to water your seeds," Grandma said. Francie came back with a big pot of water. Grandma said, "Don't just dump it, you'll wash all the seeds away. Sprinkle it like rain."

Sam wanted Francie to sprinkle water on him. He slashed his arms and legs, but Grandma wouldn't put him down.

"Bath time for Sam, say bye-bye to Francie."

Sam would not. Francie wasn't even looking at him. Grandma started walking up the driveway, and Sam yelled over Grandma's shoulder to his big sister—*look at me, look at me!*—and then she did, she looked right at Sam and lifted the big pot and dumped the water that was left over her head, soaking her hair and face and clothes, staring at Sam in surprise, gasping.

Sam banged his head forward and smacked his chin down on Grandma's shoulder. Hard. Yes. That was his big sister. *Mine.*

The bus clicked along its early morning route, almost empty, rattling. The sky was already light, flushing pink and beige, streaked with cloud, but Marietta's eyes kept closing, snapping open, closing. At this time of day, she was in an altered state, burning eyes, burning brain. She'd survived the longest hours of her shift: the middle of the night, or three o'clock in the morning, when even the restless sleep.

The book from the library said that a labyrinth could be laid down anywhere there was a clear bit of space, like a yard or a parking lot. Marietta had cracked the book open to copy the pattern she liked while sitting at the nurses' station, taking her break. The pattern began with two intersecting lines that made a lower-case T, to which were added eight dots, and then lines to connect the dots, which became expanding arcs. It looked like a brain.

Lopsided.

The book from the library said a labyrinth could be made from any available material (stones, rope, wood chips). Cigarette butts, thought Marietta. Beer bottle caps. There were plenty on the sidewalk in front of their house.

This is not a joke, she thought.

But then, what was it?

The bus window was surprisingly clean, and in the soft light the ugliness of the city's outlines snapped into focus. Marietta curled in the corner of the seat, leaned her head onto her hand, elbow supported by knee, and she gave in, drifting into a doze. When she woke up, this was her stop, coming up. Her body knew. She snapped upright, pulled the cord.

Early morning humidity coated her like breath as she stepped onto the sidewalk in front of their house. The two dead trees greeted her, two dead sentinels warning her: do not enter. Her phone was ringing, and she stood at the bottom of the driveway to answer it.

"Hey, it's me. Mikey. Will you talk to me? I'm sorry."

"I'm just getting off the bus," she said.

"But it's so early."

"Overnight shift, Mikey. I'm just home now."

"You shouldn't have to take the bus, next time call me, I'll give you a ride. Any time."

"Right," she said, "sure, whatever you say."

"I'm not afraid of Luce," he said. "That's what I'm calling to say."

"What if I told you he was listening in right now?"

Gobsmacked, petrified silence. Poor guy didn't know what to say next, and she didn't feel like helping him out.

"See?" she said. "Listen, Irene's come to stay, the kids are fine, we're fine."

"You shouldn't have to take the bus," he insisted.

"You're a good guy, Mikey."

"You deserve better, that's all."

"Maybe another time," she said vaguely, the side door was opening, Luce was coming out. "Don't call me again, I'll call you."

Her tennis shoes carried her up the driveway, toward Luce. "Who was that?" he asked.

She put Irene's car between them. "Nobody."

"Oh yeah?" The new meds made him too awake, too alert, she didn't like it.

"Wrong number," she said.

"I bet."

"Luce." She tried to look him dead in the eye, but when their eyes met, the force of his gaze repelled hers. She walked by him into the house, and she didn't take her shoes off, she just climbed the steps into the kitchen and stood there, feeling dazed, doomed, desolate.

The house was otherwise quiet.

Irene had left a bag of whole wheat flour out on the counter, its paper top rolled down. Flour, Marietta thought. Easy as pie.

She took the bag of flour outside, to the backyard, passing by Luce, who was waiting for her—or for somebody—resting his weight on the hood of his mother's car.

She searched for the pattern in her mind, dipped one hand into the flour, and began with a T, the shape of a cross. She squatted close to the grass, where the picnic table had left its shadow in yellow, and the flour ran through her fingers in a thin line. She measured out room for her feet, then created dots, followed by elbows within the arms of the cross—lines at right angles, more dots at each empty corner: an opening.

Like this.

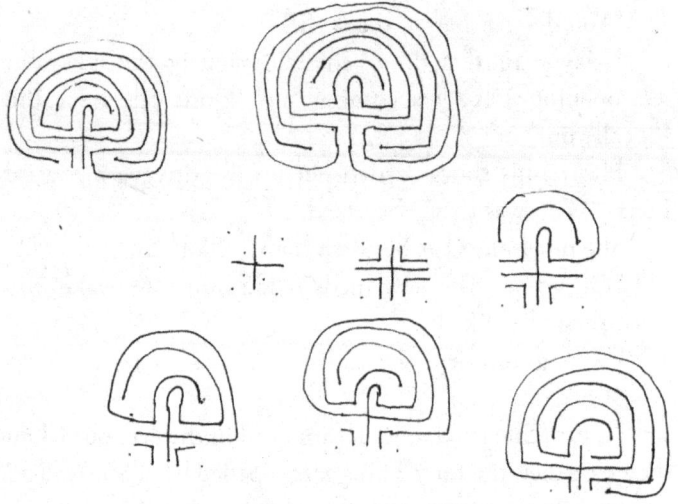

Marietta was aware that Luce had followed her, was standing behind her, leaning against the side of the house, propping up his arm in the cast with his other arm, watching as she connected lines and dots with curves that became progressively wider and wider.

Ask me, ask me what I'm doing, ask me what I'm making, ask me why.

She was scaring him, she thought. He wanted to spoil what she was making, drag his feet through it, wreck it. He didn't want the details, didn't want to know what she was lugging around on the inside, he'd never remember her favourite fast-food order from high school because he never knew it in the first place.

The lines were fixed and they were temporary.

She hoped he was watching as she stepped onto the path at its entrance. She hadn't made it wide enough, she had to balance with her arms out, room for only one foot before the other, around and around. Her next shift started at ten. Her uniform, stained under the armpits and smelling of worn-out fibres, moulded to her body like a second skin. Protective layer. Her disguise. Caregiver.

The surprise, as she neared the centre, was that the path didn't take her there directly. Instead, it led her away, to the furthest ring, the longest circle of them all. Was he watching? After this, she was pulled in, drawn in, to the very heart, where she'd wanted to be all along.

The centre.

A place to stop. A place to start.

She bent down and put her hand into the bleached grass in the middle of the circles. If you could leave something here, anything at all—

She looked up, and Luce was gone.

Someone was in the bathroom when Marietta brought the bag of flour inside. She removed her shoes and socks, the linoleum gritty under her feet. Oh well.

Click. The bathroom door opened.

Francie.

Marietta reached for Francie to pull her into a hug, her daughter's body stiffening against Marietta's touch. The child was turning feral, a kitten raising itself in the weeds outside the barn, and what was Marietta to do, to coax her closer? "Hey, let me show you something," she said.

They went outside, barefoot. The lines of flour were already beginning to fade, sinking into the grass and blowing away. Marietta felt unexpected relief to see it going of its own accord: Luce couldn't wreck something that had *self-destruct* written into its form. Maybe the thought should have given her pause? It did not.

Marietta held Francie's hand and pulled her into the labyrinth's entrance. It was okay that their feet made marks, smeared the lines, landed imperfectly, as they walked around and around. "It's called a labyrinth."

Francie followed her mother willingly enough, but though Marietta tried, she couldn't put herself into the child's mind, inside the wiry body, holding its secrets, tough as a weed. "When we get to the middle, we can leave something behind, okay? Maybe something we don't feel like carrying, something we don't want anymore, something that's too heavy."

Shut up, Marietta, shut up, it's too much, you're talking too much.

Francie didn't seem to have anything.

Marietta tried showing her. *Here, like this.* She bent down and mimed putting something into the grass.

The long shirt Francie had slept in brushed her knees as she crouched and touched the place where Marietta's hand had been. Silently, she picked the thing up, the thing that Marietta had laid down. Marietta felt panic roil her guts. *Oh no, this is not what I meant, don't do it.* Marietta yanked on her daughter's arm, pulling her up. But it was too late.

Francie held on to whatever it was, looking up at Marietta. "Mom?" she said. "Tonight is my concert. Remember?"

Oh shit. The concert.

"If I can get home in time from my shift, I'll be there, I promise," Marietta said, thinking, *well, maybe Mikey could help with this, maybe he could give me a ride.*

Francie was holding whatever that was, trying to follow the path back out again, but the lines seemed to dissolve around her.

There was no path. The path was gone.

SEVENTEEN

Gun Run Rewind

You run the film in reverse.

In silence.

You begin at the tip of the top.

Rewind: You hurry backward down the tree, barefoot, in wet jeans, you leap from your face to your feet over a fence, putting on your socks, which fly into your hands in neat balls.

Now, you run backward through trees to a stream and again into the trees, and you stop for a moment to take off the socks and slide your feet into a pair of shoes you've found here, but they are soaked, the laces knotted, and they don't exactly fit.

You move awkwardly, stumbling in the shoes, half-on, half-off, checking your shoulder every few steps.

You rush from the shadow of the trees into bright sunlight, stepping from shoes, holding them and plunging on your belly, feet first, down a slippery bank into rushing water, the gun raised over your head, and then you hop to standing, water over your ankles, and you're yanked backward at speed onto the bank, you're completely dry—startled, you look around—and put on socks, shoes.

You skid backward up the hill till you reach a small clearing.

Your running becomes erratic now, and a bullet is sucked back into the gun you are holding and BANG and the gun hits a branch which hits your face, and you are running, backward, then stopped completely, shoulders rising and falling to draw breath. Crouched low, then pulled up and out into sunlight and across a street as a police car seems to reverse away from you. You hover at the street's edge, glancing behind you as if you know you'll be pulled backward at any moment, sucked into the slipstream of time reversing—and you are, down this picturesque alley shimmering with sunshine that streams in beautiful patterns through thick green leaves.

A barking dog leaps into a house, tail first.

You stop before a stone fence, one hand to your mouth, sucking, then lowered, you pivot as a cat lifts its claws from the back of your hand. The cat moves in circles, falls gracefully into the weeds, and you stand at the fence almost wistfully looking at the yellow-sided house, but not for long—you begin to shuffle backward, hesitantly at first, then faster and faster.

You're in the street, running backward down the street, and the arm that had been under the bejewelled black t-shirt comes out and you're holding the gun.

The gun slides back under your shirt. You turn, stand firm. A woman gets into your face. She's gone. You turn again, running across a street in reverse, and another, and a man shouts from a car's open window driving backward, and the car almost hits you and speeds away, shiny rims revolving.

You're under some bushes and crawling right out the other side, where you come up running and stumble into a sand trap, pulled backward, running, again, awkwardly, then faster as the hand holding the gun draws out from underneath your t-shirt. Exposed.

You're being pulled through a terraced garden while a woman looks down at you and undials a number on her phone.

You're in another street, a cul-de-sac, and you reverse at speed, you're on the sidewalk, and the gun hangs from your hand that hangs stiffly from your arm, your shoulder, and your running becomes more and more awkward, like it's new to you, to run while holding a gun. You don't know how to do it.

And, something is happening.

You drag your feet, you fight against where this is going, time rolling and rolling and pulling you pulling you toward a fenced construction site where a new house the size of a small barn is about to be built in this smooth suburban neighbourhood where two men are waiting for you to arrive.

And one of them wants his gun back.

And you can't seem to stop the reel from bringing you here. You can't seem to stop picking this up, putting this down, carrying and dumping and burning and digging through the ashes of whatever this means to you now.

The trees you planted in childhood have grown too heavy. You cannot bring them along.

EIGHTEEN

Group Therapy Bullshit

Luce said he would go to the group therapy bullshit appointment by himself, he could get himself there.

"Are you planning to walk? It's halfway across town!"

Luce said he could take the bus like other people.

"Let me drive you," Irene said. She tried not to beg, tried not to put him off. "You're my son, after all. I'm here to help."

"That's why you're here?"

"Marietta can't handle this all by herself."

"Handle me, you mean?"

Oh, what did she mean? Could she say what she meant?

"Look at me, Ma. I'm back on my feet. I'm taking the meds. What more do you want?"

Irene looked. Her son had gotten up early this morning, he'd put a comb through his hair, fresh shirt, he'd made a pot of coffee, spilling grounds across the counter, yes, but he'd been outside to greet Marietta before the kids even woke up. She'd heard it all from her makeshift bed on the couch, and she hoped, how she hoped, for the best. But wasn't there something slippery about him, a looseness to his shoulders, his slow grin as he watched her assess him? Daring her. Call my bluff, Ma, go ahead.

Luce didn't resemble his father closely, except in certain gestures, which shocked Irene when their symmetry aligned: the way his arms flew akimbo when he was uncertain or especially pleased, the way he stuck his chin up when asking a question; and now, daring her to contradict his claim. The slow grin.

Frank—she'd married him for the lightness of his intensity, his looks were incidental, it was his ease with language, with people, that pulled Irene, like it pulled everyone. But for good.

In the son, it seemed that fluency, that looseness was used for other purposes. A superpower obscured, corrupted, abused.

Like Luce, Frank could talk to anyone. But Frank knew how to listen too. The pleasure Frank took from learning something new animated his features. Luce was better-looking, but Irene wondered whether his face had ever shone like a lantern in the night in appreciation of someone else. Had Luce ever wondered, really wondered, what made another human being so interesting, so remarkable?

For that matter, had Irene? Well, that was different— wasn't it? I'm not a curious person, she thought, and for good reason.

Frank, tell me, what should I say to your son? What would you ask him right now? I need you here to talk to him, to help me talk to him.

Luce was pulling on his boots in the front hall.

"Don't use the front door!" Irene said, regretted it immediately, both the words and the tone. She hoped she hadn't disturbed Marietta, sleeping like the dead behind her closed bedroom door, the poor woman would get only a few hours' rest between shifts today, and Irene was waiting for the right moment to tell her that she was clearly working herself to death—and that Irene wanted to help, in some way; but how? The right moment hadn't yet arrived. The right offer.

"Let me drive you, please."

Francie came out from the bathroom, drying her hands on her jeans. "Tonight is my concert," she said.

"Yes?" said Irene, distracted, and then, "Of course it is!" The tickets were stuck onto the fridge with magnets.

"Are you coming?"

"Of course! Of course I'm coming!" Irene spooned the last morsel of porridge from Sam's bowl into his mouth. She did not let him feed himself, the way Marietta did. He swung his head in protest as she wiped him with the cloth from the sink.

"Are you coming, Dad? To my concert?"

Luce walked past them in his boots and out the side door. "Where are you going?" Irene called after him, but he didn't answer. She wasn't asking the right questions, she knew. "I'm sure your dad will come too," Irene said to Francie, but she could see Francie didn't believe her, or didn't want to hear it from Irene. She wanted to hear it from Luce.

Good luck with that.

"You can't go to school with your hair looking like this, let's put it back in a ponytail," Irene said, though she managed to bite her tongue and not mention how much she disliked the child's bejewelled t-shirt.

"I don't like ponytails," said Francie. "They hurt."

"No, they don't," said Irene, "get my purse." Irene could have lived out of that purse. That gave her comfort. "Birds could make nests in this mess, do you know that?"

Francie made a sound in her throat.

"I'm going to drive your dad to his appointment, can you get yourself off to school?"

The comb snarled in a knot of matted hair that looked like it had been felted. "Ouch," Francie said. Just then, Luce came back inside, a bit dishevelled, dirt on his jeans, on his left elbow. Now Irene was worried. His footsteps were heavy on the kitchen steps, and across the linoleum.

"You're making a mess, Luce, look at the floor."

The wrong thing to say, always wrong.

"Dad, are you coming to my concert? It's tonight!" Francie had escaped, curled herself free from Irene's hands.

"I give up!" Irene laid the comb on the table. Sam was not going to last another second in his high chair. "I made you a sandwich," Irene told Francie. "It's in the fridge."

"Did you put peanut butter on?"

"No, I did not, I won't do it again." Apparently, spreading peanut butter on bread and putting it into a lunch box was akin to sending bomb-making material to school. "Don't bother your mom, let her sleep," said Irene.

Francie nodded.

"Let's go, then, Luce. Let me drive you. I've got my purse."

Irene lifted Sam out of the high chair. She flashed to the sight of baby-sized Luce being lifted out of the same chair, chubby legs, large head. *I think he's having a good life so far, don't you, Frank?* young Irene, new mother, was saying. *Yes,* young Frank, new father, was agreeing, both of them pleased and innocent, as if this was their doing, as if it were in their power to grant their baby a good life.

"Here." Luce reached for Sam, which surprised her.

"Your arm, be careful," she said automatically. Always with a warning. *That any of us allow ourselves to feel anything—that is pure miracle.*

Francie sat at the table over her bowl of porridge, long gone cold, squashing the grey substance against the side of the bowl with her spoon, spreading it thin.

"Don't play with your food," said Irene.

Luce handed the baby back to Irene. He was wearing a jacket too heavy for this warm day, she noticed, as he slipped his good hand into a pocket.

"Hey kiddo," Luce addressed Francie, "wish me luck."

"Okay," the child said, poking at the porridge.

"Big day," said Luce, and Francie said, "I know."

Irene strapped Sam into the car seat she'd borrowed from a friend's daughter at church. Ask and you shall receive.

Luce shifted in the passenger seat, scanning the radio stations.

Do you want me to come in with you? Irene decided she would wait to ask till they'd gotten there. She would wait.

In her mind, Irene listed the last-minute instructions she'd forgotten to give Francie: finish your breakfast, rinse the bowl, brush your teeth, walk safe. She thought about telling Marietta that she, Irene, approved wholeheartedly of Francie walking to school with a friend, it took a special mother these days to trust her child to be independent in the world. You are a good mother, she could almost imagine telling Marietta.

Do you want me to come in with you? No. She wouldn't say it after all.

Luce got out of the car. "Thanks, Ma." He tapped the roof.

"I'll wait." Irene leaned out her open window. "We'll wait right here."

"Ma!" Luce shook his head. "Gimme a break. I can find my own way home."

"You're going to be too warm in that jacket!"

Irene watched him walk through the doors of the out-patient clinic.

She pulled out of the parking lot and began to drive almost aimlessly, around the streets near the hospital, circling wider and wider. Luce had left the radio on a country station. Sam seemed to be asleep, soothed by the motion.

Please see my son, Irene thought toward the group therapy bullshit counsellor, whoever was in charge in there. See him. That was what she hoped for, even knowing she was hoping for too much, she was hoping for the moon. She couldn't see him herself.

Was that what you were missing, Frank?

No, came the answer, as clearly as if Frank were speaking inside her head, across the years.

Because if you'd seen me, you would have known, Frank said clearly. *You would have known what was coming for me.*

Oh.

The song on the radio landed in Irene's arms like a glass casserole dish covered in foil; she hadn't heard it before, women's voices in honeyed harmony. It sounded like a lullaby, arranged as a round, and the chorus was simple enough that Irene began to sing along. It was a song about forever. But it wasn't, was it? It was a song about love, like all the songs on the radio. To sing along was to make a promise. The same promise she'd made to Frank, she made to Luce. She had no idea what she was promising, of course, but she knew that, at least—that she had no idea.

When the song ended, Irene had to turn off the radio. She felt a bit lost.

She kept driving, the circles growing wider and wider, till she found her way back to the little house again.

There was always something, some ambush from some unexpected source, no matter the helpful letters of instruction sent home to parents, left to rot in the bottoms of backpacks. But it wouldn't matter one way or the other, because the show must go on!

"The show must go on!" Mrs. G declared. The children stood before her, arrayed on risers. A ukulele player had snapped a string, multiple children had ignored the dress code, and one of her soloists was late, but this something was a lot of nothing, at bottom. A lot of noise.

They were exceptionally noisy this afternoon. Post–lunch break.

Perhaps the sound was amplified by the polished concrete gymnasium walls. They'd escaped the confines of the music portable. They'd reached the final leg of their race. Mrs. G drank it all in, as she sipped turmeric and ginger tea, brewed at home and poured into a travel mug, the turmeric to fight inflammation, the ginger to soothe a nervous stomach. Nerves were normal, to be expected, she needed to remember to tell the children not to worry about worrying, especially her soloists.

A euphonic cacophony! Shuffling feet, whispers, laughter, pinging of strings, humming, all charged by an undercurrent, a whirring energy like the soft rush of hundreds of wings.

This could be the concert, as far as Mrs. G was concerned. Imagine the outrage.

She must remember to tell the children: if you pick your nose onstage, everyone will see.

It would be very different this evening; the performance atmosphere could not be adequately mocked up in a music portable, or even here, dress rehearsal in an empty gymnasium. When the children gathered this evening, and the lights softened and dimmed, and the wooden chairs arranged behind her in flat rows on the shiny parquet floor were filled with warm human bodies, it would be like nothing they could guess in advance.

She looked for her soloists, and saw Francie sneaking in through the double doors, shoulders hunched. She waved Francie closer. "Remember to breathe in, and remember to breathe out," she said, exhaling upon the child the spirit of turmeric and ginger. There was more advice she could offer, but she firmly believed that no child could absorb more than a handful of consecutive words in a row. "Go on," Mrs. G directed the child.

Francie stepped onto the riser, almost unwillingly, beside her friend. Both looked nervous and stiff as boards.

Good grief! Breathe, I told you, breathe!

Mrs. G gathered all her children's eyes upon her by means of sheer will, mouthing the words, "Clap if you can hear me, clap if you can hear."

Slowly enough, they began to clap, and the sound of hundreds of wings hushed.

"Raise your hand if you ate a good breakfast," she said, "and a very good lunch."

Everyone's hand shot up. How she wanted to believe them.

"Let's practise coming off the risers."

Something was going very wrong. Everyone looked green, not just Francie. Another sip of tea.

"Yasmeen!" Mrs. G called to the student teacher who was managing the lighting. "Not the green, please."

Francie would need a box to stand on, or no one would be able to see her.

Shoes squeaked on the slippery gym floor. "No running shoes tonight, please!"

Mrs. G watched as several children took a flying leap from the highest row. The shoes were the least of her problems.

The ukulele chorus had just practised gathering in their formation on the risers, while the rest of the children sat in place. "Will Francie Fultz please come to the office? Francie Fultz?"

Mrs. G could not believe her ears, she could not believe her ears! She stared at the child, baton raised. "You can't be serious! Oh no, no, no, no, no. We haven't even practised your solo yet. You are going to march down to that office and tell them—"

Yasmeen flooded the darkness with a deep-purple glow, ominous as a scene in a bad dream. *Wake me now!*

"Francie Fultz to the office, please."

Quietly, Francie slid herself down off the riser. Behind her, the other children shifted in heightened silence.

"Oh no you don't!" Mrs. G waved her arms wildly. "And not the purple, for goodness' sake, Yasmeen! Not the purple!" The light switched abruptly to red, evoking a different nightmare altogether.

Quietly, Francie trudged toward the double doors. Mrs. G's high-heeled sandals rapped loudly on the parquet floor, and the waiting choir was preternaturally still—waiting to see what would happen to one of their own. Outside the doors, in a hallway bright with sunlight, Mrs. G caught up.

"What is going on here?"

The child stared down at the running shoes she'd better not wear to the concert tonight. "It's my dad," she said at last. She looked so weary, so slack and defeated,

Mrs. G flashed to the notion that the child was drifting toward an enchanted sleep.

"I'll tell him you can't leave right now. He must know how important this is!"

The child shook her head. "It's okay," she said. "I know all the words to my song."

"Of course you do." *Well, sort of, but good enough!* Mrs. G sighed deeply, her eyes bright and wet. She shook her head. She stood with fists on hips, watching Francie walk away. "See you tonight! You'd better be here!"

NINETEEN

Gun Run

Here you are, said Alice inside Francie's mind. Francie could almost see her, climbing up through the branches. *I've found you! Come down, Francie, there's still time to get to the concert. Everyone is waiting for you.*

Everyone?

Well, not everyone.

There was always, eventually, an end, to everything, or a time that felt like the end, a last time. Sometimes you didn't know before it happened, sometimes you could see it coming, like now. *I'm not holding you anymore!* It was not so hard, after all. Francie put the gun inside the rainbow pony lunch box, she settled the lunch box inside the backpack, she zipped the backpack shut. It was nice not to see the gun. It was nice not to touch it, nice not to carry it. She broke off part of a branch, over her head—the highest branch she could reach—and she slid the loop of fabric at the top of her backpack over its stump—the tip of the tip of the top—and she hung it there.

There.

I did it, Dad. Bye, now.

Grandma hadn't seen what Dad had in his pocket. Grandma didn't know about Dad's gun, or where he kept it.

Grandma said she would drive Dad to his appointment, and Dad said okay, and Grandma carried Sam outside to the car, and Grandma didn't know that Dad had a gun in the pocket of his jacket.

Dad only wanted Francie to see.

He pulled it out of his pocket to show her, and he winked. Grandma was digging around in her purse for her car keys.

"Wish me luck, kiddo," he said, and he slipped the gun back into his pocket. "Big day."

After Grandma's car drove away, Francie stood outside Mom's bedroom door, and listened. What if she opened the door and went right up to Mom, stood silently beside her in the dark, would Mom know she was there, would Mom wake up and roll over: What is it, Francie, are you having a bad dream?

Yes.

Francie checked Grandma's sandwich before putting it into her lunch box—no peanut butter—and she stuffed her feet into her sneakers. In the front yard, she could see Dad's boot prints in their garden. It was too late to undo what was happening. It was already happening.

Alice was waiting for Francie on her front porch.

Alice smelled like licorice toothpaste. She wore black tights and a black t-shirt, her hair pulled into a high pony-tail. She said that Kate did it for her.

Francie said, "It's just the dress rehearsal. Tonight I can turn my shirt inside out for the concert."

"Hurry up," the crossing guard told them.

The morning was like a normal morning. At lunch, Francie ate all but the crusts of her sandwich. She was sorry she'd packed Grandma's cookies, they were dry in her throat, the crumbs made her choke. She walked to the gym for dress rehearsal. Her feet moved slower and slower down the hallway, but they couldn't stop her from getting to the gym. She stepped through the double doors and held her breath.

See that girl all dressed in black?

Keep on running, don't ever look back!

"Will Francie Fultz please come to the office? Francie Fultz?"

Francie's heart slowed like it would stop, and then began to hammer inside her chest. Her face felt hot, her throat was closing, she couldn't say a word when Mrs. G started yelling: "Oh no you don't!"

Francie's sneakers squeaked across the gym floor (useless for sneaking!). The coolness of everyone's eyes on her back made her feel chilly and small. She moved deliberately, taking care, one foot set down in front of the other.

"We'll march right down to the office and tell your dad you can't leave right now!"

Mrs. G didn't know Francie's dad. She didn't know about the gun. Francie felt afraid for Mrs. G.

She took a big breath and said, "It's okay, Mrs. G. I know all the words."

Dad's eyes shone like glass. "Time for your appointment," he said, loud enough for the secretary to hear.

The sun was bright—warm.

Francie didn't ask where they were going.

Dad wiped his face on the sleeve of his jacket, his hair slick underneath with sweat. Francie noticed he had cut the sleeve of the jacket to fit it over his cast. He slipped his left hand in and out of the pocket. He was gritting his teeth. They were walking very slowly.

"Dad?" she said, and tried to hold his free hand.

But it was the hand with the cast wrapped around it, their fingers brushed. "Hey." He smiled at her, and then his smile twisted up, and she knew they weren't going home. Was that good or bad?

They followed the sidewalk up into the neighbourhood behind the school. Flowering trees had dropped their blooms, the leaves were lovely and green, and they walked past garden beds of flowers, bushes, flat stones.

The street wound up and up.

Dad was having a hard time. He told Francie to walk on his other side. He held her shoulder tight with his good hand.

"Look at that house." Dad stopped. "Eats up the whole damn lot. Neighbours must be pissed—they've lost their view."

Dad pointed out the detailing in the brick, the slope of its roof, the ill-fated design decisions, the special glass in the front door, the cobbled driveway that would have cost a fortune. "Looks just like a Mikey special," he said. "This is why I can't work with that guy anymore."

Dad said he hadn't walked this far in a while. It was okay to stop and rest, right, kiddo? Francie said yes.

"Some people have money to burn," he said. He reached in his jeans pocket and offered her a mint. She chomped down hard on it, and it hurt her teeth. What should she do with the wrapper? Dad tossed it into the pristine yard and started walking again.

Up and up.

Dad stopped to rest his hands on his thighs. He pretended to be looking at a garden, but really he was catching his breath. Inside this house, behind a large window, a tiny white dog threw itself in a frenzy against the glass, like it was all alone, living inside an enormous terrarium.

Next door was an empty lot, stripped of grass, a construction site wrapped all around with metal fencing, a machine with treads instead of tires parked inside near a large pile of dirt.

And Francie knew: This was where Dad was going.

He noticed Francie looking, and he nodded. But he didn't move.

A red pickup truck drove up and over the curb and parked in the dirt outside the metal fencing, beside a grey porta-potty. A man—Mikey—climbed out of the cab. Dad's hand locked around Francie's shoulder, his fingers tightened. Had Mikey seen Dad yet? He was checking the fencing, unlocking a big padlock clamped around a heavy chain, pushing the gate open. Baseball cap, oversized t-shirt, steel-toed boots.

"Looks like it's my lucky day." Dad pushed off Francie and took a big step forward. "Hello, Mikey."

A lot of things were about to go wrong.

Francie looked down. Dad was wearing his steel-toed boots too.

"Come on," he said to her, "this won't take a minute."

Francie was partway down the tree when she met the policewoman climbing up.

The policewoman stopped when Francie saw her. She was breathing hard. "You must be Francie?" Her tone was cheerful, like this was a totally normal place to be meeting a kid.

Francie decided to keep climbing down.

The policewoman showed Francie the harness she'd carried up the tree. She wanted to strap Francie into it, to attach them together, for safety, she said. But even she didn't seem too convinced by the plan. Between them, even going down, Francie was the better climber, no matter the cuts on her feet, no matter how thirsty and tired.

Francie glanced at the woman, rustled around to the branches on the other side of the trunk, and slipped through the trap.

"Do you have a gun, Francie?" the policewoman called, climbing down after her. The woman's boots were too heavy, her buckles and pockets snagged and caught.

Just don't look down.

"It would be better if you tell me now, about the gun, I mean, because people are waiting for you down below and we don't want any surprises, any trouble. I can radio down to let them know."

Francie said nothing. *Don't look down, don't look down.*

But when she looked up, the policewoman was struggling after her, black boots on branches creaking over Francie's head. "We have reports from people who saw you with a gun, Francie. There's no reason to lie about it. You're not in any kind of trouble. We need to know, because it's a very dangerous situation, Francie, and the people on the ground, they need to know—"

A branch snapped.

"Shit," the woman said. "Oops, sorry. I haven't climbed one of these since I was a kid."

The radio on her vest crackled.

"Soon this will all be over," she said. She pressed a button and responded and Francie got a couple of extra branches on her.

"It would be better if you waited for me," the woman called down, but wouldn't it just be better for her?

Maybe Francie expected a dog, when she crawled out. What she didn't expect was yellow tape marking off a big circle around the tree. She didn't expect a man with a bull-horn who knew her name, asking to see her hands, both hands, please, Francie. "This will all be over soon." She didn't expect all this attention, trained on her, pointed at her, when, after resting for a moment in the soft, clean nest of needles, she crawled out from under the lowest branches, lifted her face, and stood up.

TWENTY

Gun

Today had been a nice day. A solid start. Good workout at the gym (legs and core), an icy-smooth protein shake from the coffee counter, chocolate with a shot of espresso, enjoyed while sitting in his truck in the parking lot and finding the guts to dial Marietta's number—and Marietta picked up! She picked up, and she said she'd call later.

A nice day. Right up till just about now.

Mikey could see the personal trainer handing him a towel for his face halfway through their 6 a.m. session. He could have used that towel right about now. He imagined the trainer pressing it against his stomach with her strong hands. She'd know what to do. The trainer liked to say it wasn't her job to make friends. She said it was okay if Mikey hated her a bit, at some point each session, she could take it, her job was to make him hurt.

Make you hurt, make you better.

Make me better, he said.

He wasn't your typical gym rat—no shit, Sherlock—but

he had to admit he enjoyed those sessions. Didn't go to the gym in between, which would have helped with his progress, the trainer told him, but he couldn't seem to get motivated without someone telling him what to do.

Like now. Like what the fuck should Mikey do now? Luce, do you want to give me some tips here? Mikey was pretty sure Luce was still over there where he'd been when he pulled the gun out of his jacket pocket, pointed, and shot: *bang, bang, bang.* There had been a third bang.

One blew out the side window of the truck—

One in the stomach—

Where was the third?

Luce, Mikey tried to say, but it sounded like a gurgle. *Not good, man, not good.*

"I believe my days are numbered," his mother liked to say, it was some kind of comfort to her. "God has written up my days in His ledger, and He will count them out for me."

This was going to kill her.

He should call her. First, he'd call Marietta, then his mom. Or his mom, then Marietta. There wasn't exactly time to be weighing this decision, not with so much blood pouring out of his middle section. All those crunches! For nothing? He was slumped in the dirt beside a smattering of glass from the window of his truck, he'd put his hand into it. He wondered why Luce hadn't just shot him in the head or the heart. Maybe Luce wasn't much of a shot, like he wasn't much of anything else.

What a shitty thing to think. Mikey hardly recognized himself. *Mister nice guy.*

Until this very moment, he hadn't known he was holding any hatred toward Luce. So much hatred. *But I'm a stand-up guy!* Standing up for Luce, from day one, every step of the way, even over these past few months, keeping him clear of work sites, keeping him away from trouble, the kind of trouble that seemed to chase Luce wherever he went.

I couldn't afford it anymore, man, I'm sorry: Mikey laid out his argument.

But that was done. That was over. That fight had been had.

Best buds, best friends, best man at Luce's wedding. Funny guy, Luce never seemed to notice or comment on Mikey's weight, which was pretty much the only Mikey-related talking point for most of the kids in grade seven, where they first met. Mikey was the new kid, his mom had divorced his dad and moved back to her hometown, which wasn't a town so much as a handful of bungalows built on either side of a busy country highway at the bottom of a valley. The bus ride was an hour one way. Mikey sat at the back of every class. He didn't expect much. He noticed Luce walking the hallway like he was the shit, but Mikey noticed everything. Noticing was what he did, interested in human nature even at the age of twelve.

He noticed when Luce picked him—Fat Mikey!—for his volleyball team in gym. He picked Mikey to be his lab partner in science. He called out to Mikey in the hallway till others noticed too, and Mikey didn't have to be Fat Mikey anymore.

Mikey slipped sideways, looking past his gut, feeling essentially appreciative of that kid that Luce was. He didn't regret much of anything, he decided, slumped here. He didn't regret defending Luce for so long. He didn't regret letting Luce cheat off his biology exam, even though it got them both flunked and suspended.

He didn't regret partnering up with Luce to build shit together.

We were going to build the best shit together.

Okay, one regret.

He never should have let Luce work alone. If Luce hadn't been working alone, someone would have stopped him from walking through that drop zone, or maybe someone would have marked the zone with cones, and Luce wouldn't have been clipped by that beam and sent sailing for a three-storey drop down below. Lucky Luce, falling into sand instead of poured concrete.

Mikey should have been working with Luce. Mikey should have put up the cones.

Why was Luce working solo?

Because no one wants to work with him.

He takes too many risks, cuts corners, he's lazy, because it's dangerous working with Luce and no one wants to do it, not even you, Mikey.

I'm sorry, man, it's going to be okay! But everyone could see it wasn't going to be okay. He'd be lucky to walk again. They'd be fined for code violations. No one would want to insure them.

I'm sorry, man, I've gotta keep you off the books.

I'm sorry, man, we don't need you at this site today.

I'm sorry, man, I can't keep paying you to stay away.

I'm sorry, man, it's time to go our separate paths.

You think so? That's what you think?

Funny thing was, when he'd seen Luce waiting here for him, Mikey had felt that familiar flutter of something—like, hey, here's something about to happen. Luce did that to a person. It was like when he chose Mikey for his team in gym class, he expected Mikey to be all in, no matter his deficiencies, Luce expected Mikey to dive, to jump, even if that meant skidding across the floor like a clown, his shirt flying up and exposing his belly. He was supposed to hate Luce sometimes, it was Luce's job, Luce could take it, it was Luce's job to make him hurt.

I'll try to find you a spot on another crew.

Fuck you, man.

I'll ask around for you, I'll put in a good word.

Fuck this. We're partners. You owe me.

What if that were true?

"You hurt, you grow," the trainer told him this morning. She meant it literally: you shred all your little muscle fibres and they repair themselves and get bigger and stronger.

It had been a nice day.

Marietta answered! She picked up! She didn't hang up on him!

He drove home in his sweaty shirt and giant basketball shorts, took a shower. He called his mother to check in like he did every morning, she said she was starting with a boiled egg on toast, and she reported on the weather, he could hear her shaking the pages of the newspaper to find it. "Twenty-five percent chance of rain, that's pretty good! Have a good day, Mikey, I love you, bye."

"Love you too, Mom."

Drive-through for brunch, two breakfast sandwiches, two hash browns, but he ordered his coffee black. Hungry an hour later. Stopped to buy a sleeve of candied nuts at a gas station. Resisted getting a soda. He had two sites personally under contract, and this one was just getting started. The palace was on its way, lots of juggling yet to be done with contractors; he liked that part of the job, making the connections, choreographing the timing, standing back with arms folded to admire the craftsmanship. But he'd hook up that fountain himself. That'll be something to see! He'd had a meeting with the woman of the household to run over the numbers. And another meeting with a prospective client. A nice country drive, windows down, halfway wishing he'd gotten the soda, halfway proud of himself for resisting. He thought of Marietta. He checked his phone to make sure the ringer was on. It was on.

She said she'd call him.

He was slumped in the dirt. His phone was in the front pocket of his shirt, over his heart.

Funny how happy he'd been to see Luce this time, considering last time, when Luce clocked him and knocked him flat. Must be some kind of Pavlovian response. Ring a bell, drool. Mikey'd pulled his truck in, bumping over the curb— was that just now, just a few minutes ago, now?—and he'd seen Luce right away, standing on the sidewalk, almost like he'd been waiting for Mikey, Mikey'd noticed the heavy jacket, and the kid, Luce's kid was with him, *Francie*, skinny, looked a lot like her mom—he should've gotten to know the kid better, spent more time, made an effort. That was on him.

Mikey had been one of their first visitors after Francie was born. He'd gone to a baby store and on the advice of a saleslady he'd purchased a shockingly expensive outfit that included a hair band with a bow, a frilly diaper cover attached to white tights, and a velveteen dress. He was pretty sure Marietta was pleasantly surprised. He'd even held the kid, walking up and down the room with her, longer than bachelor uncles were obliged to do.

Not her real uncle, of course.

But he said he'd take on the job, he'd stand in for all the missing uncles in the kid's life.

Turned out Mikey wasn't much of an uncle, past the first birthday party. What do you say to a kid? Kids made him nervous. He didn't know the first thing about kids. Or women. Or maybe, even, men.

So much for being an observer, a student of human nature.

Even while hearing the dot-dot-dot of an unspoken warning rattling inside his own head, Mikey'd pretended not to see Luce and the kid, waiting for him. He'd pulled in, parked, swung out of the cab, leaving the radio on, key in the ignition—that was an oversight, considering what happened next—unlocked the gate, pushed it open, telling himself not to rush, telling himself to stay cool, telling himself that he was just glad to see Luce alive and well—

Mikey wouldn't waste precious time reliving that.

He had been glad, that was true. He'd been glad to see Luce. He'd been Fat Mikey all along. He'd been so stupid. He'd been walking back through the gate to say hello. He was passing by his truck, on his way to walking over and sticking out his hand, and saying, Luce, good to see you looking so good, man.

Francie was staring at him, kind of an odd-looking expression, glassy-eyed but alert, he was trying to get a read on her, but like he said, he didn't know much about kids.

She flinched when Luce pulled out the gun. He pulled it out slowly and looked at it. It looked toy-size. Mikey thought, why's he got a toy gun?

Bang—window.

Bang—stomach.

Bang—FUCK!

Mikey crumpled forward and sat down hard. He looked at his hand, which came away bloody. He held it up and looked at it.

Time slowed till he thought maybe it'd stopped moving. How could he put it? He was without time, he was undying.

We just go through, he thought.

Luce had the gun pointed down at the ground. He was leaning heavy on his right leg, his bad leg. Then he held out the gun, like he was going to point it at the kid, and Mikey heard himself shout, "There's something wrong with you, man!" Like it had only just occurred to him. Because it had. This was what it took?

Call me, Marietta, call me back, call me now.

I'll give you a ride.

Luce was saying something to the kid, and the kid took the gun, her eyes locked onto some future they couldn't see, she was off and running.

Time was moving faster for the girl than it was for him, Mikey could tell. He sincerely hoped that his grotesquely dying body was no more than a blur in her periphery as she rocketed out of his frame. She was just passing through. They were all just passing through.

Some happened to pass through closer, that's all.

Marietta, the time is now.

Mikey felt relief like a big hand coming down onto his chest, pressing down—and he knew where the third bullet had gone.

Luce. It had gone into Luce. It had got him in his good leg, and he could hear Luce cursing as he dragged himself past where Mikey huddled with his eyes opened to the sky. Artery? Femoral artery? Mikey could only hope, listening to Luce crawl into the cab of Mikey's truck, where Mikey had left the key in the ignition, like a parting gift to an old friend. Mikey heard the engine roaring, tires spinning in dirt—he hoped, he hoped.

He hoped Luce wouldn't hurt anyone else.

He hoped this was Marietta calling, he could hear his phone ringing in his pocket, his hands weren't moving, couldn't move, but wouldn't that be something? Hello? Hello?

Mikey drifted back to the high school biology exam, the diagrams of veins and arteries, bones and muscles, organs. The heart. A map of a place that only existed in time and time was stretched so thin it was threadbare, it was layers of gauze unwinding, it was air, nothing but air, it was too diffuse even for that.

Exhale.

⟨⟨⟨⟨

A gun—

It had its uses. He'd been waiting for the right moment, and here it came, here it was.

Easy enough, right, kiddo?

When everything's going wrong, you just need one thing to go right.

This was the thing.

Everything lining up perfectly, no plan needed. He wasn't one for planning, never had been, never would be. He was smarter than that. He rolled with it. It was like being an inventor. Inventor of situations.

Inventor of the present moment.

He worked with what was on hand.

A gun—

Its uses hadn't been entirely clear till he'd pulled it out of his pocket—surprise! But the kid knew, smart kid. Why'd she have to look so scared? It was pissing Luce off. He didn't want his kid to be afraid of him, that's not why he brought her along.

And Mikey was shitting his pants.

Too easy!

It's not the gun you should be afraid of, Luce told Mikey. It's me.

Left hand, awkward, arm outstretched, aiming for head or heart, heart, head. Or gut. Fat larded belly. Head. Head.

A gun—

It had its uses. So use it.

Use it! Don't make another mess, man!

Hold it—hold it hold it hold it right there.

Damn, his hand was shaking. Not his right hand, his wrong hand.

Time was a tricky bastard, speeding up just when he wanted it to go slow. BANG BANG BANG. Time slowing to show him what he'd done, like it was all a big joke.

First shot, glass shattering.

Second shot, oof, in the gut.

Sorry, brother.

Third shot, FUCK.

A gun—

Couldn't stop time. Couldn't rewind. Take it, take it and run. Never stop running.

If anyone could save him, it was her, sprinting away from him with big, strong strides that reminded him of himself, running along a trail marked out with flags in the woods, being chased by every-damn-one else. Making it look so easy. Great kid, one helluva kid, that one.

TWENTY-ONE

Tree

The tree was a balsam fir. It was not quite as tall as the little girl believed it to be, but it had stood at the edge of this field, growing here, some small distance from its neighbours, for many seasons, and it had not succumbed to windstorms or falling branches or rot, despite the relative shallowness of its root system underground.

It was shaped like a tree drawn by a child, an upside-down cone. Its branches were green and thick all the way to the ground.

Its needles were soft and short, its bark blistered and sticky with sap, which smelled clean, of sweet, sharp wood resin.

When the child crawled out from under the tree's skirt of branches, she looked very small. The tree was hesitant to let her out, but it was not for the tree to decide what happened to the child. The child stood still and did not move even when a small cheer broke out among the humans gathered here.

Surrounded.

Yellow caution tape fluttered in a wide perimeter around the tree and the child, and beyond the perimeter more humans waited, including several who had lugged heavy bags and a stretcher from an ambulance parked in the gravel by the highway. The child wouldn't need that. The tree's branches were sturdy, they had held, as the tree had known they would.

The tree had never had so many visitors. The field was a more formidable barrier than it looked, swampy and wet and frothing with insects, slashing grass growing tight with thistles and prickle bushes and burrs. This is what the deer said.

The deer would stay out of sight, away from the dogs. One of the dogs had been ordered to retreat, and its owner struggled to hold on when the child emerged.

Stand here and wait.

The child did not move. Rooted. Yes.

What would happen next?

The tree wasn't interested in protocol, that tedious human word, in boxes to check, tasks to manage, notes to take, paperwork to fill out, a social worker assigned to the case, a medic with a foil blanket. The woman with boots was descending from the tree's lowest branches just now, awkwardly fighting her way out, slapped and scratched. A dog sniffed around the tree's trunk, the woman was pointing, up. The tree was neutral on the subject of the gun. It could stay where it was. But it wouldn't. Either the unnatural fibres of the backpack would erode in the sun, wind, rain, sleet, snow, and it would fall, eventually, or someone would climb up now, hopefully without spikes in the bottoms of their boots, find it, and remove it.

Well, it didn't belong here. In this world.

Not like the girl.

She belonged.

A woman with hair like a bristle of needles poking out from the back of her head was ducking under the yellow tape and no one stopped her, the woman was running to the girl, crying, pulling her close to her body, against the bones of her chest. The woman was telling the girl to leave this, leave it, leave everything, all of it, behind. Oh my baby.

The tree knew that was not how it happened, in this world.

What you carried came to you, found you, it climbed you, nested in you, left its mark on you, you shed it and it rotted and fed your roots, it grew into you. You grew circles around circles. You grew.

Concert

We had come.

The gymnasium, with its high ceiling, smooth concrete-block walls painted white, its floor shining with varnish and painted with lines and circles, was harshly lit, and we filed in, having already parked and walked further than we would have liked, having already waited for the bottleneck at the double doors, having tried and failed to remember the names of people whose children's names we knew; here we were. We'd had to wolf down our insufficient dinners. We were dressed appropriately, we hoped, though our shoes already felt uncomfortable. We shuffled down rows of stackable chairs, hoping to find the perfect sightline to see the child we'd come to see.

We trained our eyes on empty risers and waited to see the one that was ours.

We said we wouldn't have missed this for the world, though for most of us that wasn't exactly true. We said we were looking forward to this, and again, we were just saying what we believed was required of us. As if anything at all were required of us, except to come. And we had come. We were here.

The lights dimmed, all but those focused on the empty risers, and a rustle passed through us.

A pause.

It was already quite warm, and many of us began to fan ourselves with the programme, which some of us—professional school concert attendees, parents of multiple children—recognized was ominously thick. We tried to read the programme but couldn't see it in the dark.

Someone was preparing to give a speech at the podium. Few among us appreciated the seniority and authority of the person speaking, who, assuming we'd recognize him, had failed to introduce himself. He began with a joke, but went on for too long. We were waiting for one thing, and one thing only: to see the one who was ours. The fanning and rustling grew louder, until, mercifully, the director marched in, and we applauded both the speech's end and the arrival of the main event, we hoped.

Behind the director came the children, snaking in an unsteady, quietly noisy line, clad mostly in black, sneakers squeaking on the floor. We searched, leaning, straining to find the one that was ours. The risers groaned and creaked as children tramped up and across, purposeful and proud, some of them, while others were dreamy and unaware, and, oh—there she was! We spotted the white tag sticking out of the back of her inside-out shirt. There hadn't been time for her to change, and besides, she'd had nothing better at home. But most of all, this was how we'd come to know her, and we didn't want her to change.

She had to be wearing her favourite shirt.

The director raised her baton, turned, and bowed.

We were happy that the child had been placed in the front row, beside her best friend. We were happy she had a best friend. We noticed that the friend had reached for the child's hand and was holding it, and that the child, the one we'd come to see, was unable to sing the opening notes of the opening song, as if her voice were stuck in her throat, and we were worried for her. Perhaps this had been a mistake, only she'd wanted so badly to be here. It had been the only thing she seemed to want, once she'd satisfied her thirst and hunger.

At last, the child's voice joined the others, and relief poured through us. But as our bodies weakened and slumped, lumpen in the uncomfortable chairs, we were beginning to realize, some of us more slowly than others, that we were in for a long and protracted wait. There was no avoiding it, it was the nature of the school concert.

There were songs with no soloists and songs with several. A soloist wearing a bow tie was rattled but impressed us—that a boy was willing to put himself forward to sing, we were thinking, what a nice boy he must be.

The vibe in the gym grew restless, impatient, and too soon. We were beginning to think we knew what to expect from these children, this many songs in, and we no longer expected anything at all. We'd suppressed our rage at the dad who raised his video camera, viewing screen open, to record each number. We'd tried sucking on a cough candy we'd found rolling loose in a pocket. We'd attempted and failed to count each child's head.

We'd managed to forget why we'd come.

The ukulele chorus was the jolt of sloppy energy we needed. The instruments were bright orange and purple, yellow and green, and although the rhythm began as

amenable to the cause, it quickly rolled off-kilter, enough
to create interest—the interest of fresh disaster looming. The
choir, singing along, struggled to keep up, till there came a
moment when we suspected that the choir had somehow leapt
into an unlikely lead and was threatening to lap the ukuleles.

The director's baton slashed the air, increasingly desperate, but what could she do? It was clear that chaos was their
unity, and time could not be tamed.

We were all sad, truth be told, when the song came to
an end, forever unresolved.

Just then, the lights cut out—gasps; this wasn't in the
programme—and we sat in the dark. We sat for what seemed
a rather long pause. Our eyes were drawn to a door propped
open at the side of the gym, through which a rectangle of
June light shone.

What could possibly come next?

The spotlights flared yellow-gold, like a sunset, warm.
It made us feel unaccountably happy.

At last.

Our child was stepping forward. She climbed onto a
black-painted box, a microphone aimed at her face. The heat
of the stage lights mixed with breeze from the open door,
lifted loose strands of her hair, which was tangled and a bit
matted, we knew, with pine sap. We could not know who,
passing by on the sidewalk, had stopped to listen for what we
were about to hear. We could not guess the colour of their
nail polish, nor the depths of their griefs and sweet joys, as
they stopped and held their breath, and became one of us too.

The child opened her mouth and she saw what we could
not—the song alive before her, carrying her between the
rows of chairs, searching each row till she found the ones
who were hers.

Here we are!

What did she need, and could we give it to her?

But we didn't know, and we couldn't. We could only watch and wait, straining to read the child's inscrutable face.

The song went on, a call-and-response between the child and the children behind her. They stared out into the darkness that was us.

And we saw that the child was not alone.

It was enough. It had to be.

ACKNOWLEDGEMENTS

This book lived many lives before agreeing to root inside this one. I've written iterations in notebooks before sunrise; at a hotel in Kingston; on index cards in cartoon form at a Lynda Barry workshop in upstate New York; at my friend Lisa's kitchen table; in an anonymous shared office at the University of Waterloo; while my family went to Canada's Wonderland and I should have been with them; in my cluttered home studio; at Marg's cottage in the bunkie my dad built, over-looking the lake; in secret; in private; in a fugue state at the dining-room table; on a picnic blanket after biking to a child's swim lessons; in the front seat of a small white car; the back seat, too, beside a soccer field; in the woodshed at my friend Nina's farm; and everywhere in between.

I don't know how this book got made, or invented, or finished. I think it must be thanks to the support of my family and friends: fellow early morning risers Nina, Heather, Marnie; Zoe, planner of parties; Fiona, another sister; my word-of-the-year group; my teacher and friend Kasia; my X Page friends;

and Lisa, who introduced me to the joyful teaching of Lynda Barry. Thanks to my siblings too: Christian, Clifford, Karl, and Edna (and their partners); and to our parents, for the unique gifts they bestowed on us.

And gratitude beyond measure to my writing group, Tasneem Jamal and Emily Urquhart, from whom I've learned so much. You give me the courage to continue.

Several interviews and conversations helped guide the direction of the book: for their invaluable professional expertise, I thank Michael Parkinson for his public health perspective on opioid use, and Julia Forward for talking me through realistic legal outcomes for imaginary scenarios. Any errors are of my own making. Thanks also to my late stepmother, Marg Janzen, whom I consulted for legal advice on an early version of the book.

Thank you to Kevin and our kids, Angus, Annie, Flora, and Calvin, for letting me retreat to do this work, even though it meant not being with you (in spirit as much as in body). Thank you to Hilary, my agent and friend, for your visionary wisdom, and for never giving up on me, ever ever ever. Bless you, a million times over. Thank you to Lynn Henry for reviving my hope and lighting a fire, and for delivering the brightest news in the bleakest hour, and to Melanie Little for accompaniment through the gruelling labour of the final miles. Thanks to Kelly Hill for her brilliant cover design, and to John Sweet for his non-fussy copyediting, and to everyone at Knopf Canada for your welcome and your support. This book was also supported by a miraculously timed grant from the Canada Council.

Is that everyone? I'm sure that it is not, and I name you in my heart, all whose feet have walked the path with mine. So much love, and thanks!

This book began as an ode to childhood friendship. My first friend was Katie and together we climbed trees. Drifting into those memories was like swimming in a lake in the sky; and I floated on this book across some very dark lakes. Writing it brought me comfort. I hope that reading it brings you comfort too; or something else you were longing to feel. For your attention, and for reading, especially books, *thank you.*

© Hilary Gauld

CARRIE SNYDER is an award-winning Canadian writer who has published three previous books of literary fiction and two books for children. Her bestselling novel *Girl Runner* was a finalist for the Rogers Writers' Trust Fiction Prize and published in twelve countries. Her novel-in-stories, *The Juliet Stories*, was a finalist for the 2012 Governor General's Award for Fiction. She is a consulting editor for *The New Quarterly* magazine and publishes an award-winning literary blog, *Obscure CanLit Mama*. Carrie Snyder lives in Waterloo, Ontario.

carriesnyder.com